# BITTERROOT

## A Novel
### Of the Forest Service, Gold, Murder, and Mercy

By

Stephen E. McDonald

# BITTERROOT

Published by: SM & Associates, Publishers
371 E, 3700 N
Ogden, Utah 84414
801-782-4311
E-mail: smassociates@silkspin.net

ISBN:  0-7392-0310-X

Printed in the USA by

MORRIS PUBLISHING

3212 East Highway 30 • Kearney, NE 68847 • 1-800-650-7888

# DEDICATION:

To all the personnel
of the
United States Forest Service,
past and present.

# Author's Preface

This story is set in the worlds of post-Civil War placer mining in North Central Idaho, the 1960's U.S. Forest Service, and the 1980's power elite of the East Coast. It blends the ingredients of greed, violence, and deceit that normally accompany the golden metal, with the themes of human failures, triumphs, mercy, and justice.

The role of Chinese laborers and miners in the development of the western United States has never been fully appreciated. Their contributions were significant, and we still benefit from their labors. By the end of the 20th century, many of the physical vestiges of their presence have disappeared, but it was not long ago that many were still evident. I recall, as a child growing up in Lewiston, Idaho, in the 1940's, that there were several old wooden Chinese structures in the older part of town. I asked my grandmother about them. She indicated that they were "Chinese temples", but she knew little else about them.

A remote Ranger District of the United States Forest Service is the setting for the middle of this book. The life and work of a young forester in the remote woods in Idaho of the early 1960's is described, based on my personal experiences. With all the hardships and frustrations, it was still a great place to be. I am sure many of my friends and colleagues from those times agree.

In that backwater of time and place, the Forest Service was operating in the overlap between the old "custodial" world of the Forest Service (the pre-development American west) and the new, and accelerating, post-war world of expansion, growth, and development that we now consider to be "normal".

The vestiges of the "custodial era" were still there then—mules, old log cabins, old timers, crank telephones with oak cabinets, kerosene lamps, etc. In addition, because much of the land was still largely undisturbed by development, much older things were common too, like old mining ditches from the 1860's gold rush and old mining town sites.

The corrosive effects of greed, jealousy, and hate can infect any society, even a small and close-knit one like a remote Forest Service Ranger Station's people. Everywhere there are strong and weak people and good and bad people. Similarly, the human qualities of justice and mercy are eternal and profound, no matter what culture or circumstances they are found in.

The characters described in this story draw upon composites of many people I have met and known over the years. Beyond that, any similarity to actual persons, living or dead, is purely coincidental.

In this book, accurately recreating the dialogue of the times often required it to be 'adult' in nature. The reader is forewarned that the characters, herein, talk with the 'bark on'.

I wish extend my personal thanks to those that have encouraged me to complete this book, especially my wife, Shirley.

**Stephen McDonald**, Ogden, Utah, 1999

# BITTERROOT

## Contents

Dedication
Author's Preface
Contents

## 1869

## 1964

# 1988

# Bitterroot

## Section 1 - <u>1869</u>

> "The thirst for adventure is the vent that Destiny offers; a war, a crusade, a gold mine, a new country, speak to the imagination and offers swing and energy to the confined powers"
> --Ralph Waldo Emerson, 1893.

# Chapter 1 – Voyage

Huang Lee was far sicker than he had ever been before. He was so sick he wanted to die. His stomach heaved violently, but there was nothing left to vomit up. He had been sick for days, just like the other two hundred Chinese crammed in the forward hold of the Vancouver Prize. It was no wonder they were sick. The old vessel was rising and plunging forty and fifty feet in the huge swells that came all the way from a typhoon 200 miles away near Okinawa. At each plunge, the ship crabbed twenty or thirty feet as the wind pushed the reefed stormsails over until they spilled their wind and the ship rebounded. No human being's stomach could stand such treatment for long.

1

Even the veteran seamen sailing the old square-rigger were sick, sick and almost continually on deck or in the rigging, trying to keep the ship afloat. Up where the sailors worked the pitching and yawing was much worse than in the hold where the Chinese were. At least, the sailors had fresh air and light. The fetid hold was dark and the air was saturated with the stink of vomit, urine, and feces. The screaming wind and the impact of tons of seawater on the sides of the vessel were deafening.

A continual deluge of vomit and gastric juices drained from the three-tiered makeshift bunks in the hold, pouring all the way to the filthy deck. Once there, it ran through wide cracks to the next artificial wooden deck, and on to the next. There were three "decks" constructed one on top of the other to hold the Chinese "passengers". "Steerage" was too polite a term for these accommodations.

They had been at sea for fifteen days, leaving balmy Shanghai and skating smoothly eastward across a glass-smooth sea. As the hills and shore of China disappeared over the horizon, most of the Chinese passengers cried a little. After all, they were only young men in their teens and early twenties. They knew little of the world except the villages in rural China. They had never been anywhere but home. These peasant boys had walked many, many miles to the strange, noisy, crowded city to make this passage. The magnet that drew them was the promise of work in America. They had heard that America held riches impossible to achieve in China.

It all began when travelling city men came to Huang Lee's village with news of the work in America. Poverty made the peasants' ears receptive. Huang Lee had gone to the village center with his father to hear what the city man had to say. The man passed-out handbills and said, "Workers are needed in America! Workers are scarce there. White men will pay young Chinese men's way there if you agree to work for them for three summer seasons. The work is easier than farming here in China and food is plentiful! Best of all, you will be paid one

2

American dollar per day while you are working! Think of it! That is more money for one day than you can make in a good year in this village!

Remember that they only want young, strong men. You must be at the American Labor Company in Shanghai City no later than 30 days from now. The details are in the handbills that I have passed-out. Consider it carefully! This is the chance a lifetime for Chinese men and their families!"

Huang Lee and his father walked slowly home after the city man's speech. They said nothing to each other, but each knew what the other was thinking. Dinner was ready when they arrived. As usual, it was meager. Afterward, as they sat around their little fire in the mud hut they called home, his father said, "Huang Lee, you must go to America. There you must earn money and send it home to us. We will miss you, my son, but it is too good an opportunity to miss. It is the only way I can see for us to improve how we live. You all know I am not getting younger."

Huang Lee looked at his family. His mother, sisters, and brother were all weeping and his father was very sad. They did not want him to go away, but they all knew what his father had said was true. It was their only hope for a decent life. Their little plot of land simply could not produce enough food for the whole family, no matter how hard they worked. Huang Lee said to them gravely, "I will go and make the money we need. I will send home all that I can. I love you all very much. I will do the very best that I can. I will miss you very much." They all gathered round him and hugged him and they all cried.

The next day his family helped Huang Lee prepare food and his few belongings for the journey to Shanghai. Then he and his father went to the village elders and explained their plans. From the bearded old men they learned that eight other young village peasants were going to make the same trip. They also told Huang Lee how to get to the city. They assured Huang

Lee's father that he was doing the right thing for his family and for the village. They wished Huang Lee the best of luck and good fortune.

The next morning the nine young men assembled at the village center. Their families and all the well wishers of the town joined them. The young men received small presents of food, thanked everyone, and walked briskly off down the narrow dirt road that connected the little village to the rest of the world. Those remaining behind waved, shouted encouragements, and cried until the young men disappeared. Everyone realized that they probably would never see them again.

Huang Lee and the other young men were frightened and excited as they walked down the road. They knew that it led not only to Shanghai City, but also to their destinies. It was a sobering thought! Along the way, they frequently asked fellow travelers for directions. The walk took several days. They survived on the small amounts of food they carried. At night, they slept on the ground along the road. As they neared the city, they met several other groups of young men that planned to work in America.

Group after group of such young men trickled into Shanghai City from surrounding rural areas. They showed the city folk the handbills they carried and were told to go to the offices of the American Labor Company near the docks. On the way, they shuffled through the city, gaping at its strange sights. Near the docks Huang Lee's group saw their first white man - a huge, fat, dirty American with a heavy black beard and strange eyes that looked like a pig's. They all stopped and stared, each one wondering at how the man grunted and wheezed and growled as he talked.

. At the American Labor Company's reception area, all instructions came from an officious city Chinese wearing funny western-style clothes. This self-important man ordered, "Form a line here! The doctor must check your health and condition."

The disinterested Chinese doctor gave each man a perfunctory physical examination. Then the brusque man in western clothes ordered them into another line. There, each man, in turn, made his mark on a paper contract with the Company and received a numbered tag for identification.

"Now you are to go into that warehouse building and wait until I tell you to board the ship!" shouted the Chinese man in western clothes. The young men hurried to do what he ordered.

When they were all in the building, the man in western clothes climbed up onto a crate and loudly said, "The contract that you signed pledges each of you to pay for your transport to America a out of wages that you will earn after you get there. You have also agreed to be available to the Company as laborers for three year's time. After this three-year's indenture you will be on your own. The pay is to be one American dollar per day, paid at the mines. The cost of shelter, food, and other necessities will come out of your earnings before you are paid. The work is from daylight to dark, seven days a week. You will not be paid for days that you are unable to work, of course. Now, stay here until I come to get you." Without waiting for questions the man jumped down from the crate and left the building.

At dawn the next day they were moved from the old warehouse to the ship, moored to a shabby pier. The vessel was immense. The masts seemed to reach right up into the clouds above. They were nervous and excited as they boarded the gangway. Once aboard, they were directed to the forward main deck.

There they met by a chubby middle- aged Chinese man. "I am Mr. Liu," He announced. "The Company has hired me to accompany you to America. I will see that you safely reach the Company offices at Fort Vancouver, Oregon Territory. If you have questions, about anything, during the voyage direct them to me. Do not speak to the ship's crewmembers or any of the officers. I will do that. I speak English and none of you do.

While you are on the ship, remain in your bunks in the lower part of the ship at all times unless approved to come up to this deck. Normally, when the weather is calm, you will be allowed to come up, but <u>only</u> then! I will tell you when. The exception is that you can go to the "head", or toilet, anytime. However, only four of you are allowed up at once, maximum." The head was a wooden shack on the main deck; a portion of it projected over the side of the ship). Mr. Liu stopped and pointed at the wooden structure.

He went on, "If bad weather forces the crew to seal the hatch cover, containers will be provided, below decks, for your toilet needs. Above all, you are never to get in the way of the ship's crewmen or to bother them in any way."

He continued, "Food will be provided on each of the three decks where you are housed, twice a day. There is a fresh water tap on the second tier deck, below. It will be on four hours a day. Use this fresh water only for drinking! Use seawater for cleaning. In good weather, when you are on the main deck, get seawater for cleaning by slinging those buckets (he pointed to where the buckets were) over the sides of the ship."

Mr. Liu paused for breath. Then he continued, "The Captain is the sole and final authority for anything that happens on the ship. Any stealing, fighting, insubordination, etc., will be dealt-with in the harshest terms. The Captain expects the trip to take about forty days, depending on the wind (for this was a sailing ship and an old one at that). Finally, I say again, you are to come to me, no one else, if you have questions or concerns. If you obey these simple rules, we will have a good voyage. Now go through this entry port (he pointed to a set of descending steps) into the forward hold and find yourself a bunk on one of the three decks below." With that, Mr. Liu disappeared.

A cursing American crewman motioned for them to go down the stairwell cut into the hatch cover of the forward hold. It was very dark below. They groped their way down the wooden stairs. There was no provision for light entering the hold. The only glimmer of light to see by came from a few candles.

Once in the hold, Huang Lee selected a bunk as best he could in the gloom. The bunks were triple tiered and made of lashed bamboo poles. Each bunk was two feet wide and had a rope bottom. They were packed in as tightly as possible. A man, walking sideways, could just squeeze through the aisles between them.

Finding a bunk took a lot of talking and jostling. They had never seen a "bunk" before, but they reasoned how it was used after awhile. Finally, after they had spread their meager property- none had much more than a little added clothing and a clay rice bowl to eat from- on the bunk to identify it as theirs, they drifted back up to the deck.

There they became acquainted. Most of them were from the same province. They could, consequently, speak the same dialect. They were all from poor peasant families, just like Huang Lee's. They marveled at what they had seen and at their ship and the strange men on it. They discussed the details of all that had been seen, each man adding something the others might not have noticed. A few knew, from Mr. Liu, that the first destination was to be a place called Fort Vancouver in the Oregon Territory (from there they would travel up the Columbia River to Idaho). Later they would learn that this strange word, "Idaho", meant "the land of the shining mountains" in the native Nezperce Indian language. The Indians pronounced it "EE' DA HOW."

Huang Lee, like the others, was excited enough just to be on this great ship going to mysterious America. As they talked and talked, they watched, with rapt fascination, the loading and other preparations being made for the ship's departure.

Three days out of Shanghai the weather worsened and a great storm began. They were sealed below decks so the sea could not enter the hold as it burst over the bows and ran back

7

along the deck. Below decks, the lack of space confined them to the bunks and there they lay, sick as dogs, while the ship slowly struggled through monstrous seas toward America. The wind, spawned by a distant typhoon, was nearly on the beam, so they made slow progress. The moist, fetid air of the hold, combined with the stench from vomit, urine, and excrement, was almost intolerable.

Men began to sicken and, after several days, some died. Those that passed away remained in their bunks. There was no way to move them. No one had the strength to do it anyway. Finally, after two weeks of extreme misery, the wind began to veer abaft of the beam and gradually diminish. The ship's more rapid movement through the water and the quartering wind smoothed the way of the vessel. Huang Lee began to think he might live after all!

The next day the wind had dropped more. The ocean swells stopped coming aboard over the bow. The weary crew of the Vancouver Prize removed the seal on the top of the forward hold to see if any Chinese were still alive. Surprisingly most of them were. They began to stagger up the stairs into the light; blinking, pale, and filthy, like prisoners emerging from a dungeon.

They had had no food for several days. Huang Lee knew he was starving. Mr. Liu saw to it that the cook brought buckets of boiled rice forward and served it out. Huang Lee was so hungry and relieved that he wept as he wolfed the rice down.

When they finished eating, the stronger ones carried rice to those too weak to climb the stairs to the main deck. As they recovered over the next week, the strongest cleaned up below decks with what tools and containers they had. Mr. Liu gave them buckets, a shovel, and a mop.

All the while the weather moderated. Gradually the air became warmer. At the same time, the waves became smaller, and the sun came out. Ten men had died in the forward hold of the Vancouver Prize during the storm. The bodies were brought up from below and were buried over the side with no ceremony. No one even knew them. Mr. Liu did check their numbers off the ship's manifest. The surprising thing was that so many had lived, but, then, they were young men at the height of their recuperative powers.

At Mr. Liu's urging—he was worried about the cargo he had to preserve—the Captain allowed the forward hatch cover to be fully removed to allow light and air below. Several days passed in this pleasant way while the ship sailed across the cobalt blue Pacific. The weather soured again on the forty-first day and the Chinese were put below decks again. The sky had turned cloudy and gray.

Three days later the cook and his mates, who brought the rice buckets below each day, said there was land off the larboard side of the ship and that it was still rainy and cloudy. It was the coast of America at last! Huang Lee hoped he would leave this hellhole ship in a few days' time!

Up on the quarterdeck the Captain scanned the rocky tree-covered shore through a powerful telescope. He was looking at the Quinalt headland. He was about 75 nautical miles north of the mouth of the Columbia River. He secretly congratulated himself on a good landfall. Now he had to enter the River.

Although he had done it many times before, it was always a risky proposition crossing the "bar" at the mouth of the Columbia. At the River's mouth the rip of the current along the rugged shore piled up the sand and debris that the mighty stream brought down to the sea. This barrier caused the onshore swell to mount to prodigious heights when the tide was low and the sea was running ashore. The trick was to be there at high tide and ride over the bar without scraping the ship's keel!

The Captain had to judge wind, off shore currents and the tide to bring him inshore at the right angle, speed, and time to get over the "bar". He also had to weather the headlands north

9

and south of the river. If he misjudged any of these factors, or took them lightly, the ship could be lost, and many had.

In anticipation of all this, the Captain, and his First Mate had carefully calculated and timed their approach to the River's mouth long before critical point was reached. He hoped the wind would stay as it was; slightly onshore and moderate, but not so strong that he couldn't claw off the shore if he had to. Once more, he carefully checked his table of tides and the chronometer. He had already made a good landfall and identified his position. They should be over the bar about noon on the tide and, if the wind held in the River's mouth, they would be at Fort Vancouver's docks twenty-four hours later.

While the Captain of the Vancouver Prize was fretting about crossing the Columbia Bar, Mr. Ian Campbell stoked the smoldering wood fire in the iron stove in his office. A lanky, red haired Scot, he was the American Labor Company's Agent at Fort Vancouver. When the flames began to dance to his liking, he turned and sat down on the chair at his old wooden desk. He put his feet up on it and thought about lunch.

He was hungry, having risen late enough to miss breakfast. Too much of the "water of life" last night, but it has been a good, unblended whiskey from Glen Morangie in the 'auld' country. He had not been able to resist drinking more of it than was wise. Yes, he remembered that beautiful Glen well and had visited that very distillery not ten years back. Homesick, his eyes watered in spite of himself. How in the Hell had he wound up here in soggy Oregon Territory, he mused? It was tough not dying of boredom between shipments. This Goddam gray, cold, wet climate sure didn't help!

He looked at the ticking clock on the opposite wall and was glad to see that lunchtime had arrived, finally. After carefully locking the drawer of his desk with a brass key he kept on his watchchain, he rose, donned an oiled canvas rain slicker, and walked out of the Company's rough log office building.

10

Misty rain was falling, just as it was when he had arrived earlier. Navigating gingerly over wet and slimy wooden duckboards, he managed to keep from sinking into the street's gooey mud. He headed for McGinty's Restaurant.

As he picked his way over the slippery boards, he thought about the Company and his job. He had been working for the Company for about a year now, having left the Hudson's Bay Company up in British Columbia after five years. Most of this job was easy. Just arrange to move the incoming Chinese to where they were wanted. The real work was when they arrived. He had to see they were equipped, fed, and sent along. It boiled down to a few days of frantic activity and then a long wait for another ship to arrive.

The biggest difficulty was getting reliable men to take the Chinese to the delivery point in Idaho. He had lined up a man named Barlow to take this group of Chinese to Idaho. He didn't know Barlow very well. He knew that he had been around the Territory for awhile, but he was relatively new to this Company. Barlow seemed to be bright enough all right, but he had the air of a rogue, too. Well, he had to chance it. His other 'deliverymen' were not due back in Vancouver from Idaho for sometime. It was Barlow or nobody.

In addition, the damned ship was now long overdue. The last China ship to come in had reported a big storm making up in the Pacific. The Vancouver Prize might have sunk. In any event, he knew he was ready for them, if and when they made it in. That was comforting.

The restaurant he entered was a ramshackle place run by a huge, and extremely ugly, Irishwoman, Kathleen McGinty. She looked up as he entered. Her hands were full of dirty dishes she was clearing off a table. She motioned with her head to a small table near the kitchen. Campbell removed his heavy, wet slicker, hung it on a peg near the door, and went to the crude little table and chair and sat down. The menu for the day was scrawled in

11

chalk on a board nailed to the wall next to the kitchen door. Elk stew, one of Ian's favorites, was available today!

Mrs.McGinty came by with a load of food for another table. He said to her, with an affected County Cork accent, as she passed, "Acusla, Oi'll be haavin' your foine elk stew, if you please, Daarlin' Deer."

She stopped just long enough by his table to say, "Don't be givin' me any 'a yur fake Irish dribble, you bloody murderin' Highland fugitive from justice! Just for that blarney you git the part a' the stew meat wi' the hair 'a the animal still upon it!"

"Aye," he said loudly to her disappearing back, "I'll be takin' anythin' you ha' in th' kitchen, Lassie. I'm badly starved or I would no be here!"

He really liked Mrs. McGinty and she like him. Some hot stew with real red meat in it would taste good! He was tired of clams, oysters, and especially, salmon. As he waited for his lunch, his mind drifted back to business. He wondered again when the Vancouver Prize would arrive and, for that matter, if she would at all.

Miles to the west the Vancouver Prize's Captain could clearly see where the Columbia's bar was by the way the sea's waves broke. He could feel the change in the ship's motion as it responded to the main Pacific Ocean swells and the stronger and stronger return washes from the shore. He sensed it, but was unconscious of it. After so many years at sea it was part of the overall impression. It interlocked properly. When he had this feeling, things were right. He checked the set of the sails for the hundredth time as the mate said, "Cape Disappointment is abreast the starboard beam, Sir."

The Captain nodded, but made no other answer to the obvious.

In the forward hold, the Chinese were quietly of excited. The motions of the ship were more irregular, they could tell, and they knew from what the cook had said that land was nearby. Perhaps, in a few hours or days, they would be back on solid ground and breathing fresh air! Suddenly the ship began to pitch in an erratic, jerky fashion. Huang Lee grabbed the sides of his bunk. Then the whole vessel tipped forward slightly and accelerated. Just as quickly, it settled back to level.

A little while later Mr. Liu entered the hold and announced that they were sailing on the Columbia River and should be at Fort Vancouver the next morning if the wind held. He then said, "Come on deck if you want to see America!"

Clambering eagerly up the steep stairs to the deck, they were greeted by a gray sky filled with mist and low, gray clouds. A brisk cool breeze whipped small white caps up on the water. Dark evergreen-covered hills rose from the River's edge on each side of the ship. In the distance they saw a canoe with some Indians in it. A great skein of honking geese came winging by. The wind carried a fine, misty rain. So this was America, Huang Lee thought. It was so different from home—so wet, dark, and cold!

The following morning, as soon as the ship moored alongside the rude log wharf in Vancouver, Mr. Liu began to unload the Chinese. Ian Campbell had met the ship, mounted the gangway, and solemnly shook hands with Mr. Liu and the Captain. Mr. Liu told him that, due to the storm they encountered, they had suffered ten deaths and two serious injuries enroute.

A couple of Campbell's assistants were noisily directing the disembarking Chinese to a low log warehouse building nearby. The warehouse was where they were to spend the night. Meanwhile, in the Captain's spartan cabin, Campbell paid the Captain for the delivery of the laborers. Then, with no further formalities than a parting handshake and a grunt of farewell, he and Mr. Liu left the ship and silently walked through the misty rain and mud to the Company's office building.

Once inside and free of their wet coats, Liu produced the cargo manifest papers for Campbell. Sitting down at his battered desk, the Agent carefully reviewed them. He said, "The papers all appear to be in order". He signed a receipt for the 190 men (two injured) and gave it to Liu, along with a bag of coins that constituted Liu's payment for his services. Then he said, "I have a fellow named Barlow coming in the morning for this group. Your job is done, Liu."

Mr. Liu shook Campbell's hand, and said, "Thank you, Sir. Goodbye. See you on the next trip!" He immediately threw on his coat and left the office. He hurried to the warehouse to fulfil his last duty of this shipment. Entering the crude building, he saw that the Chinese were all sitting on the dirt floor in the large front room. He knew this place well. He had been there many times before with other cargoes. He called for their attention and said, "My work is done. I am leaving you here. You will be spending the night in this room. In the morning you will be issued work clothes and the necessary equipment for the trip inland to the work site. From this point on a white man, Mr. Barlow, will be responsible for your transport. You will meet him in the morning. Tonight your dinner will be brought to this warehouse by the cook and cook's mates of the Vancouver Prize. I wish you good luck. Goodbye". With that, Mr. Liu turned and disappeared in the direction of the ship. They never saw him again.

The Chinese went about finding places in the dank warehouse to spend the night. They discovered an elderly American Indian sitting by the door. He made motions that they were to stay inside. When he talked, they could not understand. He sounded like he was just clicking his tongue, not talking.

Most of them walked strangely after so many weeks at sea. Indeed, the ground felt overly solid, even hard. Huang Lee wondered if he would always feel this way on land now. When he eventually reclined in his blanket, he felt even stranger. The floor seemed to rise and fall like the ocean's waves. Even so, it was wonderful to be able to freely move around and stretch out and to breathe the fresh, cool air. Darkness fell and a cold, penetrating chill came with it. They could hear the rain pattering steadily on the wooden roof and then dripping from the eaves into puddles on the ground outside. They were glad to be inside, cozy, and dry. It had been an exciting day. Best of all, they were in America! Soon they were all sound asleep.

# Chapter 2 - To Idaho

Jacob Barlow awoke to the pounding of rain on the cedar shake roof over his head. The cabin was pitch black, damp, and cold. "Goddamn this fuckin' endless rain!" he swore aloud to no one in particular. He snuggled down in the warm Hudson's Bay blankets to go back to sleep for awhile. Then he remembered he had to get 200 shittin' Chinese headed up the trail to Idaho, and moaned. Well, anyway it would be good to get upriver. It would be warmer and drier there, he reflected fuzzily. Then he grunted loudly and poked the snoring Clatsop woman lying next to him. "Make fire!" he ordered.

Without a word, she obediently rose, lit a candle, and began to split the red cedar kindling needed to start a fire. Barlow pulled the heavy wool trade blanket up to his chin. Chink (his Chinese assistant and interpreter) had better have the damned wagon and supplies ready to go or there would be Hell to pay, he thought! The fire began to crackle and pop. Flickering firelight illuminated the inside of the small log cabin. The Indian woman climbed back into bed beside him to wait for the fire to warm the room. God she stinks, he thought! These Clatsops and Chinooks always stink like the half-rotten salmon they eat. He liked the NezPerce women up in Idaho better. They smelled better and didn't flatten their heads like the Clatsops did. These damned fools thought it made them beautiful! He wiggled his toes, cleared his throat, and, in spite of the burning cedar's noisy crackling from the hearth, drifted back to sleep.

Chin Pang was already drinking his second a cup of tea when Ian Campbell arrived at the Company office. Chin, who was called "Chink" by his boss, Jacob Barlow, quickly jumped up, poured a steaming cup of tea for Campbell, and handed it to him. Then, in heavily accented Americanized English, he said to him, " Mr. Campbell, I have seen to breakfast for the Chinese cargo just as you ordered. They should be finished by now"

Campbell grunted recognition and slouched into a chair by the stove. With both cold hands curled around the steaming tea mug, he slowly sipped its contents. After warming up some, he went over to his desk. He unlocked the center drawer, opened it, reached in, and drew out a large iron key. He tossed the key to Chin and said, "You need to issue each of the new Chinese a set of work clothes and a "pack" for the trip."

Chin did not move, for he knew that he needed some other things to get the men ready to go. So did Campbell.

Campbell thumbed through the papers that had come with the cargo. He found the manifest list with the name and number for each Chinese. He gave the list and a pencil to Chin. "Be sure that each of 'em signs for his goods, Chin", he said with emphasis. Chin, who knew this exercise by heart, assured him that he would, gulped down the last of his tea, and hurried out to the warehouse.

When his turn came, Huang Lee marked an "X" where Chin Lee pointed on a paper and walked away with his clothes and "pack". Returning to where he had slept on the floor the night before, he examined his new possessions. There was a padded heavy cotton work coat and corresponding work pants, the same as they used in China, a new pair of the type of heavy work sandals he was already familiar with, and the "pack". The pack contained two wool blankets, two cotton shirts from China, a large tin cup, a knife, and a few other items. Since the weather was cool, but not severe, he decided to wear the coat today and keep the heavy pants for later. As Mr. Chin had suggested, he rolled everything he was not wearing into the blankets in a tube-like fashion. He then tied each end of the tube with a piece of hemp rope that had been provided. This done, he could easily sling the circle of rolled blanket and rope across his shoulders to carry it. He was ready. Soon the others were too.

Mr. Chin, returning to the Company office, saw that Mr. Barlow had arrived and was drinking tea with Mr. Campbell. Barlow looked up at him and said, "They ready Chink?"

Mr. Chin nodded and said, "Yes, Boss".

"The supplies and camp gear?" Barlow added.

Mr. Chin nodded 'yes' again.

"Then get everything in the lugger and let's get outta this fuckin' swamp while we have the up-river wind!" Barlow said, dismissing him. When Chin was gone Barlow turned to Campbell and said, "Chink is pretty good at this now that he knows the routine."

Campbell, hugely unimpressed, gave Barlow the manifest and related account book. Then he had him make his mark for the cargo, supplies, and the pack stock. He also handed him 25 U.S. silver dollars for financial necessities along the way. "You are to deliver these Chinese to Mr. Edward Johnson at Moose City on the North Fork of the Clearwater." Campbell said. "Be sure he gets the manifest and the account book, too. Most important, be sure he pays you 20 dollars in gold for each Chinese laborer as agreed!"

Barlow grunted assent. Hell, he knew what to do. He sure as Hell didn't need any guff this morning from a dumb horse's ass like Campbell. Thrusting the papers and money into the parfleche at his side, he said, "See ya' in about six weeks, Ian! Stay dry if ya' can and don't catch a dose screwin' the squaws around here." Suppressing a chortle, he rose and lumbered out the door, slamming it loudly behind him.

18

Campbell looked after him. He sometimes wondered if Barlow was in the human race. He quickly opened a window to air out the office. Damn that man stank!

Two days later Barlow, Chin, the Chinese, and all their supplies, disembarked from the river lugger "Celilo" at the head of the Columbia Gorge at a place called "The Dalles". Here the River became unnavigable because of the huge Celilo Falls just above the town. Chin and Barlow mantied up the supplies for the trip and loaded the canvas-covered parcels onto mules the Company kept at the Dalles. Then they saddled their horses and headed up river. The Chinese and the mules trailed in a long line behind.

It was much warmer and drier now that they were east of the crest of the Cascade Range. They climbed a steep, grassy sidehill up out of the Gorge and traveled east through ponderosa pine covered highlands south of the River's main canyon. Soon they left the trees behind. They were now in dry steppe country. The ground was covered with grass, sage, and prickly pear cactus. That evening they stopped at a much used camping ground, cooked a meal, ate it, and then went to sleep under the stars. Coyotes' howling bothered the Chinese some. The howls were entirely new to them.

Soon the walking, stopping, eating, sleeping cycle became familiar and habitual. After a few days, the broad Columbia turned north abruptly. They left it and began to parallel the tributary Snake River that came from due east. After several days more hard travelling up and down, across dry, rocky side canyons that fed into the Snake, they came to a broad valley. Here the Snake turned straight south. The smaller Clearwater River came in from the east. At the Rivers' junction was a small settlement named Lewiston, so called because Lewis and Clark had come down the Clearwater and camped nearby in 1805. It was no more than a trading post for the surrounding

19

Indian tribes and a supply dump for the miners working in the backcountry, but it was the "Capital" of the Idaho Territory.

Barlow had Chink settle the Company party into a campsite in the shady groves of cottonwood trees along the Clearwater. Then he walked over to the crude log trading post at the center of the village. Several Nezperce Indians were gathered outside the post. One of them, a tall man with gray strands in his dark black hair, waved to Barlow as he approached and said in an elevated monotone, "Barlow! Barlow! How! How! Good see you, Barlow!"

Barlow smiled and shook the Indian's hand, saying, "How! How! Are you going to Moose City with me this time, Yellow Bear?"

The Indian looked sad and said, "No, Barlow. I much sick. Food gives me no strength. My oldest son, Twisted Grass, will go with you."

"I am sorry you cannot go. I hope you get well soon, old friend. I will be glad to have Twisted Hair along, though," Barlow said. "Tell him we leave tomorrow at sunup." He turned from the Indian, went into the post, and sat down, with a grunt, at a crude table in one corner of the grubby room.

The heavily bearded owner took a glass and a bottle from a rude backbar, and put them on the table in front of Barlow. "How many this time?" he asked.

"One-ninety", said Barlow, as he downed a shot of the liquid from the bottle. His breath caught in his throat. He wheezed and shivered involuntarily all over. When he could talk again he gasped, "Goddamn it, Murdock, where in the Hell do you find this panther piss?"

"Straight out of the finest distilleries in old Kentucky! It is specially distilled and bottled for my high-tone establishment!" the owner seriously replied as he carefully wiped the only other glass he owned with a filthy rag.

20

That doesn't deserve a response, Barlow decided. He poured himself another belt. Carefully sipping the whiskey, he leaned back and considered the rest of the trip ahead. Twisted Grass would be a good man to have along. It got rough from here on and choosing a wrong path could cost a party days of backtracking. Besides, paying a Nezperce guide was good business even if he was not needed, just to have the friendship of the tribe. The NezPerce were good people, Barlow reflected, — handsome and honest, for Indians. They had been friendly to Lewis and Clark a long time ago and to all white men around here, right up to today. Usually, on the return trip, he would stay with them for a week or so down around Ahsahka. It was a beautiful place. One old Indian there had told him that he had watched Lewis and Clark's men make yellow pine log canoes and paddle off down the River to the Pacific. Yes, the NezPerce had been good to him the last three years. They had made his job taking supplies, miners, and Chinese laborers into the Idaho backcountry a lot easier. He liked them. He hoped that the damned greedy miners didn't rile them up too much and make 'em mean.

Down by the River the Chinese were finished setting up camp. It had become a simple and rapid ritual. Huang Lee had toughened up. So had the others. He had softened physically during the long and rough voyage across the Pacific. Now the constant hiking, fresh air, plentiful food, and the powers of youth had brought all the Chinese back to a good state of fitness. The trip from Fort Vancouver had been full of wonder and adventure. They had seen strange wild animals and a huge country nearly devoid of people except for the Indians and their strange spotted-rump horses. It was all marvelous to the wide-eyed youths. So different from home! They all loved to eat the rich salmon trout that Mr. Chin bought from the Indians. Cooked over a fire and mixed with their rice ration the fish was delicious! Mr. Chin had told them that the hard part of the trip was coming now. They would have to go up into the mountains where the gold mines were. He told them it would be colder and wetter. Undeterred, Huang Lee and the others were eager to get to work. The sooner they could earn money, the sooner they could send some home to their families. They also had other thoughts. They had seen several "free" Chinese in Fort Vancouver. These Chinese were free of the indenture that had paid their way to America. A Chinese visitor in Vancouver had told them that many Chinese had become businessmen here and some worked for others, like Mr. Chin did for Barlow. What surprised the newcomers the most was when he told them that some Chinese were prospectors and miners in their own right. Some had become very rich mining gold! Alerted to this, Huang Lee noted several Chinese merchants at the Dalles and in Lewiston. Indeed, he saw that Lewiston had a small community of Chinese. Some of them had settled on rich land near the Clearwater River. Ever the farmer's son, he saw they had extensive, rich vegetable gardens!

At dawn the next morning, the party set out again up the Clearwater. They would be in the drainage of this River from now on, Mr. Chin said. The sun warmed them and they were soon sweating freely as they climbed out of the River canyon a few miles east of Lewiston. They emerged on a huge prairie to the south of the River. On the horizon to the east, north, and south, were high mountaintops covered with dark evergreen trees and patches of snow. Mr. Chin said that these Mountains were called the "Bitterroot's" because of the bitter taste of an edible plant root that grew in the area. He went on to say that they would be living and working in the Bitterroot Mountains.

Huang Lee noticed a young Indian was travelling with them. He rode a beautiful horse with strange white and black spots across its rump. Huang Lee had noticed these markings on some other Indian ponies, too. The Indian rode with Mr. Barlow. They talked a lot in a strange Indian tongue and using hand motions.

After a few days progress east, they left the prairie and descended a brushy canyon to the River again. The River split here into two forks. They waded across a shallow, wide ford to the north side of the main branch. Mr. Chin called the place "Ahsahka". Upstream a few miles more, at the mouth of a creek coming out of a steep, deep canyon to the north, was a tent town. It was called "Orofino". They camped there.

That night, around a roaring bonfire, Mr. Chin explained, "Orofino means "fine gold" in Spanish, one of the languages of the white man. Several years ago, some miners found very fine gold dust here in the creek. It was the first gold discovery in the Clearwater. From here, other miners went up into the Bitterroot Mountains looking for the source of the gold at Orofino. They set up mines in the headwaters of the River. It is these mines where you will be working. Orofino is the last settlement you will see. From here on we will be travelling through real wilderness."

It was during a day's rest at Orofino that they first saw gold. It was a heavy dust kept in small leather bags carefully tied shut with leather thongs. Dirty, rough-looking men paid for supplies and whiskey with it. The merchants used balance beam scales to weigh out small amounts of the precious stuff. The miners were fierce, bearded fellows who talked loud and gestured wildly. They carried big knives at their sides and wore pistols in belts around their waists. The Chinese stayed out of their way!

There was a constant procession of mule strings in and out of town: those headed for the mines loaded with supplies, and those coming out of the backcountry loaded with small iron-bound wooden boxes full of gold dust. That night, from their camp along the River, the Chinese could hear shouting and faint sounds of music from the town. Twice there were gunshots; the shots did not interrupt the shouting and the music.

While fog was still thick in the valley bottom the next morning, they broke camp and headed up a wide, heavily used trail that climbed a steep ridge to the northeast of Orofino. After climbing up grass-covered slopes and across brush-filled draws, they emerged onto a flat, grassy prairie. The next day they crossed it all day in a northeasterly direction. Gradually, clumps of trees became more frequent and, by that evening, they were in a level forest of scrubby pines. Another day brought them into a land of ridges and ravines. Only occasional thickets of low shrubs broke the heavy evergreen forest. Soon they were continually either climbing or descending over very broken, steep ground.

The air was much cooler. They caught sight or an occasional patch of unmelted snow on north slopes although this was late July. The mountains seem endless. From the high ridges they crossed all they could see for miles was a series of identical mountains in all directions.

The next morning there was frost on the grass in the small meadow where they camped. The air did not warm up until nearly noon. Mr. Chin told them that this was normal in the canyons of the Bitterroots. Huang Lee wondered what winter must be like in this wild place.

During the day, they often met mule strings going in the other direction. All the animals were loaded with small ironbound gold boxes. Each string had several tough-looking men with it. The men were always armed to the teeth.

On the fifth day in the mountains, they camped on a mid-slope bench. The area had been burned by a recent wildfire. The lack of trees allowed them to see some distance to the east up a deep and magnificently wooded canyon. Mr. Chin noticed them looking into the canyon and he said, "That is the main canyon of the North Fork of the Clearwater River. Our destination is near the head of the it, twenty-five miles away." They were happy to hear this. Everyone was growing weary of arduous travel.

A little later, after they had set up camp, two rough looking white strangers rode in from the east. They were also employees of the American Labor Company. Their names were Matthew Brown and Jerome Whittaker. Barlow knew them well. Tethering their horses nearby, the men sauntered to Barlow's campfire. As they walked up Barlow said, "Sit. Coffee?"

"Sure", said Brown, and both men sat down on the ground by the fire. Barlow filled two tin cups and handed them over.

After sipping the steaming coffee for awhile, Whittaker said, "Any trouble?"

Barlow responded, "No, but Swede Olson got shot dead three days ago in Orofino. His grip is with the Company man there. You probably should take it down to Vancouver to Campbell to be sure accounts are straight. Be sure to tell him to let Swede's folks know."

"Too bad. 'Ol Swede was a good un'," Brown murmured.

"They need your Chinamen at Moose City real bad," said Whittaker. "The buggers keep dyin' off and they're short a' help. The pickin's is still there fur the takin'. All's they need is water at the claims to wash the gravel out."

"How bad do they need 'em?" Barlow said, raising his head for the first time since they began.

"Well, I heared they was down ta' 500 diggers. I figgur they need 'bout 'a thousand to take out what they want to by winter. I reckon you could ask $35 bucks a head and get it, easy," said Brown.

"What about Johnson?" said Barlow, alluding to the contractor that the Company had a deal with for this group of Chinese. "He still there?"

"Still there. Catshit mean. He'll be expectin' us tuh' come through, as promised." Whittaker said, grinning.

"That's all good to know. Thanks", said Barlow. "Come and have some grub. Shot an elk today. Got some fine steaks cookin'!"

Early the next morning they broke camp and headed east again. Barlow waved to Whittaker and Brown as they rode out of sight going the opposite direction. Very late in the day they descended to a broad flat alongside the North Fork where a tributary came into the River from the east. They spent the night on the lush flat.

In the morning they went up the smaller, easterly stream Its rocky shoreline soon narrowed to nothing and the trail left the river and climbed the steep canyon wall. Huang Lee noticed the remains of several mules far below in the canyon bottom. The trail snaked along a series of narrow benches until the canyon widened again. They descended to the canyon's bottom. By this time, it was already getting dark in the deep, rocky canyon.

They camped on a small rocky flat where another, smaller stream came in from the north. "That's Moose Creek", Mr. Chin confided to them over dinner, "and a half a day up that Creek is your destination". Huang Lee heard this. He was relieved. It seemed like he had been traveling forever!

# Chapter 3 - Moose City

Moose City would not have been name a "city" anywhere in the world except in a howling wilderness like the Bitterroot Mountains of the 1860's. Nevertheless, at this place and at this time, only four years after end of the Civil War, its existence was a miracle. It had sprung up in just about a year, beginning in the summer of 1868. Two prospectors, Tom O'Brien and Bill Shapard, had discovered rich placer gold deposits on Moose Creek that summer. When they eventually took their accumulation of gold dust to Lewiston to "cash in", the word spread. A mad stampede to Moose City, and its general area, ensued. Many of the miners had been at earlier Idaho strikes and some of the old timers had even been in on the California rush before the War. For many of them, such stampedes had become a way of life. In 1869, with all the feverish activity at this place, it was hard to imagine that Moose City would be a ghost town in just a few years.

The town was not much to look at, to put it mildly. On a semi-flat area, clearings had been hacked into a wet, dense evergreen forest. Huge western red cedar and grand fir trees grew everywhere around the clearing. Several small streams converged nearby to form Moose Creek. The "structures" of the city were mostly tents placed on raised earthen platforms. There were a few log buildings. A smattering of these had floors of split logs. There was a store, a jail, saloon, stable, blacksmith's shop and forge, and two canvas hotels of sorts. That was city "center". About 600 men and 5 tough women called it home. Up the several small creeks that converged near the "city", miner's tent camps and claims ran for miles.

At "city center" mud was a foot deep and the stench of pit toilets and mule dung hung in the air. Mule strings constantly came and went. Dirty, bearded men hurried back and forth on errands. A banjo twanged in the saloon. Four filthy men, standing in the mud in front it, were arguing loudly. The whole place seethed with activity and vitality.

When the American Labor Company party arrived, Barlow had Chink put the Chinese in a cleared area near the corrals and a creek. Then he walked wearily over to store. The "store" was the largest, most permanent structure in Moose City. The roof was made of split red cedar shakes. The walls were a mixture of logs, cedar shakes, and canvas. The floor was puncheon with canvas stretched over it. It was big enough to house a fair collection of canned goods and hardware. There was a rack of soft goods, too. At one side stood an imposing black safe and a prominent set of balance beam scales for weighing gold. At the makeshift counter stood the proprietor, Mr. Levitz. He was one of the few people in Moose City who was really getting rich.

"Well, hello, Barlow!" Levitz said as Barlow entered. "Everyone will be glad to see you. They badly need the Chinese laborers you undoubtedly brought!"

"Seen Johnson lately?" Barlow asked.

"Yeah, just yesterday he was in and bought some grub," replied Levitz, "and he asked about you—wanted to know if the laborers had arrived yet."

"He still up in Prospect Gulch?" Barlow asked.

Levitz replied, "Yep".

Barlow nodded, turned, and left the store. He walked back over to the corral area to talk to Chin. "Chink, bed 'em down for the night over there nearer the creek and keep the locals away from 'em", he said in a hushed tone. "Johnson's not in town so I'll have to look him up tomorrow if he doesn't show tonight. I'm goin' to get a drink." Without waiting for an answer from Chin, Barlow turned and strode over to the crowded canvas covered "saloon". He entered through the open tent flap, found an empty chair, and ordered a whiskey. Less than an hour later a tall, dark, lean, wolf-like man entered, saw Barlow, and came to sit down by him.

"Whiskey for me and bring my friend, here, another," the wolfish man yelled to the barkeep over the drone of others' talk. He then turned to Barlow and said, leaning forward on the table and speaking confidentially, "Jesus, you took your time, Barlow! I'm down to 200 Chinamen and half of them are sick with the grippe. I have contracts with these miners to get water to their claims. I'm late and they are plenty pissed-off! Did you bring the shovels and picks for them, too? I suppose you stopped to fuck every squaw along the way!"

Barlow frowned, then slowly leaned forward and brought his nose within four inches of Johnson's. In a loud rasping whisper he said, "Johnson, you may run a lot of Chinamen around like animals here, but, if you try to pull that crap on me I'll kick the livin' shit outta' you right here and right now. By any chance in Creepin' Jesus Hell, can you possibly remember how far it is from Vancouver to this God-forsaken pisshole?"

Johnson swallowed, looked down, away, and then back at Barlow. He licked his lips, took a short swig of whiskey and said, "Well, yeah. I do. Sorry. Do you have the full 200?"

"No, 190. Ten died on the ship in a storm," said Barlow as he leaned back to his former relaxed position. "I got the tools too. I figure you owe the Company 7, 500 dollars, gold. I want to leave in the morning."

Johnson, half into a swallow of whiskey, gagged and choked. Then he reared back and shouted, "Where in the Hell did you come up with that figure? I have a contract with the

Company! Twenty dollars a head! Let's see, that's 3800 bucks. With the tools at $5.00 each that's another $950, so I owe the Company 4,750 bucks, not any friggin' 7,500!"

Barlow took a small sip from his glass and looked hard into Johnson's bulging eyes. He had him, he thought! "Well, you are right about the Company agreement, but I figure I will have a surcharge for me this time. It's 10 dollars per head and 5 dollars per tool. I figure fall's commin', and you are screwed if you don't get the Chinks now. The nearest law is a long, long way away. I'm not gettin any younger or richer and I'm sick and tired of sleepin' on the ground like a savage so assholes like you and Levitz will be able to live in luxury the rest of your lives."

Johnson jumped up, knocking his chair over backwards, wildly waved his arms, and shrieked, "That's Goddamn highway robbery! A violation of the contract I have with your Company, Barlow!" All talk stopped in the saloon and everyone was looking at Johnson and Barlow.

"Take it or leave it," said Barlow evenly. He rose from his chair and walked toward the door. Over his shoulder he said, "Have the gold here in the morning. If you don't show, I'll sell the Chink laborers to the miners for 35 bucks each at noon."

Johnson stared open mouthed at the receding back of Barlow until he disappeared behind the tent flap. That low life Sonofabitch, he thought! Extortion was what it was! Well, we'll see Mr. "High and Mighty" Barlow! We'll see! Without a word he quickly paid for the drinks, left the saloon, and vanished into Moose City's chilly, gathering twilight.

Barlow left the saloon and walked up to the campfire where Chink and Twisted Grass were sitting. The Chinese were gathered around several other nearby fires. Squatting by the fire, Barlow said, "Chink, you and Twisted Hair keep a sharp eye out for trouble after dark. Johnson doesn't want to pay the Company price and I figure he might try to take 'em from us later on." With that he rolled in his blankets and, shortly, began to snore.

Twisted Hair looked intently at Chin and said "I be near, no worry". He silently disappeared into the darkness away from the fires.

Chin did worry. He assembled all of the Chinese and told them, "Some men here would like to steal you and not pay the Company. They may come in the dark tonight. We must not let this happen so you and the Company will be paid what is right. I am going to post sentries. If they sound the alarm, rise quickly and go to them and help them defend the camp." Then, selecting ten men from among the group, he told them, "You ten are the watchmen for the camp tonight. Be alert and make a big noise if you see or hear intruders! We all will come quickly to help if you do!" He then had the ten get their blankets and packs and motioned them to come with him. He placed them around the perimeter of the camp, beyond the light of the fires and spaced-out, so the whole perimeter was watched. Mr. Chin then went back to his fire, wrapped a blanket around his shoulders, and drank some coffee. He would stay awake throughout the night.

Huang Lee was one of the sentries. He was scared to death and he and the others did not like this place. He sat down with his back to a large tree and wrapped a blanket around himself to keep off the chill. The noises from the saloon gradually died away. Moose City settled down for the night. The campfires slowly died down. All the Chinese, except the "sentries" and Mr. Chin, were soon asleep. An owl hooted in the forest and Huang could hear the down-canyon night breeze rustle the tops of the huge trees around him. When he became drowsy, he kept himself awake by pinching the tender skin on the inside of his upper arms. Somewhere in the woods two trees rubbed together as the breeze flowed through them. It sounded like a human grunt, or so Huang thought. Otherwise, it was very quiet except for the regular gurgle of the nearby streams.

Huang passed the time randomly reviewing the events of the trip he had just completed. This world was so different from the one he had known. The white men were generally crude and cruel, but rich and fat. The rice that they had had on the ship was very good and he had had all he wanted for the first time in his life. The bunks had been so much better than his straw pallet on the floor at home. Still, he missed his family, especially his sister, Nee Loo. She was a year younger than he was. They had been very close all their lives. He hoped she was all right. He hoped that they all were all right. He really missed them. He missed home. He wished that he had money to send to them right now. He would soon. Mr. Chin had said so.

His thoughts wandered to Mr. Barlow. He was a strange man. He seemed to hate what he did and the Chinese, but he always was the one who forcefully protected the group and he settled disturbances fairly. All the Chinese respected him, even if they did not understand what he said. Huang noticed the moon was three-fourths of the way across the night sky. It should be light in awhile. He drifted back to his reverie. The biggest surprise in America had been the "free" Chinese. It seemed they could go anywhere and do anything that they wanted-to, unlike at home. He had seen several groups of Chinese freely come and go here at Moose City already. Then he remembered the gardeners at Lewiston. He had envied them the rich bottomland they were tilling along the River. The vegetables they were growing looked magnificent. He wondered if he could have a claim of his own and mine his own gold someday. He wondered if he could buy good land like those men he had seen working in their fields in Lewiston.

Johnson had invited ten tough miners to his tent in Prospect Gulch that evening. They were anxious men who needed to get water to their sluice boxes as soon as possible. They understood that they would not get it unless they helped Johnson. Johnson had asked them over early that evening and explained the situation. They had shared several of bottles of whiskey in his large tent. Then they played a little penny-ante poker. During the game, Johnson detailed the interaction he and Barlow had earlier that day. He told them he could not afford the extra money for the Chinese and that Barlow planned to sell the

32

laborer's services on the open market tomorrow. This meant the men in the tent would not get the water they needed to sluice their paydirt. The whiskey bottles went around again. The men decided to hold the Company to its promise. They also decided to kill Barlow, the thief and brigand, and take the Chinese by force. By this time it was getting late. They agreed to return to their respective camps, arm themselves, and meet back at Johnson's in about an hour.

When they were all reassembled and fortified with another bottle of rotgut whiskey, they trooped down Prospect Gulch toward Moose City. They planned to approach Barlow's camp from the uphill side, with the town to their left, to minimize the chance of shooting anyone in town by accident. As they neared Barlow's camp they deployed in a rough semi-circle that was about the width of the campsite below. Then they crept slowly and, they thought, stealthily, down the hill.

Barlow woke with a jump. There was a hand on his shoulder and one over his mouth. He heard Twisted Grass whisper, "Men come down creek to here."

The hand came away from his mouth and Barlow whispered back, "How many?"

Twisted Grass held up both ands to signify ten men.

Barlow nodded and said, "You go 'round the right side and I will go 'round to the left. Let's run 'em off without killin' any if we can." Without another word between them, the two men silently rose and left the camp in opposite directions.

Huang Lee and the two other "sentries" nearest him heard them coming first. They quickly rose and ran into the camp yelling, "Men coming! Get ready to fight!" The Chinese sprang to their feet, facing the direction Huang pointed-to. A prolonged scream came from the darkness; then a gunshot. Someone yelled in the darkness, "Get Owens. He's been hit!" There was a great deal of rustling and crashing about in the dark bushes and sounds of men running, falling down, and cussing. The sounds gradually became fainter and then completely died away. The Chinese had never moved.

"Is it over?" asked Huang.

From the back of the group Mr. Chin said, "Yes. Go back to sleep now."

They went back to their blankets and were soon asleep. Several minutes later Twisted Hair and Barlow silently emerged from the shadows and sat down by Barlow's fire. "Twisted Hair, you earned your keep tonight," Barlow said softly, smiling at the Indian.

Twisted Hair nodded slowly and seriously. "Hard for white man to walk with arrow in butt," he said in a low monotone. Barlow chuckled for awhile at that and even Twisted Hair cracked a little smile, in spite of himself. Then they both rolled in their blankets and went to sleep.

They awakened to Mr. Chin's usual call of, "Breakfast ready, Mr. Barlow!" Soon they were eating hot flapjacks and drinking scalding coffee. Mr. Chin and Barlow made plans for the necessary mule shoeing to be done for the return trip to the Dalles. Barlow then walked over to the store, entered, and asked Levitz, "Anything you want me to haul outta here? I plan on leaving this afternoon."

Levitz looked up from some paperwork he was doing and said, "Not that I know of. No pelts, bodies, or gold right now, but I'll ask around to be sure. By the way, what was that ruckus early this morning?"

"Just a bear looking for scraps," replied Barlow.

"Well, it sure sounded like a big 'un!" said Levitz, with a slight smile. "I never heard a bear scream bloody murder or cuss like that, neither!"

Well, funny things happen in the woods", Barlow laconically responded and he turned and left the store.

Levitz looked back at his inventory sheet, but he was thinking that he would soon hear the whole story in the saloon from Shorty Simmons, the camp's busy body.

About eleven o'clock, a one armed Chinese man, who served as Johnson's assistant and interpreter, found Barlow busy mending his riding bridle. In Pidgin English, he asked Barlow to come to the saloon where Mr. Johnson was waiting for him.

"Tell him I will be there in a few minutes," said Barlow, without even looking up. After the man had left, Barlow laid down the bridle and methodically checked his pistol, making sure all the cylinders were loaded and the percussion caps in place. He then stood up, put the pistol in his belt, and walked over to the saloon. Johnson was sitting at a table, alone. He motioned to Barlow to come over and sit down. He pushed a bottle of whiskey and a glass across the table as Barlow sat down.

"Mornin. It's early, but have a drink anyway," he said, with a manner of a friendly, but scared, dog.

Barlow said, "Don't mind if I do", and poured himself a glassful.

Johnson allowed time for Barlow to sip the drink and said, "Barlow, I know you're taking advantage of me on the price for these Chinese, but I need them bad, so I'm prepared to pay what you asked-for. I don't like it. I plan to tell the Company what you are doing, but for right now you have me over a barrel."

Barlow looked up at him and said, "Good. Where's the gold?"

"In the safe in Levitz' store", said Johnson.

Barlow said, "All right, let's go and get it. You can sign for the Chinese at the same time. I have the papers with me."

35

They quickly finished their whiskies and went out the door.

A little later, they were both standing outside the store watching Chin and Twisted Hair carry a small, heavy, wooden box toward Barlow's camp. "I'll pick up the Chinese in about an hour," said Johnson.

"Fine", said Barlow. Johnson stuck out his hand to shake. Barlow took it and held it while he delivered a crushing left to Johnson's chin. Johnson went down into the muddy street like a pole-axed ox. Barlow waited for Johnson's senses to return and then pulled him to his feet by his shirtfront. With his nose to Johnson's, Barlow growled, "You try to bushwhack me again, you chickenshit Sonofabitch, and I'll kill you! Got that? As for squealing to the Company about this deal, go right ahead. I'll see you go up for attempted murder!"

Johnson feebly nodded that he understood and slumped back to the mud as Barlow let him go. Jacob Barlow stalked away without a backward look.

# Chapter 4 - The Work

Huang Lee was in a long line of Chinese slowly winding out of Johnson's work camp in Prospect Gulch. Each carried a shovel or a pick. A few had axes for chopping down trees. As they walked, the early morning sun shot rays of light down through the branches of the giant trees around them. Although it was August in the Bitterroots, Huang had seen frost on the grass that morning at their camp in the bottom of the Gulch. When they reached the ridge above, the air gradually became warmer and the sun's rays warmed their shoulders. This was the fifth day on the job for the new arrivals. They were sore, and the sun's rays were a balm to their sore muscles.

They walked into the neighboring Deception Creek drainage. Deception Creek contained the water destined for the sluices of several miner's claims. Their job was to dig the contouring ditches that would bring the needed water to the placer mines in the Gulch. The ditches had to be three feet deep and two feet wide at the bottom.

One Arm, the Chinese amputee foreman, who oversaw the work for Mr. Johnson, had explained to them that the water was essential to the mining operations and that part of Mr. Johnson's share of the gold that came from the miner's water driven sluices was what paid their wages. He also explained how the ditches had to meet certain standards of size and smoothness, or Mr. Johnson, and they, would not be paid for the work. The work was hard, but no harder than they were used to at home. One Arm coached them. Each day passed, he had to coach less to get the ditch quality that was needed. They were learning fast. Other Chinese men, who were more experienced at this work, provided helpful hints to the newcomers about how to work faster and with less effort.

They were being fed well too, by their austere standards. They had rice three times a day and were issued dried salmon trout and salt to go with it. They occasionally were given some wheat flour and salt pork or bacon. There was little wild game in the area except an occasional grouse, so wild meat was a rarity. Once or twice a week they brewed a huge kettle of green tea and drank it, with happiness and memories of home. They slept in lean-to's they had made of sapling poles and evergreen boughs. These were not water proof, of course, but the crude shelters broke the cold night breeze and kept the frost away. There was little rain to worry about this time of year in the Bitterroots.

One Arm made a mark in the pay-book by each man's number for each day worked. If a man could not work for some reason, he did not get a mark for that day. They could take Sundays off if they wanted-to, but, since the work and the pay were available, they all worked on Sunday. To them it was another day.

A favorite discussion topic among them was how the money they were earning would be used. Each man kept a total of the days he had worked and toted up the money that he had coming. Their talk and calculations indicated that each would gross about 70-80 dollars by the time winter came. Out of this, they had to pay Mr. Johnson for their transport, clothes, packs, and food. About the size of these expenses, they had little idea, but One Arm assured them that they would be treated fairly. Most estimated they should enter the winter with 50 American dollars. If true, it was a tremendous amount of money by their standards.

Huang Lee knew that he had to send most of his earnings home, but he also knew that he had to reserve enough to survive the coming winter. After dinner one evening One Arm had said to them all, "When and if you take the trip home it will cost each of view about fifty dollars, depending on the ship and the Captain you go with. Now, winter weather will force us out of the Bitterroots in two or three months. Remember, when you send money home this fall, to save enough so you can live until the work season comes again in the spring."

The result of all this was that these Chinese men felt good about what they were doing. They were young and strong. They worked hard and slept the sound sleep of exhausted young men. Although sanitation was primitive, they were remarkably resistant to the dysentery and influenza that sickened many of the miners. Outside of a cut or a broken bone here or there, they were healthy.

It was apparent to Huang Lee that what the city man had said in his village was true. With luck, in three year's time he would be able to return to China rich, by peasant standards. Each day he made soil, rocks, and tree roots fly from the ditches. So did the others. In a remarkably brief time, water from a Creek would flow through a new ditch to the waiting sluice boxes. Then, somewhere in Prospect Gulch, the miners would process the gold bearing sand and gravel had been deposited by an ancient river millions of years before. Usually, when the water arrived, the miners ran the sluices all day. Then, all night, by the light of wooden torches. Some miners rented Chinese labor from Mr. Johnson to accelerate the movement of the "paydirt" from the banks and streambeds to the sluice boxes.

All summer, bags of gold dust from the workings in the area poured into Moose City. Mr. Levitz assayed it, weighed it, and credited it to the miner it belonged-to. Mule trains, as Huang Lee saw on the trip up River, carried the bags of gold, in strongboxes, overland to the coast. Between transfers to Moose City, the bags of gold accumulated in the miner's camps.

Where more than one miner worked a claim, which was the normal case, each one had a secret cache with his share in it. All this wealth in and around the claims, coupled with long and hard workdays, made for short tempers and suspicions among the miners. These tensions sometimes erupted into fights and outright murders. In addition, the claims were constantly changing hands as one owner decided to leave and another arrived. Free Chinese had made numerous claims in the area, but they supposedly had no legal right to them, not being white men. Bands of whites often took over Chinese claims. The free Chinese only held their claims by being able to present overwhelming numbers to blunt the white's take over attempts

Moose City had a thriving business in claim registrations, sales and exchanges. There were also constant fights about where boundaries of claims were, including many accusations of moving boundary stakes surreptitiously. In the middle of all this fuss and flux, the contract Chinese of the American Labor Company were an omnipresent, stable commodity of production. Most Chinese never had a chance to be "bitten by the gold bug" and were just happy to have good work for good wages. They viewed the arguments, fights, and general tumult of the miners in the camps with astonishment and, as they became used to it, tolerance.

The miners, for their part, considered the Chinese, both free and contract, as little better than dumb animals capable of hard work, but little other human activity. If a Chinese happened to be shot in the middle of a ruckus, little was thought of it, except to settle a property account with Johnson.

All this new knowledge was coursing through Huang's mind as they walked to the job on another fine, sunny day. When they arrived where the ditch was to be extended, the workers distributed themselves out along the line. Without ceremony, they began digging. They worked steadily and with great economy of motion. The work went somewhat slowly at first, until their muscles warmed fully, and then to settled into a faster rhythmic, regular pace; a pace that they would sustain throughout the day. Periodically, as a stretch of ditch was deemed complete by One Arm, the whole crew moved to the next stretch of ditch line to be constructed. So it continued day in and day out through the rest of August and into September.

The fall of the year brought rain showers and colder temperatures to the Bitterroot country. Huang Lee began to wear the heavy pair of padded work pants he had been issued in Fort Vancouver. Most days he wore the heavy coat too. On especially wet or cold nights the men kept bonfires going all night in front of their lean-tos. From somewhere, One Arm provided them with pieces of tarred canvas. They put these over the tops of the lean-to's to keep the icy water out. It was a tremendous improvement. They also had hot tea more often as it became colder.

All of these things were furnished as necessary expenses to keep the work going. They had no illusions about Johnson being their friend. He made that clear in his visits. To him they were tools to be kept functional, just like the replacement of broken pick handles and the regular sharpening of axes and shovels. Soon it was apparent that daytime was rapidly shortening. When they crested ridges on the walks to work, they could see fresh snow on the ridge tops. Cold rain came almost every day and it was sometimes mixed with ice crystals.

One day ten new Chinese joined the work-gang. They had signed up with Johnson because they had lost their claims in nearby China Creek. A tough miner named Dave Graham, backed by several other white men with an arsenal of guns and knives, had told them that they could either leave their claims or die where they stood, so they left. At least working for Johnson would provide food and shelter and a bit of money for winter, they told the others. One of these miners was named Chu Pong. For some reason, he and Huang Lee became friends. They talked about prospecting, mining, and Chu's other experiences in America. Chu had begun as a contract laborer five years before. Huang sensed he could learn much from him.

One wet, chilly morning, as they prepared to leave camp for the ditches, One Arm announced that he needed three men to work for some miners in nearby Independence Creek. He

41

selected three of the laborers for the detail. Huang Lee was one of them. Another was Chu. One Arm motioned for them to come with him. He led them to where two burley miners were standing in the rain, waiting.

One Arm said to the three Chinese, "You are to go with these men today. Their names are Mr. Burbidge and Mr. Jenkins. Take shovels. Note the trail you go on so you can return by it tonight. You will be working for them for the next week."

The three Chinese collected shovels from the tool dump nearby and followed the two white men up the Gulch on the winding, muddy trail to Independence Creek. They welcomed the change in routine and the change in scenery. The trail wound north through the head of Prospect Gulch, over a low, broad saddle covered on the south side with ponderosa and lodgepole pine trees, and then down into the dark, steep canyon of Independence Creek. The trail forked several directions in the saddle and Burbidge and Jenkins led them down one that descended the left side of the canyon. The claim they arrived at was alongside the creek, about a mile below the saddle.

At the claim, a sluice was set up near the Creek. Thirty feet away was the claim's "diggings" in an ancient sand deposit in the canyon's wall. Burbidge busied himself with the sluice and Jenkins motioned them to follow him. He seized a shovel, walked to the diggings, and dug out some of the sandy earth. He then selected one of several large metal buckets that were lying about, filled it with the sandy soil, lifted the bucket, carried it to the head of the sluice box, and poured it into a large wooden hopper atop the high end of the box. The Chinese imitated Jenkins. Soon, the sandy soil from the digging pit was flowing steadily, bucket by bucket, into the hopper.

Jenkins and Burbidge worked on each side of the sluice. They controlled a gate so that the right amount of water was flowing through it. At the same time they dropped amounts of the soil from the hopper into the head of the sluice and worked the soil and water over the notched boards in the bottom of the

42

sluice box. They busily picked out larger rocks and pebbles and threw them aside. Every once in awhile they would stop the water, lift the boards out of the bottom of the sluice box and carefully scrape the material caught in the notches in the boards into a large, shallow pan. Then they would return the boards to their places in the sluice box, allow the water to begin flowing through it again, and drop new soil down from the hopper above.

Both white men paid little attention to the Chinese except to direct them where to dig once in awhile. Otherwise, they focused on the operation of the sluice box. As the day went on, a pyramid of wet, black, sandy material accumulated in the large, shallow pan near the sluice. The Chinese noticed that the white men talked more and seemed to become more excited as the black sand in the pan accumulated. Throughout the day the cold rain did not stop, but its intensity decreased to just a fine mist. The steep canyon walls were covered with dark, wet spruce, cedar, and fir trees. It was a gloomy day and a gloomy place. A gray Clark's Jay flew in and lighted on the ridgepole of the miners' tent nearby. It harshly scolded the workers. After seeing there were no scraps of food around the camp, the bird flew off to look elsewhere.

Huang Lee watched all this as he worked. This was the first time he had seen an actual mining operation. It was fascinating. He did not understand all that he was seeing, but he could compare what he saw at the sluice box to the rice winnowing process at home. He reasoned that Burbidge and Jenkins were winnowing grain from chaff except that here it was winnowing the black sand from the soil! They did it with water instead of a breeze. Chu confirmed this similarity. The black sand had to be valuable because the white men treated it very carefully as they removed it from the notches in the boards. It must contain the gold.

After lunch, Huang saw that Mr. Burbidge had left the sluice and was carefully putting some of the black sand from the large, shallow pan into a smaller pan. He carried this over to the

43

creek near where there was a small box with rockers, like those on a child's cradle, on the bottom of it. Burbidge squatted down by the box and ladled a small amount of the black sand into it. Huang could not see all that he was doing, but he did see Mr. Burbidge begin to rock the small box back and forth with one hand while he poured water into it with the other.

It was nearly dark when Mr. Jenkins motioned to them to stop digging. He showed them where to put their shovels and motioned them to go home. The rain picked up as they left the claim. They said little as they climbed the steep, muddy trail. It took all their concentration to avoid slipping and falling. After a hard hour's walk, they arrived at Johnson's camp. Warming themselves by the crackling, hissing bonfires, they each filled their cups from a steaming cauldron of scalding green tea. They could smell cooking rice and their mouths watered. They sat together on a log near a fire and sipped their tea.

Huang told the others what he had seen that day. They agreed with him that his reasoning was correct. Chu explained in detail how the process generated gold dust. He had done it himself. Huang asked how the white men knew where to dig and Chu assured him it was just by observation, experience, and luck. Chu said that the miners would take gold dust out of the small rocker, put it into tightly sewn small leather bags, split it between themselves, and hide the bags around the campsite. Later they would take the gold to Moose City and put it into their accounts. Someone cried out that the rice was ready! They rose quickly, grabbed their eating tins, and got into the rapidly forming dinner line.

"Abe, Abe!" Burbidge yelled at Jenkins, soon after the Chinese had left.

Jenkins, who was in the middle of making dinner for the two of them, replied testily, "What do you want? I got biscuits 'bout to come outta' the Dutch oven!"

"GodAlmighty, forget the friggin' biscuits, we're gettin' rich!" replied Burbidge, with a high pitched chortle.

Jenkins yanked the Dutch oven out of the coals, sat it down, and ran to where Burbidge squatted, staring, with bugging eyes and open mouth, into the little rocker box. "Holy Shit!" Jenkins said, as he saw the little piles of gold in the ridges of the separator board in the bottom of the rocker. "Holy Shit! How long has this been going on?"

"About an hour!" said Burbidge. "Look at that!" He whooped. He pointed to several bulging leather pouches near his knee. "I've never seen anything like it. We just hit a pocket! I'd guess we got about a thousand dollars already and I ain't even dented the "fines" we got outta the sluice today!"

Abe Jenkins couldn't help dancing in a little circle. Then he started crying in spite of himself. So did Burbidge, who rose to his feet, grabbed Jenkins by the shoulders, and hugged him. They stood there in the cold rain, leaning against each other for awhile. They had been through many tough, lean times together over the last two years. Gradually they both regained their composure.

Burbidge spoke first, "Here's what I figure we do right now! First, stop and eat dinner. Then make some good pitch torches, come back here, and work this rocker as hard as we can as long as we can tonight. Whaddya' say, Abe?"

"Hell, yes!" said Jenkins, his eyes gleaming with excitement. "Who knows how much there is in that sandbank over there. Let's get the rest of these "fines" separated tonight and be ready to run this rocker to beat Hell all day tomorrow! Sam, we could be millionaires by tomorrow evening if these pickings stay this good another day!" They both giggled like lunatics, giddy with fatigue and delight.

The next morning One Arm saw to it that Huang Lee and his two fellow workers headed for Burbidge and Jenkins' claim at the same time the others left camp to dig ditch. More cold, misty rain was falling. The air was cold and penetrating as the three Chinese walked up the muddy trail toward Independence Saddle. Huang noted the gold color was fading from the big leaves of the thimbleberry bushes. The scarlet was also fading from the mountain maples' leaves. Winter was certainly on its way!

When the Chinese entered the miners' camp, Jenkins and Burbidge were sitting by the fire drinking steaming coffee. Both were bleary eyed with fatigue, but they cheerily said, "Mornin' boys!" to the Chinese. They gave Huang and the other two Chinese each a cup of the hot coffee to warm them. When they were all ready, they went to work following the same routine as the day before, except that either Jenkins or Burbidge were continuously operating the small rocking box next to the creek.

Huang noted that both the white men were talking more today and that they had excited tones in their voices. He could only conclude that they were finding gold. The fact that they furtively carried small leather bags from the box to the tent, periodically, convinced him of it.

After working several days for Burbidge and Jenkins, the three Chinese returned to their regular work on the ditches. Each day gave new signs that winter was coming. The Chinese knew that the work would soon end and they would be leaving the Bitterroot country for the winter. They were eager to be paid off. They had little reason to expect the violent trouble that would soon occur in Prospect Gulch.

# Chapter 5 - Revolt

It all began with the reckoning of the individual accounts for each Chinese laborer in the Johnson Camp. The weather was announcing that end of the season was near. One arm and Johnson were working busily at the paperwork needed to pay off the Chinese. The results, on the surface, were favorable for the August-arriving 190 Chinese. Although they had arrived a bit late in the season, the average gross amount each had earned still amounted to about 75 dollars. This was a large sum of cash to anyone in 1869. However, the debts the Chinese had accrued had to be deducted.

The contractor needed to pay himself back for the original fees paid the American Labor Company, in this case 30 dollars per man, which covered his recruitment, transport and equipment prior to arriving at Moose City. Then there was the food and shelter expense accrued while working for Johnson. Johnson reckoned the true cost of his expenses, per man in the Camp, was about 10 dollars. All of this amounted, in reality, to about 40 dollars of costs for each of the 190 Chinese. Legitimately, each had about 35 dollars coming. Johnson's take from the miners for his August crew's services for the period was roughly 100 dollars per man. Johnson stood to make, net, about 5,000 dollars for the two and a half month's efforts of the August Chinese crew— more than most American men earned in twenty years! That didn't even count the income from the other 200 men he had had all season!

The problem was that Johnson was greedy, and greed often overcomes wisdom. Johnson wanted as much of the

Chinese net of 35 dollars as he thought he could get away with, so the critical calculation was how little he thought the Chinese would take without a violent riot. He also wanted them to willingly work for him again in the spring. He figured that each of them would need two dollars a month for crummy winter's lodging in Lewiston, so they would each need a total of about ten dollars for that. He also figured that each man would need about one and a half dollars per month to eat, at a bare subsistence level, and that would amount to seven and a half dollars for the winter. Therefore, food and lodging would cost at least 17.50 dollars for the winter.

The upshot was that Johnson figured he could squeeze another fifteen to seventeen bucks out of each Chinese and still have them survive for spring work. Without much further thought, he padded the food expenses another 17 dollars for each man. Then he and One Arm discussed what they would say to the August Chinese crew on the morrow.

While Johnson and One-Arm were conniving to defraud them, the Chinese, in their camp nearby, were speculating about their pay and the necessary winter arrangements. The ten laborers, who had been run off their claims in China Creek in October by Davy Graham, provided the larger group with their counsel. These men, naturally, had grievances against white men. Their advice conveyed a general distrust of, and disdain for, white men. They gave the newcomers several important bits of unsettling information.

The main one was that the white men were rich and lived like kings during the winter in the city of San Francisco. They also told their comrades that living the winter in Lewiston was the thing to do, but that it was costly. Nearly all the food had to be shipped in by mulestring or small river steamers from the lower Columbia.

These observations and the discrimination they had seen themselves, led them all to be suspicious of their employer. However, they all felt that, as honorable men, they would see

48

what happened. Each man had a total of the days he had worked. Each man also knew about what the staples of rice and dried salmon cost at the store in Moose City.

The next day they completed work on the last ditch in late afternoon. One Arm told them that this was the last work for the season. They returned to camp and turned in their tools. One Arm had told them to assemble at Johnson's tent in an hour. When they arrived, Mr. Johnson was sitting at a rough table in front of the tent. A ledger book was open on the table. There was a small strong box on the table too. One Arm stood by the table waiting for them all to assemble and become quiet.

After the last of them arrived, he began, "Mr. Johnson has asked me to tell you what is going to happen now. I will also give you some advice for living this winter. In a few minutes you will be paid for the work you have done since August. As agreed, when you signed the labor contract in Shanghai, you will be paid one dollar for each day you have worked. Some of you have been sick and you will not be paid for the days you did not work, so all of you will not be paid exactly the same amount.

Out of the amount you have earned you owe Mr. Johnson for the cost of getting you here from China and the cost of food and shelter while you have been here. The cost of your transport was 30 dollars per man. This is a one time cost; the next two years you work under this contract will see no further deduction from your pay for transport." One arm paused.

The Chinese looked at one another. It seemed fair to them and they expected it.

One Arm went on, "Since you arrived in August the cost of your provisions and shelter has been $27.50. Mr. Johnson knows that this may seem high to you. He wants you to know that shipping food and other equipment to Moose City is very expensive."

At this declaration, there was a stirring and murmur among the assembled Chinese. This could not be true! This was much more than they had expected to pay for food—more than twice as much! They knew what the price was for food at the store in Moose City and, even that was much cheaper than this!

Johnson looked up at the sound from the Chinese. All eyes were on him. He said in a loud voice, "Show yourselves, boys, so they know you are there". Ten white men stepped into view from behind the trees around the camp. Each was armed and had his gun at the ready. Johnson slowly and calmly reached below the table and pulled out two Navy Colt revolvers. He cocked them and laid them on the table by the ledger book.

The murmuring died down after the Chinese saw the armed men. They looked either at the ground or glared at Johnson. One Arm cleared his throat nervously and continued, "Now to come get your pay. Form a line to the left."

After some hesitation, they did what he asked. Each man received approximately $17.50 in United States paper currency and coin after he had made a mark beside his name and number in the ledger book. A few who had been sick got less. There was a sullen silence during the whole process and a number of very hard stares at Mr. Johnson as they passed him, one by one.

After they all had been paid, One Arm told them, "Since it is so late in the day already, I suggest that you go back to your camp for the night. Mr. Johnson has arranged dinner for you there, free of charge. Tomorrow you are on your own. I suggest you go to the store and purchase enough provisions to subsist you while you are walking to Lewiston. The last packstring to arrive told us that there is already three feet of snow on the Orogrande divide between the North Fork and the Weippe Prairie, so you need to leave soon to avoid being snowed-in. You will see many leaving here soon! That is all. We will see you in Lewiston in the spring about May 1."

Dismissed, the angry Chinese slowly left the clearing and walked the short distance packed to their camp, heads down.

After the last Chinese laborers had left, Johnson totaled up the book and closed it. He then closed and locked the strong box and put both it and the ledger into the tent behind him. Coming out of the tent he turned to One Arm and said, "Go over to the Chinamen's camp and see the cook gives them all the rice they can hold. Try to use up the last of that dried salmon too, and, uh, give them plenty of tea to brew." One Arm nodded 'yes' and headed for the camp. He wondered if Mr. Johnson was having twinges of guilt about robbing the workers of half of their earnings.

As One Arm disappeared into the gathering darkness Johnson looked at his ten white accomplices, now standing by the fire. He said, "Thanks, boys, for the help. I got a case of good whiskey in the tent that needs drinkin' and we got a quarter of an elk just 'bout to come outta a barbecue pit in back a the tent! It's been a great year and we might as well celebrate a bit!" The men around the fire agreed loudly and hurried to get the whiskey and help the cook retrieve the meat from the cooking pit.

At the nearby laborers' camp, the mood was quite different. With somber faces and little said, the fires were built up. A steaming cauldron of green tea was boiled. They dipped in their cups and sat around the fire drinking the brew. Nearby, the cook was boiling the rice. Chu Pong, the miner from China Creek and Huang's best friend, spoke first, "You better get used to white men. I've seen it happen over and over."

Then one of the young workers stood up and said indignantly, "Do they think we are stupid? Do they think, because they have guns, that we are afraid?"

One of the other ex-miners said, "Yes they do, and I am. If I didn't have some gold hidden in a cache for the winter it would be very hard."

51

Huang Lee said, "I cannot send money to my family until the end of next year!" He began to weep. So did several others.

The cook yelled that the rice was ready. They got their dinner, returned to their warming fires, and quietly ate. Then they drifted, one by one, to their lean-tos and to bed.

From the darkness, outside the circle of light cast by the fires, One Arm looked into the camp. No trouble here, he thought. He turned to retrace his steps to Johnson's tent to make his report. He had walked about fifty feet when he was suddenly thrown to the ground and pinned there. Powerful, callused hands covered his mouth. A rag was stuffed in his mouth and he was swiftly bound with rope. He was hoisted like a side of beef and carried away into the darkness. Chu, Huang, and five other Chinese carried One Arm far enough away from the camp so that his screams could not be heard. Then they unbound him, except for his hands, and removed the rag from his mouth. He quickly screamed, "Help! Help!"

Chu Pong punched One Arm hard in the belly and the screaming turned into retching and vomiting. "Shut up, whore of the white man", said Chu.

One Arm, recovering quickly out of desperation, looked up at them and squealed, "What do you want?"

"The truth about our pay!" said Huang Lee.

"You got what was coming to you!" yelped One Arm.

With that, Chu dragged One Arm to a pool in a nearby creek and shoved his head under the water. One Arm struggled wildly for awhile, then went limp. Chu pulled him from the water. One Arm began coughing and choking and gradually became fully conscious again.

"Now, the truth!" Huang Lee repeated.

"Johnson will kill me!" One Arm sputtered.

"Then you will die now or later!" said Chu.

One Arm looked wildly about, seeking a way out, but there was none. Reconciled, he slowly said, "You had thirty-five dollars coming. Mr. Johnson added $17.50 to the food bill for each of you."

Before One Arm could draw another breath, Chu thrust his head under the water and held it there until bubbles stopped coming up. One Arm's body twitched and was still.

"He could have told us where our money is!" said Huang Lee.

"Perhaps," said Chu, "but we know where it probably is! It's in the safe at Levitz' store."

Abe Jenkins had never eaten such delicious elk roast as Johnson's cook had prepared for them that night. His partner, Sam Burbidge, was lying by the fire next to him smiling and looking at the stars in the night sky. Sam said, to nobody in particular, "Boys, I don't think it gets any better than this, do you?"

There was a general grunt of agreement. They were full of Johnson's whiskey and prime elk meat. It was the end of the mining season. They had made some good money. Soon they would be heading down river for the winter and on to the good times in Seattle or San Francisco.

Johnson, sitting in his chair by the fire, took another drink of whiskey. Then he sighed, and said what they were all thinking, "You are right about that, Sam. Sometimes I wish it could go on forever. We are as free as any men could be. We have the Chinamen to do the shit work. We celebrate all winter in the city and we come back to this beautiful country for the summer. Yep, we got it made!" Plentiful whiskey and bellies full of rich, barbecued meat pushed the men into a heavy, alcoholic sleep.

Soon, two hundred angry Chinese emerged, like vengeful ghosts, from the shadows around the sleeping, snoring men. The firearms were moved out of their reach. Then each man was pinned to the ground by many hands and kept silent while his throat was cut and he bled to death. Soon the only white man left alive was Johnson, sleeping peacefully in his chair by the fire.

Chu prodded Johnson gently with a rifle barrel. Johnson stirred and lifted his head to look, blearily, into the fire. Slowly he became aware that a sea of grim Chinese faces surrounded him.

He sat up straight and said, in a puzzled tone, "What the Hell?" What had happened, he thought, his muddled mind racing? Why are these Chinese here? "One Arm, what the Hell is going on here?" He shouted. There was no answer. The crackling of the fire and the sizzling of the wooden torches the Chinese held were the only sounds. Standing up abruptly, Johnson said, "What to you want?"

Chu Pong, who was standing by the chair, and who spoke a bit of English, said, "Our money!" He shoved Johnson back down into the chair.

"You got your damned money!" Johnson retorted. "Where's One Arm?"

There was no answer. Johnson's suddenly noticed the bodies around the fire and saw the pools of blood by each one. His eyes bugged and his mouth sagged in disbelief and terror. "One Arm, One Arm!" he cried in a terrified voice and tried to rise. Chu and another Chinese shoved Johnson back down into the chair. Chu raised a knife in front of Johnson's face.

Chu said, "Your whoreman, One Arm, is dead. Give us our money or you die!"

Johnson gulped and swallowed hard. He said to Chu, in a strange, half-strangled voice, "Jesus Christ! You can have the money. It's in the safe in the Store in town. Please don't kill me! You need me to get the money in town!"

Chu turned to the other Chinese and translated, "He says it's in the iron box in the store in Moose City." All the Chinese began talking at once. Someone put a rope around Johnson's neck. Johnson stared at the ten bodies in horror and disbelief.

The Chinese finally decided that they needed Johnson to get the money in town. He had to tell Mr. Levitz to open the iron box in the store. He and they would have to go there. In addition, they all would have to go to show force or the white men there would simply overwhelm them. They also knew that, once the white men knew that ten of their kind had been slaughtered, they would want revenge and would kill as many Chinese as they could. They had to keep the killings secret until they had the money and could get away.

This decided, Chu told Johnson, "We will all go to town. You will get the money and give each of us $17.00." They then forced the shocked and trembling Johnson to his feet, tied his hands behind his back and led him, by the rope around his neck, down the trail to Moose City.

As the group funneled out of Johnson's camp and down the trail to town, Huang Lee gently drew Chu Pong aside. He put his mouth close to Chu's ear and said, "Burbidge and Jenkins, the men with the mine in Independence Creek, are dead by the fire. I think that there is a lot of gold at their camp. Should we go there now, or go to town with the rest?"

Chu Pong looked at Huang blankly for several seconds. He had been so focused on the pay situation that he had trouble thinking immediately of anything else. Then he blinked his eyes and said, "It is a good idea, but, if we do, we will have to find the gold. They have probably hidden it well."

Almost all the other Chinese were out of the camp and on their way to town. Chu and Huang had to make a decision now. Chu said, "There are 600 white men in Moose City and I am not sure they will let us to have any money from the safe. There maybe more killing too. Let's go to the Independence camp and

55

try to find the gold. If we find it, we will be richer than we ever dreamed. If we don't find it we can use the dead miners' supplies and tent to make the trip to Lewiston."

Huang nodded. It made sense to him. Before leaving they went into Johnson's tent and found two rifles, powder, and bullets. They shouldered the rifles and set off on the trail to Independence Creek. None of the other Chinese saw them leave.

It was lucky for Chu Pong and Huang Lee that there was a full moon that fateful night. They could make out the Independence Creek trail clearly, once their eyes had adjusted to the darkness. Soon they were at Burbidge and Jenkins' claim. They did not light a fire for fear that someone in the nearby claims would see it. They carefully went through the tent, feeling more than seeing. They found three small leather bags of gold dust. They were elated at this, for, with gold at $20.00 an ounce, they already had much more than their full pay from Johnson. Evidently, Burbidge and Jenkins had not yet split this gold between them. They also found clothing, packsacks, and plenty of food for the trip out of the backcountry. The light of early dawn was beginning to creep up the eastern sky. As they waited for the light, they tried to figure out where the miners would have put their caches.

Huang Lee said, "They would put it relatively close to camp and certainly within the boundaries of the claim."

Chu Pong responded, "Yes. It would also be someplace not too hard to get to, but easily made inconspicuous."

They decided that Huang would look below the camp along the stream. Chu would look above the camp in the trees and brush. They made a quick breakfast of some cold biscuits and jerked elk meat that they found in the grub box. By that time there was enough light to begin the search.

Before they separated, Chu said, "Whatever happens in Moose City, when the white men find the dead bodies at Johnson's camp they will begin shooting Chinese on sight. If we

56

find this gold, it must be within a couple of hours. Then we will have to hurry away from here. We also will have to travel off the regular trails, too!"

Huang looked at his friend and nodded 'yes'. He really appreciated Chu's common sense approach to these things. They separated and began to look for the hidden gold caches. Huang Lee went down to the Creek and slowly side-hilled along the bank of the stream. He looked hard for telltale indications of someone walking back and forth or for disturbed forest floor duff or bushes. He slowly went down stream about 100 yards. He found nothing. Turning back to the direction of the camp, he climbed up on a big downed spruce log so he could scan the surrounding area.

The old log had lain on the ground so long that it was very rotten and tended to crumble beneath his feet, but it held his weight enough to allow him to walk its length. He looked the area over carefully as he walked up the rotten log. It ended where it had broken off its ancient stump. A small opening in the forest surrounded the stump. The ground in the opening was covered with three-foot high bracken ferns. Looking hard, he thought he saw a line created by a few beaten-down ferns, but was not sure. It could just be a game trail. He had seen many of those here in Idaho.

The line in the ferns seemed to lead away from where he stood on the log, so he jumped down and began to follow the trace. After about 70 feet he left the fern patch and was under a canopy of sapling cedars. There seemed to be no trace of a path or anything. He slowly retraced his steps to the edge of the fern glade. He looked carefully at the faint trace he had first seen. His eyes followed the faint line back across the glade. It ended at the rotten stump he had been standing-on. Could it be the cache?

His heart began to beat faster. Rotten wood would be a good place to hide something and cover it up. It already looked disturbed because of the way it fell apart over time! He walked quickly across the fern-covered opening to the huge stump and stopped. He stood for awhile, looking for signs of unnatural disturbance. He saw nothing unusual. Thousands of small cubes of degraded wood littered the ground around the stump. He noticed that pine squirrels had used the top of the stump for an eating place. They had sat on the top of it and torn pinecones apart to extract the seeds that they hungered-for. The scales of hundreds of pinecones littered the top of the stump and flowed down its sides. They were piled all around it, on top of the underlying rotted wood. His eyes took in all of this.

The cone scales around the bottom of the stump formed a layer over the rotted wood beneath, except for one area between two roots! There he saw only rotten wood. In a flash, he was on his knees scraping the rotten wood away from the area between the two root bulges on the stump's side. His breath was coming in quick gasps. His fingers made the rotten wood fly! Suddenly they caught on something. Huang stopped digging and looked at what his fingers had snagged. He thought it was a small root, but then he saw that it was a leather thong!

Chu was very quietly poking his way through the undergrowth of the forest above the camp. He had been at it for about an hour and was beginning to lose hope of ever finding either Jenkin's or Burbidge's caches. Then he heard a thudding on the ground and the snapping of twigs and branches. The noise was coming closer. He squatted and hid behind a huge cedar tree's trunk. Probably an elk had been alarmed, he thought. He had seen and heard them before, but it could be white men after Chinese. He cautiously peered around the tree as the noise came closer and closer. It was Huang Lee! He was bloody from running though the sharp lower branches of trees and from falling down. He was looking wildly around, sweating, and gasping for air. Chu stepped out into sight and hissed, "Huang!"

It took Huang a moment to locate the source of the sound, then he ran to Chu and grabbed him and knocked him to the forest floor. Between gasps for air he wheezed, "Found...gold! Much gold!"

Chu disentangled himself from Huang and got up. Brushing himself off, he said, "Where? Show me!" Huang had to lie on the ground for several minutes before he had the strength to rise and lead the way.

There was more gold than the two of them could carry. They could not hire men with mules to transport it out to Lewiston because they were fugitives. There was no choice but to take what they could carry in their packsacks and bury the rest. They also had to take some food for the trip. They knew they would have to go cross-country and avoid the heavily traveled main trails. All this forced them to hide the gold that they could not carry.

There was a lot of it. They planned to return the next year to get the rest. The new cache had to be of a more permanent nature than the miner's was. For a permanent landmark, they found a big boulder that protruded from the canyon-side about 100 yards above the camp. They dug a deep hole at its base. In the hole they deposited the excess gold and laid some boards from a packing case over it. Then they shoveled the hole full of dirt and carefully returned the duff of the forest floor to where it had been when they started the digging. It was a perfect camouflage.

Both Huang and Chu were very nervous. They had been here too long. The white men might come anytime! They hurried back to the camp and hastily tried to hide any evidence that they had been there. Then they each shouldered a heavy pack and headed straight up the hill, away from the creek, claims, and Moose City.

That evening in the Moose City Saloon, Edwin Johnson took another sip of whisky and said, "I'll tell you, Boys, I was scared shit-less when I saw all those men on the ground with their throats cut. Shows you just can't trust those Chinks, ever." He winced as he shifted his bandaged left arm in its sling.

Dave Graham was sitting next to Johnson at the table. He said, "Yep, but there's twenty of 'em layin' out front that you'll never have to worry about again. The rest of 'em won't make it far without food in this cold weather, neither. We sent a posse down the trail to Orofino to take care of any they run onto on the way. They'll also tell the townspeople below to be on alert for starvin' Chinese murderers comin' outta' the woods."

Mr. Levitz, who was standing nearby, spoke up, "Tomorrow we'll get the dead men at your camp buried proper, Johnson, and then auction off their claims. There was a rumor that Jenkins and Burbidge had had hit some gold, but I can't vouch for it. They never brought much in. After that, I reckon' we all had better pack up and head for the low country or we'll be snowed in here."

The discussion of the day's events wound on as the men in the saloon reviewed the details of the exciting day repeatedly over their whiskey. Outside the saloon, it began to snow big fluffy, wet flakes. In the chill darkness, the snow slowly covered the scattered bodies of the Chinese laborers shot in the revolt. Around the Moose City saloon, the snowflakes glowed from the light coming through the canvas roof. Someone began playing a fiddle inside and some of the miners began to sing, "I danced with the girl with the hole in her stockin'; we danced and danced till our heels took to rockin'; all by the light a' the moon; all by the light of the moon!"

# Section 2 - <u>1964</u>

> "Tragedy is like strong acid—it dissolves away all but the very gold of truth".
> —D. H. Lawrence, 1911.

# Chapter 6 - Forester

Joe McCulloch wondered, for the one-thousandth time, why he put up with the horseshit the Forest Service handed out. He had been through four long, tough years of forestry school at the U. of Montana; years his new wife had had to provide most of their support by working long hours in a drug store.

Then, in 1960, when he finished school and landed a job with the Forest Service, they had moved to this God-forsaken Ranger District 50 miles from the nearest town. They had been assigned an ancient, ramshackle two-room log cabin to live in. They shared the cabin with its permanent residents: a family of large and very noisy pack rats.

He also resented the long hours, many unpaid, that he had to put in just to measure up to the Outfit's gung-ho expectations. On top of that, the pay was pitiful and the cost of living in the middle of nowhere was high. All that stuff rankled the shit out of him, but it was not what <u>really</u> pissed him off.

What really pissed him off about working for "The Green Machine" was the nit-picking Goddamned trivial bullshit you had to put up with for the "privilege" of working your guts out.

For example, Joe often left the Ranger Station in his old green Jeep about 6:15 or 6:30 in the morning. He had to do that to meet the logging superintendent of the Gravy Creek sale, on site, by 8:00 o'clock. However, the damned regulations said he could not enter anything on his timesheet earlier than 7:30 a.m.

Evidently, there was a big bureaucratic fear that the cheating, sneaky and untrustworthy Federal employees would be sneaking in to work early! Perhaps to, illicitly, use a Federal typewriter for personal business or something! The assumption was always that the Federal grunts were up to something bad, so some idiot in Washington, D.C., had put all these petty, stupid rules in the books to drive everyone nuts. Like no radios in the damned pickups—right? Those simple bastards sure wouldn't want anything to keep you awake at the wheel coming home in the dark after a 14 hour day for 8 hours pay!

Joe also knew, deep down, that this kind of crap would never end. Even if he eventually became "Gawd-Almighty" in the friggin' Outfit, he would still have to put up with all this silly crap, just like the lowest grunt Forester in the Service!

He was mulling all this over as he headed back home after a thirteen-hour day thrashing around in the woods marking out a clearcut boundary. His face, speckled with yellow tree marking paint, was a testament to his efforts. He knew the road he was driving well. He had been over it hundreds of times. It was designated as "lane and a half, gravel" by the Forest Service's civil engineers and was so recorded in the road log of the Forest. This translated, in reality, to a narrow one-lane dirt track with huge washboards that nearly jarred your teeth out.

All the gravel had long ago been kicked into the ditches by the skidding wheels of a thousand trucks. It had been graded once that summer—Uncle's idea of maintenance!

The solution to these inhospitable roads, that Joe and his young colleagues had quickly learned to apply, was, simply, to drive like hell. The theory was that, if you went fast enough, the tires could only touch the tops of the washboards. The big trick was to drift the corners just right, like the dirt track racers did all the time, while avoiding losing control and sliding sideways off the road. They all mastered this skill. They also were experts at avoiding on-coming logging trucks on blind corners and backing out of twisting one lane dead end spur roads at 45 miles per hour!

Joe was tired. He rubbed the thigh of his right leg where he had fallen on a stob that morning. The muscle throbbed and quivered in response. It was like after being in a fight when you came out of the brush; knicks and scratches all over you. It was usually nothing serious, just painful.

He artfully slid the old Jeep into a wide spot just in time to let a huge Autocar logging truck pass going the other way. He paused a few seconds to let the billowing clouds of dust, stirred up by the huge truck, settle. When it had settled enough, and he could see the road again, he revved-up the anemic four cylinder engine of the Jeep, engaged the clutch, and wrenched the vehicle onto the road.

He rapidly accelerated, shifting to second and third gear just as the engine's pistons and rods promised to tear loose from the crankshaft. All the doors, fenders and bumpers of the Jeep flopped, banged and rattled as he hurtled along, but he was used to it. He heard none of it. He was deep in thought.

He was thinking that he had been at this for four long years now. He might get to be an Assistant Ranger in another three. Working outdoors in the trees was all right—what he had wanted—but the rest was pretty bad. Hell, he could make more money doing about any straight manual labor job in town. And what about Mary, his wife? Didn't she deserve something better than a boring, hard scrabble existence out here in the middle of nowhere?

As he rounded a sharp curve, the rear wheels of the Jeep came loose from the ribs of solid rock they had been bouncing over. The Jeep slid sideways into a marshy ditch and stopped abruptly. Like a tired rhino mired in a watering hole, it tilted and sank down on one side.

"Goddamned Sonofabitch!" shouted Joe to creation. He jammed the transfer case lever into four wheel drive, low range, gunned the engine, dropped the clutch, and the growling, groaning Jeep slowly climbed from the muddy morass. Back on the road he stopped, flipped the lever out of four-wheel drive, and soon had the Jeep screaming and banging along as before.

Drawing a pack of Viceroys from his shirt pocket, he tapped the pack on the center of the steering wheel. One cigarette slid out a bit. He took its filter into his lips, returned the box to the pocket, dug out his Zippo lighter, and lit the cigarette. He puffed deeply. All this happened automatically, without slowing the screaming, wildly bounding Jeep in the slightest.

He returned to his prior train of thought. Yeah, what about Mary and little Joe? Little Joe was a year old now. Soon he would need friends his own age to play with, not the District compound's complement of flea-bitten ground squirrels. He should have a "normal" neighborhood environment to grow up in.

As he visualized an idyllic suburban neighborhood for his family, his thermos bottle bounced off the seat next to him and began rolling back and forth across the floor of the Jeep. Driving and bending over to get it at the same time, he adroitly caught it and laid it back beside him. Good thing it was a stainless steel Stanley, he thought to himself. He had had several cheaper ones that were glass inside, but they didn't last long in this rough environment. This one had been expensive, but he figured it would last for years. On bulldozers, next to the catskinner who operated the tractor, he had seen some that had big dents, all the paint chipped off them, and they still didn't leak. There it was again: why should he have to worry about the cost of a damned thermos bottle, as hard as he worked? Well, a measly 150-dollar Government check twice a month didn't go far, that was for damned sure!

He rounded the final curve of the Moose Creek road and decelerated into the center of the dilapidated Moose Creek Ranger Station. It was located where Moose Creek and Kelly Creek came together. This was some of the only flat ground in this part of the country, so the Forest Service put a permanent Station here in the thirties when the CCC's had built the first road in. From this tiny enclave, five forestry professionals of the District managed nearly 500,000 wild acres of U.S. National Forest in the headwaters of the Clearwater River drainage.

The Ranger Station—what the Forest Service called an "administrative site"—was a motley collection of buildings. They ranged from rotting old log cabins put up in the 1920's, like the one Joe McCulloch lived in, to some peeling dark green frame bunkhouses constructed in the mid-1930's. There were several old aluminum trailer houses, two smallish shake-sided bungalow-type houses, and a small office building of dark brown shingles. It had been put up in the early 1950's. Finally, there were several portable aluminum covered boxes that looked like miniature cabooses. In fact, these were the cookhouse, shower, and laundry buildings. Over across the main creek was a pole and shingle barn and generator house. All the paths and roads on the site were dirt. A few boardwalks ran between some buildings. Jury-rigged wires running from poles set in the ground at different angles carried the sometime electricity from the generator to the buildings. Joe thought it looked like a cross between a small, abandoned World War I military installation and a raggedy-assed Gypsy camp.

He swung the Jeep into a parking place with a small wooden sign that said 3651—the Jeep's number—and eased out stiffly until he was standing upright beside the vehicle. He reached into the Jeep and pulled out his paint-speckled cruiser's vest, Black Bear woolen jacket, thermos, and lunchbox. Then he took a minute to record the mileage for the day in the vehicle's logbook, as he had to do. He threw the logbook into the glove box and slammed shut the Jeep's door. Then he began walking the slow, round-shouldered walk of a tired and dirty man toward the log shack he and his family rented from the Service.

By the Office the District's Dispatcher, Al Fife, yelled out the door, "You're kinda late, Joe! Any trouble?"

"Nope," said Joe, continuing to walk slowly, "just the same old shit—too much work and not enough time. See ya' in the mornin', Al." He walked on, thinking that Al Fife was not a bad guy for being such a suck-up prick with ears.

Mary McCulloch never knew when Joe would make it home. She tried to cook dinners that could sit on the stove for awhile without going bad. Mary was a petite, slim young woman of 23. She normally dressed in blue jeans and cotton shirts like today. Looking out the front window of the tiny cabin for the tenth time, she was relieved to see her husband getting out of his Jeep and heading home. She took a minute to really look at him.

What she saw was a tall man of medium build, wearing black baggy Frisco jeans and a gray cotton JC Penny's work shirt. His dented orange hard hat was tilted back on his head. His pants were raggedly cut off ("stagged", the foresters called it, for freedom of movement) about halfway to his knees. Below that were the trademarks of his trade: big, black, high-topped leather logging boots. He had his tan cruiser's vest and coat slung back over one shoulder.

She thought, 'how handsome he is'. She didn't care what other women might think. He was also kind and loved their son, Little Joe to death. She loved him very much.

She could tell he was tired, bone tired. He had been depressed lately and she knew it was about the job and this place. Well, a good, hot meal would help, she thought, and she turned and went to the door to meet him.

Al Fife had been the Dispatcher at Moose Creek for about ten years. Before that he had been a seasonally employed trail foreman and firefighter. It was August and the high fire danger this time of year always made him nervous. The drier the woods got, the more nervous he became. If there was a wildfire, he was the one who had to call in the human and material resources to combat it. The fact of the matter was that he was unsure of his judgement and dispatching capabilities. However, he would never have admitted that to anyone else.

After speaking to Joe McCulloch, he seated himself back at the big varnished plywood Dispatcher's desk. He put his feet up, drew a bag of Bull Durham tobacco out of his pocked, and began to meticulously roll a 'make-your –own' cigarette. It was past working hours, but he always hung around the office later than he needed-to. It was more comfortable than the small travel trailer he lived-in, anyway.

His interaction with Joe McCulloch a few moments before had grated on him a bit. While he and Joe got on, day to day, Joe had let him know early on in their relationship that he was not about to take any guff from him. Al, who stood just five feet tall, had a need to try to bluff and run people, if he could. He considered Joe arrogant and insubordinate.

That was mainly because last summer he had been showing off in front of the District Ranger and unwisely and crudely ordered Joe to load a pickup with firepacks. Joe had told him to stuff them up his butt right there in front of God and everybody! To Al's dismay, God had laughed!

By God, McCulloch will learn someday, Al thought, that in emergencies you did what you are ordered to do! He lit the carefully rolled cigarette with a large, flaring stick match and shook the match to extinguish it. Then, when he leaned over the desk to get his coffee cup, loose, burning tobacco spilled out of the front of the roll-your-own. The embers burned three holes in his shirtfront and ignited some hairs on his chest. He jumped up and beat at the sparks, yelling to nobody in particular,

"Goddamned Sonofabitch!" He was very glad no one was in the office to see it happen.

Joe McCulloch was in the process of removing his heavy logging boots—the best part of his day. He sat on the front steps of the old cabin and slowly unwound the long, greasy leather laces. He pulled the boots off one at a time and sat wiggling his stockinged toes in the cool air. The sound of Moose Creek gurgling nearby was soothing. Mary had greeted him when he walked up and given him a kiss and, just that fast, the day was much better. Now he had those tight boots off at last! Little Joe toddled to the hole-ridden screen door behind him and said "Dada!"

Joe rose and shuffled, stocking footed, into the cabin. He hoisted the giggling Little Joe high to the ceiling as he did. Then holding the little boy with one arm, he hugged his wife with the other and kissed her on the cheek. "Be right out after I clean up," he said. He sat the baby down and headed for the bedroom and the shower beyond it. In the shower, he washed the layers of sweat and grime from the road and the woods, from his body. The dirt ran down the drain at his feet in thick, muddy rivulets.

After dinner, Joe helped Mary put the baby to bed and finish the dishes. Then they both sat down on an old rust-colored frieze couch and relaxed for a short while before they went to bed. Short because they both rose very early. Bedtime was no later then 9:00 p.m.

Sometimes, if the mosquitoes were not too bad, they would sit for a little while on the tumbledown porch of the cabin. Joe would usually tell Mary about his day, especially the interesting or unusual parts. It might be about an accident. It might be a funny story he heard from the loggers, or a tale about wildlife that he had seen that day.

She would, in turn, tell him the scuttlebutt that was going around the Station among the women, and anything that had happened that day that was different. These events often involved the critical failure of the old washing machine that all the women used for laundry, the once a week delivery of groceries from Montana, a stoppage of the unbelievably Jerry-built Ranger Station water system, or the latest failure of the eternally ill and decrepit Army surplus electrical generator.

Of course they often talked of the baby and his development and their wishes and dreams for the life ahead of them. These latter wishes and dreams were modest, for they had no illusions about the pecuniary prospects of a young forester or, indeed, those of an old forester either.

Tonight, Mary continued to sense the subsurface depression in her husband that had only come the last few months, so she asked him, "Joe, are you happy here?" It was not the first time she had asked this. Normally he just tossed it off with a, "Sure, why do you ask? Are you unhappy?" She always said she was happy, although she considered the Station to be the absolute armpit of the universe.

Tonight, it was different. He lowered his head and responded, "Mary, I've been doing this for four years. Ninety-five percent of the work is technician's work, not professional work. The Service makes it clear, everyday, that foresters like me are a dime a dozen and that there are six more men like me lined-up waiting for my job. I look at the Assistant Ranger and the Ranger and see that they are little better off than we are after years and years of doing this stuff. I enjoy being in the woods some days, but those are rare, what with the bad weather and the constant pressure to get more done every day. This cabin we live in is a dump. Most of our friends outside the Outfit would never consider living in such a horrible shack. Little Joe will soon need a better home and some friends his age around to play with. And you need a halfway normal life, not living like a social outcast way out here in the Idaho woods. I'm sorry to unload like this, but I'm giving serious thought to leaving the Forest Service and finding a regular job that pays better. I want us to live a normal life in town."

Mary was shocked at his candor and the seriousness of his manner. "Oh, Joe," she said, "we worked so hard to get your forestry degree. I hate to see you leave the Forest Service. Little Joe and I don't want to be the reason you decide to give this up. I have to admit, though, that I have some of the same concerns you do about the long run in this career, but most of all, I don't want to see you unhappy. You know that I will go along with whatever you decide, Darling. I'm here to talk it through whenever you want to discuss it, too."

His head had been hanging low until she said that. Slowly his head came up. He looked into her eyes and he knew, again, why he loved her so. He gathered her into his arms and held her close and murmured, "Honey, anything I do will work out and be fine as long as I have you by my side. I love you more than you can possibly know. Whatever we do we will decide together." He kissed her gently on the lips and said, with a suggestive smile, as he pulled away, "Ready to go to bed? I am!"

Before the sun was up the next morning Joe came out of the door of the cabin, dressed and ready for work. As the rickety screen door slammed shut behind him, he stopped and slipped on his plaid wool coat. Although it was August, there was a coat of frost on the grass and the vehicles in the compound. In rapid, long strides bespeaking conditioning and balance only a field forester has, he crossed the bridge over Moose Creek and swung into the District Office building.

Inside he threw his vest and lunch on the old desk he shared with Billy Rae, the other young Forester on the District. No one was in the office. It was too early for everyone else. As usual, he headed for the cookshack for coffee. Well, not really for coffee, for he knew there would be two people there and they were favorites of his.

As he entered a voice boomed, "Well I'll be damned! The kiddy brigade is finally crawling out of their fart sacks today! Mornin', Mr. McCulloch!" The voice belonged to Marlin Stelges, the bull-shaped "bull" cook of the camp. Marlin was a

70

retired 'old time' logger now making a living cooking for Uncle Sam. He was preparing a huge tray of bacon for frying.

Joe, who loved this repartee, said to Marlin, "I had some coffee at home, but I need some battery acid for the Jeep so I came for a cup of your terrible, cheap-ass Government coffee".

Marlin turned away at this to hide a grin.

Joe grabbed a cup, filled it, and went into the front of the cookhouse to the nearest table. There, sitting propped in a corner with his back against the wall and enveloped in a cloud of blue Bull Durham tobacco smoke, sat Orrin West. Orrin was the District's animal packer. He looked like a leather woodcut of an old, old cowboy. He _was_ old. Nobody knew for sure just how old. He was the District's Animal Packer, but, more important, he was the moral conscience and living history of this little place. He also had been a double for William S. Hart in silent western films long, long before Joe had been born. Orrin had worked on this District, off and on, since the mid-1920's.

He did not look up as Joe entered. He had his old dirty Stetson pulled down over his forehead and was seriously contemplating the official U.S. Forest Service coffee mug cradled between his two huge, horny hands. Joe sat down across the table from him and said, "Mornin', Orrin".

Orrin squinted at Joe and, when he was sure Marlin could hear him in the nearby kitchen, said, "When you get battery acid in this cookhouse, son, you gotta' water it down 'bout half and half with pure water so's it don't eat the side outta' the battery case."

From the kitchen nearby came the booming retort, "Orrin West, I let you come in here every morning and drink the U.S. Government's coffee, free. Now you damn well know the damn cheap Government issue coffee we get is swept outta the bottom of the Spic latrines at the coffee plants down in Gratamala (he could not say Guatemala, and wouldn't, if he could have). So you know what it is and still you come in here every fuckin' day

71

to soak it up like it was th' nectar of th' gods. What in the Hell would any sane person think of a man that did that? Hell, I make it and I refuse to drink the crap!"

By this time, Joe was suppressing a laugh and Orrin's head was bobbing up and down slightly over a little smile. They silently sipped their coffee for awhile. Then Orrin said, raising his head, and looking directly at Joe for the first time, "Where's it to today?"

Joe replied, "Same as yesterday. I've got to finish marking the boundary of Block 6 up in the head of Independence Creek or Rankin will chew my ass (Tom Rankin was the Assistant District Ranger, responsible for natural resource management on the District.). You ever see how thick those Yew patches are up there? You have to get right up and walk on 'em to get through. How about you?"

"Takin' half a string loaded with grub up to the trail crew in Newsome Meadows today. Reckon I'll be back early. It's not far an' I'm already packed up an' ready to go," said Orrin.

From out of the kitchen came another explosion of sound, "GodAlmighty Damn! I wish all me and Elron (the name of Marlin's gnarled and diminutive Cook's Helper) had to do was go out and play in the woods like a coupla' cub bears. If you boys had to take the crap the Forest Service gives me and make it into something edible, like I do every damn day, now you'd be doin' something!"

At this Orrin West slowly uncoiled from his seat, stood up, and put his coffee mug into the dirty dish tub. Joe did the same. Orrin then said loudly to Joe, "I gotta go check the stock. I just heard one of them let a huge fart and I think he might be hurt or dead. Did you hear it, Joe?"

They laughed quietly and went out the door to go to work. Before the screen door at the front of the cookhouse slammed, though, they heard Marlin bellow after them, "You forgot the acid for your shitty old Jeep, McCulloch, and you're sure not particular about the company you keep, neither!" They both knew he was really meant, "Be careful out there today, fellows, and come back tomorrow morning."

Joe waited for the Jeep's engine to stop missing and run smoothly. It was a cold starter. You always had to put in full choke and then very gradually slip it off as the engine warmed up. He threw the shift stick into reverse, backed out of the parking place, and drove slowly through the compound. Billie Rae was walking slowly to his old Chevy pickup truck, dragging his ragged paint-dappled Filson vest in the dust. He looked up and waved to Joe. Joe stopped next to him. Billie said, "Goin' to Independence again?"

Joe nodded 'yes'.

Billie said, "Its awful steep in that canyon. If you break a leg, remember I am in China Creek today. I figure you can crawl the three miles to there, easy. If you make it I might give you a ride home."

Joe replied, "You are all heart, Rae. All heart", and gunned the Jeep slowly away. Mary waved good-bye from the cabin's porch and he tooted the Jeep's funny little horn in reply. As he turned to go up the Moose Creek road he saw the Ranger, Kermit Kaiser, alias "The Tin God", come out of his house and head for the Office. Well, at least the shithead is getting out of bed early enough to see some of us go to work, Joe thought.

# Chapter 7 - Tin God

United States Forest Service District Ranger Kermit Kaiser was a legend in his own mind. He had been the Ranger at Moose Creek for four years and he had been in the Forest Service for eleven years. He had worked on two other National Forests before coming to Moose Creek Ranger District on the Clearwater National Forest of Idaho. The Clearwater was one of sixteen National Forests in Region 1 (actually named the "Northern Region") of the Forest Service.

All of Kermit's willingness to move around and accretion of rank and responsibility from Forester to Assistant Ranger and on to District Ranger meant that, in the eyes of the Forest Service, Kermit Kaiser was a success and an "up and comer". Indeed, the position of "District Ranger" (often called just "Ranger") was important in the Agency. It was the first level of actual "Line" authority, meaning a direct line of authority from Ranger to Forest Supervisor to Regional Forester to the top level—the Chief—in Washington, D.C. In effect, then, Kermit Kaiser only had two line officer levels between himself and the Chief. Therefore, the position was important in rank as well as in responsibility.

Kermit Kaiser had the sole responsibility for the management and protection of a District that covered one-half a million acres of Federal land. He reported directly to the Forest Supervisor, Ralph Seward, at Forest Headquarters in Orofino, as did the other four Rangers on the Forest. The position and title also carried a mystique that it inherited from the traditions of

74

incorruptibility and faithfulness to duty established by the old time Forest Rangers of the Forest Service, early in the century. These lonely and far-ranging men established Federal control and protection over the huge parts of the old "Federal Domain" that were designated by President Theodore Roosevelt to be National Forests. Their legacy was known to by many in the west, particularly by their heirs in the Forest Service.

A District Ranger, like Kermit Kaiser, has considerable administrative power to make resource decisions about his District and to direct the staff that was placed at his disposal. The staff on the Moose Creek R.D., very representative of the times, was composed of a primary assistant to Kermit, Tom Rankin (the aforementioned Assistant District Ranger), a couple of professional foresters (Billie Rae and Joe McCulloch), and a number of technical and non-professional specialists. These included the District Clerk (Teresa Jacks), the Fire Control Officer (F.C.O.) (Vic Castellano), the Fire Dispatcher (Al Fife), two forestry technicians, and the District Packer (Orrin West).

Most of these people worked all, or a good part, of the year for the District and had permanent Civil Service appointments with the Forest Service. Beyond these specialists were a number of people that worked on a seasonal, year to year, basis in the summers. These "seasonals" included the Cook and Cook's helper, the Trail Crew Boss, the Brush Crew Boss, the Timber Crew Foreman, and the Lookouts up on the fire towers in four places on the District. At the bottom of the order were the workers who labored on the trails, timber, and brush crews. In mid-summer the total personnel - permanent and seasonal - on the District would total about 36 - 38 people, of whom only nine were permanent Federal employees. Of the nine "permanents" on the Staff, only six had full time year-round appointments.

Kermit Kaiser was the little 'tin God' of this remote forest kingdom. He had sole responsibility for what went on in it every day and he determined if the young professionals under him would have good performance reports or not. These reports, in turn, decided if the young person's career would be a success or not. He also had veto power over who his subordinates chose to hire for seasonal work each year. Since he was, essentially, the sole District contact with the Forest Supervisor too, this connection increased his power considerably. Therefore, Kermit Kaiser was a very important man to the vassals of his backwoods 'Kingdom' and to a greater extent, in his own mind's eye.

He expected respect, even if it was not merited by accomplishment or behavior on his part, simply because he held the exalted position of "Ranger". After all, he had put in his time and the Agency had seen fit to give him this important job! Kermit also knew, as everyone in the Agency knew, being given an important position in the Service meant that you obviously must be superior, in almost every way, to those subordinate to you!

Kermit saw a brilliant Federal career for himself from here on. He expected to become Regional Forester of this or another Region, eventually. Therefore, when Kermit Kaiser strode from his modest Forest Service bungalow, across the concrete bridge over Moose Creek, and into the small, crummy District Office, he walked and acted like the local reigning royalty that he was. He worked hard at projecting an air of omniscient power and knowledge. To complete the image he wanted to project, he always made sure his black jeans and tan work shirt were perfectly clean and pressed to perfection. His custom-made White's logging boots were clean and shiny with Hubbard's boot grease, and his silver aluminum Bullard "cruiser's" hard hat was polished and positioned just so on his head.

Al Fife looked up from his desk as the Ranger entered the District Office. He knew, from long experience, the sound of Kermit Kaiser's step. He jumped up from his chair and met the Ranger by the front counter and reported, "The fire index is 71 today. No storms forecast. We should be O.K. unless we get a man-caused."

76

"Thank-you. Al," said Kermit, without stopping or looking at Fife. He went right on into his office and closed the door behind him. Al Fife hesitated awkwardly for a moment by the front counter. He never went into the Ranger's office unless asked. He knew Kaiser didn't like to have people barge into his office unannounced, even if it was an emergency. Al's habit, when uncertain in about any way, was to seek reassurance from Tom Rankin, so he got his coffee cup and walked down the short hall to Rankin's tiny office.

Tom had been working at his gray metal desk for a half-hour on some minor paper work. He looked up when Al entered. The smoke from the Lucky Strike in his mouth curled into his calm gray eyes and made him squint as his eyes burned and watered. Al announced, "Well, the index is 71. No storms forecast. We ought to be O.K. unless we get a man-caused."

Rankin was a kind man, so he just said in his usual laconic way, "That right?" He slowly leaned back and took the cigarette from his lips. He considered Fife to be an incompetent idiot, but a harmless one. However, Tom Rankin was the type of person that never said such things to anyone.

Al continued, "Yep, but its gettin' mighty dry! I wish that trail crew was here instead of out there 20 miles away."

"Don't worry, Al, you can always call in the jumpers if we get hit", Rankin reassured him. "They can be here in 30 minutes from Missoula."

Fife nodded and hesitated for a few minutes then wandered aimlessly back toward the Dispatcher's desk. As he did, he wondered why lithe and lean Tom Rankin inspired so much respect in everyone he met. The fact was that, although Tom was laconic and quiet, but he exuded quiet confidence and capability. Fife, like everyone else on the District, knew that, if the shit hit the fan, Tom would be there to take charge and do the right things. Al sensed, rather than reasoned, that Tom was the 'glue of the outfit'. Reaching the Dispatcher' desk, he sat down, put his legs up, and carefully settled his ornate Justin cowboy boots on the desk. Then, with a carefully contrived air of nonchalance, he began to try, once again, to make a roll-your-own cigarette the way Orrin West did it.

After Al Fife left, Tom Rankin scribbled a few more words and a number on the bottom of a memo from the Supervisor's Office and threw it into a wire basket labeled "Out". How the Hell was he supposed to know how many pocket gophers there were on the 500,000 acre District, he thought? Well, it must be about a million; 1,354,908 to be exact, for that was what he had written down! He chuckled to himself for a moment, visualizing some Wildlife Staffer in Missoula adding up all these fictitious numbers for a report to Washington, D.C.

Still smiling to himself, he went down the hall and, after a light knock on the door and short pause, he entered the Ranger's office. "Morning Kermit," he said. "Unless you need me for something else, I'm going into China Creek today to see how Rae is doing. Should be back about three this afternoon."

Kaiser had been looking out the window apparently in deep thought, but he quickly turned to Rankin and said, "Go ahead and go, Tom. Will you also check with Pete Arnold up at the Cedars Camp to see how fast they plan to go on logging out the Gravy Creek sale? As far as I know, we are just barely keeping ahead of them on road and block boundary layout. I'm trapped here all day on paper work. I'd like to go to the field today, but if I do, I'll just have to burn the midnight oil tonight. I don't want to be doing that again."

"O.K., I'll stop and see Pete," said Rankin. "I'll see you about three." With that he turned and headed out the door toward his old green pickup truck.

After the door closed behind Rankin, Kermit Kaiser reflected for a moment on the man. A good man, he thought. Tom is reliable, competent, and easy to get along with. You can count on him. Also, he knew his place, like a good Executive

Officer on a ship. He really understands who the Captain is. God he wanted some coffee! He lived alone so he never made any at his house. Hadn't since his wife had left him three years ago up on the Kaniksu. Memories of her flooded back and he wrenched them from his consciousness, mumbling to himself: "all over, dammit, all over!" He clenched his hands into fists at this self-control effort.

A soft knock at the door brought him back to the present. He said, "Come in." Teresa Jacks, the District Clerk, entered carrying a steaming cup of coffee. "Good morning, Teresa", Kaiser said brightly. "Thank you for bringing in my coffee. I was just thinking how good some coffee would taste."

"You are very welcome, Kermit. I just made it fresh," she said, with a beautiful 'tooth paste advertisement' smile. This ritual had become habitual for both of them in the last month. Teresa liked the opportunity to see the Ranger and get her instructions for the day, first thing. Her job as District Clerk meant she was the primary administrative assistant to the Ranger regarding District business affairs. She had worked for the Forest Service for five years, ever since she had graduated from Weippe High School. She also thought Kermit was a very sexy man and, better yet, a bachelor!

Kermit took the offered coffee cup from her hand and said, "Please sit down for a minute". He sipped the coffee as she turned and sat down in a chair opposite the desk. He noticed that her jeans were particularly snug today. He sat down the hot cup and said, "Teresa, I don't need to tell you this is timeslip day. Have you got all the timesheets for all our people?"

"Yes," she said, "and for the trail crew, too. I fill theirs out for them when they are out in the woods." While she said this she adjusted her posture in the chair, straightening her back and thrusting her more than ample breasts against the thin white woolen knit of her sweater.

Kermit Kaiser observed this over the top of his steaming coffee cup, licked his lips nervously, and then muttered, "Oh, I know I do not need to ask. You always have these things well in hand. I plan to stay in the office all day today. As you can see by looking at these papers in my inbox, there is a lot of work to do. I'll ask you if I have any questions as to form. You are always such a good helper to me, I don't know how the District would get along without you, Teresa."

Teresa smiled sweetly at him for the compliment and said, "Kermit, you know I will always do my best to make your job as easy as I can". She adjusted her peroxided blond hair with one hand as she said this.

"I appreciate that, Teresa," Kermit said. "I will call you if I need anything." At that signal she rose, smoothed her sweater, and went out. She closed the door softly behind her.

Damn, Kermit Kaiser thought, a beautiful girl like that should not be on a District where there are single men, and especially single Rangers. Most of the District clerks he knew were men. The few women clerks that there were usually were either dowdy and middle aged or immature, pimply-faced teenagers. Teresa, in contrast, was built like a brick shithouse and moved with the calculated grace of a high fashion model. Her high cheekbones, red full lips, and expressive brown eyes often transfixed the young men on the summer crews when she walked by. He could not help wondering how it would be to make love to her, although he knew it might cost him his job, if word got out. Yet, she seemed to be inviting him to make advances, or, at least, seemed to want a closer friendship. Well, Hell, he was a fair looking chap, wasn't he? That sweater today was a real come-on with the top buttons undone. She did not wear it that way by chance, that was for damned sure. If he did try to make a move on her, it would have to be very discrete and at her initiation, he decided.

To get his mind off the girl and the tension in his groin, he picked up the pile of papers on his desk and began to sort through them. Same old shit here, he thought. Reports due on this and on that. Most of them were sent just to give those dickheads in Orofino and the Regional Office in Missoula something to do. He grabbed a tablet of ruled paper and began to write out a reply to the first report request. They wanted to know why the District had such high expenses for electrical generator operation and repair. That's easy to answer, he thought. It's because the goddamn generator was built for, and worn out in, the Spanish-American War and is qualified to be an antique in the Smithsonian! He didn't write that down, though. Instead, he wrote a standard, innocuous bureaucratic reply that, he knew by experience, would make the 'dickheads' happy.

Teresa Jacks returned to her oak desk in the front of the office by the entrance counter. She was still secretly smiling to herself at the way Kermit Kaiser's eyes had bugged when she arched her back as she sat in the chair opposite him. He knew a good set of boobs when he saw them! She looked out the window by her desk. She loved this spot. She could see out into the compound and observe everything that went on there.

Although she had worked for the Service for all of the five years since she graduated from high school, she still found the operations and people of the District fascinating. Increasingly she was finding Kermit Kaiser fascinating too. She wasn't sure why. He was not particularly good looking or intelligent. Perhaps, she thought, it is because he seemed to always be in control. Of course, he also had the power in this place and the prospect of her influencing that power and being near to it had a certain aphrodisiac effect on her. She wondered what he looked like with his clothes off. While she was thinking about this she absent-mindedly sharpened a half dozen pencils and put a new supply of typing paper into the paper holder on her desk. She made it a habit to always appear to be busy.

She decided that Kermit Kaiser was not as physically appealing to her as Joe McCulloch. He was nearer her age, but was not available and he had no real established position to offer.

It was a puzzle to her, anyway, what Joe McCulloch saw in his little mousy wife, Mary. Teresa Jacks and Mary visited often, so she knew Mary well. Their relationship was based on the lack of others of the same age to visit with in this remote place. Consequently, they spent more time together than they normally would have under other circumstances. Teresa felt that Mary was too passive and too dependent on her husband. Mary seemed to have no personal goals outside of her marriage and the family she was part-of. Teresa Jacks, on the other hand, fully intended to use her brains and physical attributes to get what she wanted: wealth, security, and happiness. Teresa felt that if she had to be calculating, even deceitful, about getting what she wanted, so be it.

She had seen too many nice young Idaho girls marry some ape of a logger because he had large muscles and a big bulge in his pants. Most of these girls, she had observed, wound up living in old trailer houses in the sticks with a half dozen snot-nosed kids and a big, slobbery-mouthed bird dog to care for all day. It wasn't going to happen to her! One reason she liked the Forest Service was that there were real professional men around, not the uneducated morons she was raised around in Weippe!

In the nearby Dispatcher's Office Al Fife was jarred awake by a voice blaring from the radio speaker in front of him. He quickly pulled his feet to the floor and leaned forward to grasp the "talk" button on the pedestal microphone. The voice, with a tinge of irritation, came from the speaker again. "Moose Creek, this is Orofino! Come in!"

Al swallowed and pressed the button on the mike and said, "Orofino this is Moose Creek".

"Al, this is Herb Wallace," reported the brusque voice from the speaker box. "Is Kermit in the office? I need to talk to him."

Al replied, "10-4, I'll get him on!" He jumped up, hurried to the Ranger's office, knocked, and entered.

"Herb is on the radio for you," he said to Kermit.

Without a word Kermit rose and went to the radio. As he did he thought, that Goddam Wallace is always pissing and moaning about something and he loves to do it first thing in the morning, the asshole!

Herb Wallace was the Forest Administrative Officer, responsible for all business management of the Forest. He was also an obsessive-compulsive workaholic who was paranoid about being wrong about the smallest detail of the Forest's operations. He worked untold hours a week. However, he dutifully sacrificed three hours on Sunday afternoons to his family.

"Herb, this is Kermit," Kermit announced into the mike.

"Kermit", said Wallace, "I want you to explain something to me about last week's fuel report for Moose Creek. How come you got a delivery of gas from Hanson's Petroleum on August 10 and its not shown on the log report of the fuel tank for your District that we just got?"

Kermit answered, " Herb, I'm not sure without checking the report and the log book for the pump. I'm sure it is just an oversight of some sort that is easily explained. Let me look into it today and I'll be back to you."

There was a short pause and Herb's voice came back on the radio again, saying sarcastically, "Kermit, 575 gallons of gasoline is no small matter, you know. If we were audited right now, you and I would be in real trouble. Find out what the deal is and get back to me right away!"

"Sure will, Herb. Moose Creek clear," said Kermit, keeping his anger out of his voice.

Al Fife, who was standing nearby, saw the Ranger was flushed and angry. He quickly left the room, coffee cup in hand.

Kermit stood, glaring at the radio. That monster asshole, he thought! He knows that our only communication with the S.O. is the Forest-wide radio and he knows everyone on the friggin' Forest can hear everything that is said over it. Why does he have to do these trivial takedowns of the Rangers in public like that, just to feed his fuckin' ego? This happens too often. I'm going to bring it up with the Supervisor next time I see him, for sure. As he was thinking this, he heard Wallace on the radio berating the neighboring Canyon District Ranger for getting an accident report in three days late. Well, Kermit Kaiser thought, he does get around to everyone, the pathetic horse's butt!

When Kermit passed Teresa's desk on the way back to his office he said, "Teresa, grab the gas record sheets and delivery invoices and come into my office, please."

Teresa had heard the entire interaction on the radio. She had already gathered what was needed and figured out why Wallace was concerned. She followed Kermit Kaiser into his office and said, "I've got it right here, Kermit. There is no problem, really. What happened was that the log book summary went in the morning of the 10th and the delivery arrived that afternoon. There was no way the delivery could have been reported on the log sheet."

Kermit Kaiser motioned her to sit down at the small oak conference table in the corner and closed the office door. He sat down in the other chair by the table, folded his hands on the table and said, looking at the wall opposite him, "Teresa, why do sonsabitches like Wallace have to do things like that?"

Teresa, who had seen this sort of thing over and over and had thought about the reasons, said, "Kermit, I think he's just a weak man who grabs every opportunity to feed his ego and intimidate others. I've seen it before in others besides Herb. Don't let him bother you. If you retaliate, he has won."

Kermit looked up at her. She is bright, and wise beyond her years, he thought. He said, "You're right, of course, but it sure gets old afterwhile. I'm going to talk to the Supervisor privately about it. Don't you think it has a corrosive effect on the esprit of Forest?"

She was flattered by his sharing and wanted to tell him he was dead right. However, she said, to avoid seeming presumptuous, "I don't know. Only you and the other Rangers can judge that. Just don't let it get to you, personally." Then she reached over the put her hand on his.

At the pressure of her hand his heart jumped. He looked her in the eyes and she steadily returned his look. "Teresa," he said, after a few moments, " it's good to have you to talk to about these things. Sometimes it's tough to be in charge and be all alone. Sometimes I wonder if my judgement is good or not."

"I know about the loneliness, Kermit," she said. "You know, I am alone too."

Just then a knock at the door startled them both and they hastily drew back in their chairs, breaking the intimacy of the moment. Kermit glanced quickly at Teresa, then looked at the door and said, "Come in".

Vic Castellano, the District's Fire Control Officer, stuck his head in the half-opened door and said, "Kermit, gotta' minute?"

Kermit said, "Sure". Turning to Teresa, he said, "Please call Herb on the radio and tell him what happened. No, don't do that. Call Sarah Pestolich and tell her. She's the fleet accountant and is the one that should be doing this work, not the Administrative Officer of the Forest. Ask her to tell 'ol Herbie we have his big problem straightened out!"

Teresa smiled and rose to leave, saying as she did, "That will be a pleasure that is all mine, Sir!"

When she left, Vic entered and sat down in the chair she

had vacated at the little table. Vic was the complete opposite of Kermit Kaiser. Where Kermit was a medium build, immaculately groomed and bordered on being delicate, Vic was a huge, burley man with abundant body hair that erupted in black, fuzzy fountains around his open shirt collar. He wore a smelly red and black checked wool shirt over black Australian wool long johns. His size 44 black Frisco jeans were stagged off high and had chainsaw bar oil embedded in the legs like a football player's thigh guards. His well-developed beer belly cantilevered several inches beyond a tightly cinched heavy black belt and seemed to be held from adipose avalanche only by his wide red "Homelite" logger's suspenders.

He laid his hands on the table like two big, hairy hams. Then he leaned forward on the table, looked Kermit right in the eyes, and said, "Got a coupla' things for ya', Boss. First, the brush crew is about two weeks behind what they should be. The way it is, they will never catch up piling the slash in lower Independence Creek by snowtime. That means it will not get torched this fall and we will have to live with the hazard all next summer. I suggest we put the trail crew to piling brush for at least a week when they get back outta' Newsome meadows next week. Second, I plan to send Orrin and one crewman over to fix the corrals at Lundy Lake this week."

Kermit Kaiser leaned back to get away from the vicious Skoal snuce and coffee breath that Vic exhaled on him. He put his hands together, and said, "Vic, that sounds fine to me. Go ahead and use your judgement. I appreciate you checking with me. Continue to use trail money for the brush piling the trail crew does, since we have to use that money up this fiscal year and the brush deposit money can hold over. Just don't tell anyone but me and Teresa, or the bean counters will have our asses."

Vic stood up and hooked his thumbs in his suspenders. He said, "No sweat, Boss. Consider it done! Thanks for your time." He disappeared out the door in a flash. Kermit Kaiser looked at the closed door. He was always amazed at Castellano's agility and ability to move so fast and noiselessly. It seemed impossible such a big man could do that. Vic only talked business with him and it was always brief, utterly competent, and to the point, like this. It seemed incongruous that a physical mess like Vic Castellano could be so efficient and effective, but he was. Kermit Kaiser sat down at his desk and resumed the paperwork that he had, so far, been prevented from getting to that morning.

# Chapter 8 - Discovery

Joe McCulloch crunched the Jeep's transmission into second gear to keep his speed up as he climbed the steep, deeply rutted road to Independence Saddle. The huge tires of logging trucks had cut up the road badly after a recent rainstorm. The little Jeep lurched wildly from side to side across the wide ruts that its narrow tread did not fit. Joe had to hold the wheel tight to keep it from being ripped from his hands. The doors, hood, bumpers and tailgate rattled and banged, the suspension groaned and creaked, and the engine roared.

As usual, Joe was completely oblivious to all this. His corrections to the direction of the Jeep were automatic. After several minutes, he crested the Divide and throttled back to coast into the Saddle. From here the main road began to go down Independence Creek on the right side of the drainage and descended steeply to the North Fork of the Clearwater. Joe turned left at the saddle and took a narrow, nearly brush-filled, old logging spur road that angled near the top of the Deception Creek side of the divide. He drove about a half mile, the brush whipping the sides of the Jeep all the while. He parked the Jeep in an opening in the tall alder brush.

Shutting the Jeep's engine off, he grabbed his steel thermos and poured hot coffee into the small stainless steel cup that also served as the top of the thermos. He gingerly sat the burning hot little cup on the top of the Jeep's transmission housing and lit a cigarette. He relaxed as he smoked and sipped the hot coffee. He had already been on the job for two hours. It was 8 o'clock.

Fifteen minutes later he was climbing over a gently rising hogback between where the Jeep was parked in Deception Creek and the Independence Creek drainage. The ground was covered with second growth Douglas-fir and light brush. It was easy going. Once over the top of the divide he began to descend into the steep Independence side of the drainage and soon intersected the line of yellow-painted tree trunks where he had ended his marking of the clear-cut boundary the day before. He was now in a thick stand of virgin western white pine and Engelmann spruce.

Below him, towards the creek bottom, were dense groves of western red cedars and a few fern glades. Joe sat down and pulled off the khaki Filson cruiser's vest he had on. The vest was full of pockets that held the tools of his trade - Silva compass, maps, aerial photos, pencils, an Abney level, plastic flagging and waterproof paper in a covered aluminum clipboard. From the large pocket on the back of the vest, he pulled a one-quart can of yellow tree marking paint. He gave the can a vigorous shaking, removed the cap, and inserted the bottom of a metal marking paint gun into the can. He screwed the gun tightly on the head of the can.

He looked at his watch and noted it was 9:00 a.m. Good time, he thought. Should finish today, easy. He untied the leather laces of his boots and carefully pulled the laces very tight from bottom to top of the boot so his ankles were rigidly supported. Then he retied the laces, finishing with double square knots at the top. He pulled an aerial photo from the inside pocket of the vest. The planned clearcut boundary was marked in red pencil on the photo. Looking about, and at the photo, he noted where he was and where he had to go. He guessed there was another ½ mile of contour marking until he neared Independence Saddle. Then he would have to turn down into the drainage, roughly paralleling the Creek, but up from it far enough to leave the mandatory 'buffer' strip to protect the stream from sedimentation during and after the logging. About a thousand yards of that and he would hit the bottom line of the clearcut where he had begun the marking yesterday. The parallel along the creek would be the hard part. It was brushy and had a lot of down logs, but, at least, it wasn't raining today!

By noon he was well down the Creek. He stopped for lunch by the stream where there was a small flat area. It was evident that there had been some human activity here long ago, but he didn't pay much attention. He was used to seeing the faint remains of such activity. Most of it was from the old gold-mining days back in the 1860's. He did keep an eye out for relics like old guns, but all he had ever found were some old pieces of iron and a couple of old glass bottles the sun had turned green.

He sat on an old down spruce log, pulled off his vest, and extracted a sandwich and boiled egg from the large rear pocket of the vest. He opened a small pocket on the bottom front of the vest and took out a small folding aluminum cup. He filled it with water from the Creek. While he ate and drank he could hear the logging trucks pulling up the grade far above him on the opposite side of the canyon. In the stream near his feet he saw a dark gray water ouzel walking up the stream bottom underwater, feeding on aquatic insects as it went. What a strange bird, he thought.

After eating, he smoked a cigarette. Why was it, he thought, that cigarettes always tasted better in the woods than anywhere else? Taking a last puff from the smoke, he flipped it into the creek. He put another can of paint on the marking gun, tested it for stoppages and when it worked fine, climbed back up to where he had stopped the paint line before lunch and went to back to work.

Before long he could see yesterday's beginning of the boundary line down the Creek. He continued marking until he arrived at it. Another job done, he thought. He capped the paint gun. Now how to get back to the rig? Perhaps, for once, he could get home early. Mary would be surprised. He pulled the aerial photo from the inner pocket of the vest. The best and quickest way to the Jeep seemed to be a straight-line approximately kitty-cornered across the block of timber he had marked. It meant side hilling nearly all the way, but the brush was not too bad and the hillside was not very rocky. He stuffed the photo back in the vest and set out back the way he had come, but at the same time, slightly climbing the sideslope all the while. If he did it right he would come out on the upper boundary line about where he had started that morning. Then it would be a short walk over the top of the ridge to the Jeep.

After going several hundred yards, he was about 100 yards above the steam bottom—right for the trajectory he wanted to the ridge-top. He crossed a large fern patch and entered a patch of red cedar trees. Emerging from them on the other side, a large, isolated boulder blocked his path. Because of the steepness of the ground and the small trees growing around the top of the rock, Joe decided to detour below it. After going no more than 20 feet around the bottom of it, the ground collapsed beneath the weight of his step. With the crunch of rotten wood, one leg sank into a deep hole half way up to his hip. He fell. Used to slipping on uncertain footing, he turned expertly to the side and caught himself on his hands, avoiding a painful knee injury.

"What the Hell?" Joe grunted. He was already wondering where the paint gun he had been holding went. He slowly rolled to the side, extricating his leg from the hole little by little. A broken leg out here in the boondocks would be just great, he thought. He remembered Billie Rae's teasing that morning about just that. Leg retrieved, Joe sat up and flexed his knee and massaged his lower leg muscles. "All O.K., I guess", Joe said to no one in particular. I sure never saw that coming, he thought, and heaved himself to his feet.

He looked at the hole he had fallen into. There appeared to be a cavity below the surface. Strange, he thought. He wondered what had made it. It was not an animal burrow. Alongside it, there was a piece of old wooden board. It must have been pulled out when he pulled his leg free. He reached out picked it up. How did it get here, he wondered? Kneeling by the hole, he explored its edges. There was a layer of crumbly dry wood below the surface of the forest's duff layer of needles and

91

moss. It was man made. Maybe there were some artifacts, like guns or tools, inside. Was it an old miner's cache? He reached in. The space below was deeper than he could reach. Joe enlarged the hole by tearing back the edges of it. Rotten wood, moss, grass and conifer needles flew.

He found that the original hole was about three feet across, but deeper than that. Inside it was pitch dark. He could see nothing, especially in the gloom under the forest canopy of huge trees. Flicking open his Zippo lighter, he rasped the steel-striking wheel against the flint. Lighter lit, Joe thrust it into the hole along with his right shoulder and head. Blind at first, his eyes gradually adjusted to the dimness. Below his outstretched arm, he saw several rows of dirty gray-brown lumps of old leather and pieces of rotten wooden boards. It must be an old cache. This was old stuff. What had he discovered? What was it doing here on this hillside?

Stretching as far as possible into the hole, he rested the lighter on a piece of old board and grabbed at one of the gray lumps. It was wedged among the others, but he freed it by working it back and forth and pulling upward. It was heavy. In the awkward position he is in it was impossible to pull it and himself to the surface. He sat the heavy little bag aside, part way back to his body, grabbed the still burning lighter and pulled his head and arm from the hole.

The sunlight was blinding. Joe closed the lighter, pocketed it, and reached back into the hole far enough to retrieve the little gray bag. Pulling it into the light, he saw it was made of heavy, mildewed leather. The top was tied shut with a leather thong! There were no markings on it. It weighed about fifteen pounds, he guessed. Opening his pocketknife, he cut the old thong tie. It was still tough and he had to saw at it for a second or two, but it finally fell away. Gingerly opening the bag, he peered in. It seemed to be filled with sand. Fine, heavy sand. Oh, my God, he thought! He poured a little into his hand. As the sun's rays hit the sand, even in the relatively dim light of the forest

floor, it reflected the unmistakable bright yellow color of------
GOLD!

His hands were suddenly shaking. Joe carefully poured
the gold dust in his hand back into the little leather bag and retied
the thong around the mouth of the bag. Then he sat back to
collect his thoughts. GodAlmighty! If the other bags are filled
like this one, there is a fortune here! This one bag, weighing say,
fifteen pounds. With gold at $35.00 an ounce it was worth about
$8500! Enough for two new Buicks!

His mind began to randomly race over the things he could
do with it and what he would get his family. Then he thought
about leaving this job and going back to school. Hell, why not
send Mary to school so she would have her chance to grow! A
trust fund for Little Joe! Life insurance to protect them! He could
do all the things impossible until now! Slowly he came back to
where he was. What should he do now? This wealth was not in
the bank yet, that was for sure. What if he lost it now? He began
to shake with excitement and worry combined. Too late to do
much today. In addition, he had to hide his excitement from
everyone. Even Mary! He had to hide what he had discovered, as
well as his excitement, until the gold was safely in the Bank or
somewhere else safe. He had to remove it from here and put it
somewhere safe and secret. No time today! So, he would cover it
up—hide it right here for now and come back tomorrow!

He took the lighter out, lit it, and looked into the hole
again. He could count 25 bags like the one he had already
retrieved. About quarter million dollars worth, even if there are
no more below these on the surface! Hell, earning $5200 a year
like he did, it would take him 50 years to earn what was in this
little hole in the ground. He began to shake and sweat all over
again. Then he began to laugh. He sat by the hole with his back
against the boulder and laughed until tears rolled down his face.

Mary watched for Joe's Jeep although it was only four
o'clock. Normally he never arrived home until about six. But
today he had told her he should be home early. Little Joe was

taking a nap and she was having a cup of tea and relaxing a bit. She had done laundry that day. Half way through the job the old District communal washing machine had quit. The machine was an old, old Maytag wringer washer that was powered, not by an electric motor, but by an ancient gasoline one. When it suddenly quit, she had checked to see if it was out of gas, but the tank was nearly full. She cranked it a few times with no result, so she walked to the office and asked Al Fife if he would check it for her.

Al had no luck getting it going either, even after he had given it a powerful tongue lashing for its recalcitrance. She and Al were carrying the partially washed clothes back to the cabin when Kermit Kaiser came by, returning from his lunch. He asked what the matter was, heard the problem, and promptly suggested Mary use the automatic washer in his house. She jumped at this and thanked him profusely. She and Al loaded the wet clothes into the back of the McCulloch's elderly Chevrolet sedan and she drove to the Ranger's house and finished the washing. All that, and having to tend Little Joe too, had left her tired. She had just taken her second sip of hot tea when Joe's Jeep came into sight.

Joe McCulloch parked his Jeep, gathered his tools and lunchbox, and walked over to the office. It was four o'clock. Teresa Jacks looked up as he came in and noted he was early, for Joe. She commented, "My, you are back early today. Good for you, Joe!"

Joe replied, "Got done up in Independence. It helps make up for the extra hours this last several weeks." He wanted to be sure she understood that he had the time coming. "And by the way", he added as he turned to go down the hall to his office, "I plan to take tomorrow off, too. Think I'll go fishing."

Rankin was in so Joe stuck his head in the door and said, "O.K. if I take tomorrow off, Tom?"

"Sure," said Rankin, squinting up through his usual cloud of Lucky Strike smoke, "and Joe, don't charge the time to your annual leave. Just show it as work time on the time sheet at the end of the week. You've already worked enough hours for two weeks this week."

"Thanks, Tom", Joe said, and went on to the office he shared with Billy Rae. Throwing his stuff on the old plywood-topped desk they shared, Joe sat down in the gray metal chair by it. He wanted to collect his thoughts before heading home. He looked about the ramshackle office, noting the dirt on the floor tracked in the lugs of the Vibram soles of their boots, the dirty, smelly cruiser's vests hanging from an old oak costumer in the corner, and the beat up gray old metal file cabinets. In a few days this will be history for me, he thought, and a bit of melancholy rippled through him. He quickly discounted it and began to think about the problem he had with the treasure.

He had to remove the gold from the cache and see just how much there was. Then he had to move it to a location near the Station and hide it until he could get it to town. He must not arouse the curiosity of the others. What would he do with the gold in town? Who bought gold? How could he keep the sale quiet? He suspected if the Government heard about it they would certainly want all or part of the wealth. He remembered that Vic Castellano panned gold for a hobby. He might know how to dispose of gold!

Mary, glancing out the front window of the cabin, saw her husband come out of the office. She noted that he was walking with a bouncy, vibrant step and whistling. What a change a day makes, she thought. She picked up Little Joe and met him at the door. He gave them each a big hug and announced he was taking the day off tomorrow to go fishing.

"Joe, I'm so happy that you are taking some time for yourself", she responded.

95

He kissed her and hugged her again and said, "Honey, don't worry about what I said last night. Everything is going to be fine! I'm going in to shower and clean up." He disappeared behind the bedroom curtain and, soon she heard the shower running and Joe singing off key under the hot water. She was happy that he was happy, but she wondered at the sudden change in his mood.

# Chapter 9 - Teresa Jacks

The next morning Joe McCulloch assembled his fishing gear and drove off up the Moose Creek road in his old Chevrolet sedan. Mary McCulloch busied herself with cleaning the cabin and ironing the clothes she had washed the day before. Most of Joe's gray J.C. Penny workshirts were dappled with spots of yellow tree marking paint that would never wash out, but she ironed them to perfection anyway. Her husband would always have clean, pressed shirts, even if they were rags! When she finished the last shirt, she took off her apron, picked up Little Joe, and walked over to the District Office. Teresa Jacks saw her coming and was standing at the counter when Mary entered. She held out her arms for Little Joe. "Hi, sweetie!" she said as Mary handed him to her. "Oh, you are getting to be such a big boy! Aunt Teresa hasn't seen you for soooo long."

Mary McCulloch smiled. She reflected that every young unmarried woman she knew vicariously made every baby their own. She said, "Any mail?"

"No," said Teresa, "but it is due in today. A supply truck is coming from Orofino this afternoon." Teresa held the baby close and rubbed his back.

"I've got a fresh pot of coffee in the cabin. Can you get away for a break now?" said Mary.

"Sure," responded Teresa. "Let me tell Al where I will be." She walked into the dispatcher's office and announced to Al Fife, "Al, I'm going with Mary to the cabin for coffee. O.K.?"

Al looked up from the ornate doodle he was creating and said, "Sure, Teresa. I'll catch the phone if it rings. If Kermit needs you I can run across and get you. Take as long as you want."

Little Joe rattled the sides of his wooden playpen as the women sat at the McCulloch's battered wooden kitchen table. They were waiting for the coffee to cool to drinking temperature. Teresa Jacks leaned forward and said, seriously and earnestly, "Mary, do you think Kermit Kaiser would make a good husband?"

Mary, a little taken aback, said, "Well, I guess I never gave it much thought. Certainly he has a good job and a bright future in the Agency."

Teresa said, "Yes, I thought of that. You know, Kermit and I have worked together for two years. We seem to get along well and he has always been very nice and considerate."

Having had a moment to think, Mary asked, "Do you know if he is looking for a relationship?"

Teresa replied, "I know he is lonely. He has told me that. I think he likes me and the door is open to a more serious relationship if I want one, but I need your advice, Mary." They both paused to silently and solemnly sip their coffees, conscious that this was a big powwow, with, possibly, great ramifications for Teresa.

After a minute or so, Mary said, "I'm not the world's authority on men, that's for sure, Teresa. Joe is the only man I have known. I think I chose well, but it could have been dumb luck that I found him. I do know that I love him completely and, I guess, that is what you need to be sure of—that it's real love."

Teresa nodded slowly and said, "But Mary, I have to also look out for myself. All I have is my looks. I have no education or money. I can't just fall for the first set of muscles that lights my fire. I've seen too many girls do that and wind up in deep dodo. That's one of the reasons I am looking at Kermit. I like him and I think I could love him too, but it's not like he automatically sets me afire when I am around him."

Mary, suddenly feeling like an old lady, lifted her cup of coffee to her lips again, sipped the contents, and swallowed. Then she said, "Teresa, I guess sometimes it comes like a shot and you just know, but I would guess that, more often and probably best, a woman decides based on a whole bunch of things. I knew Joe was a solid, honest, hard working man. He was on his way to being a professional when I married him. It was more than just animal attraction, it was the whole package. What I am saying is, I think, it is O.K. to consider all the things you are thinking about. It's a big decision. It shouldn't be just slam-bam, you know. Don't feel funny being somewhat calculating about it. If all the pieces seem to fit together for you and Kermit, then take the next step."

"That is what I have been trying to figure out, Mary," said Teresa. "I want to make a good decision for the whole future, not just for now, you know."

"That seems very wise," said Mary. She continued, "By the way, Joe seems very upbeat recently, don't you think? I have been worried because he has been so 'down' recently."

"He has been working very hard, Mary," Teresa said. "Everyone knows that. Yes, he seemed very happy yesterday when he came in. It's the first time I have heard him whistling in months. Oh, it's nearly eleven o'clock! I have to get back! Thank you so much for the coffee and the great advice, Mary. You are a real friend." They both stood up. Teresa hugged Mary before she went out the door.

Two hours later Teresa was in the little travel trailer she lived in. She had had a small lunch of a few crackers and a bit of cheddar cheese and was sipping a bottle of Coke. She had a Ray Conniff LP record playing softly on her hi-fi. She was deep, deep in thought about her life and Kermit Kaiser. There were probably more exciting candidates than Kermit. Like most bachelors, he probably had some bad habits and would be inconsiderate at times. Overall, though, she could see no one better on the horizon. Oh, there was Roy Bolton over on the Lochsa District and Ray Price in the S.O., but Roy drank too much and Ray's career was high centered on his prickly penchant for always winning every argument he got into.

In this part of Idaho, marital pickings for a young woman, no matter how beautiful she was, were poor. Eligible professional men without serious warts were just plain hard to find. In addition, Kermit was a Ranger! She would be a Ranger's wife! That meant rank and status that few women had in this part of the country. She and Alice Rankin would be friends and they would be attending the Forestry Wives Club together in Orofino. She had heard that was where the old broads verbally hacked up the young, beautiful ones, mainly because the old girls were over the hill and knew it. She smiled to herself at the thought. She knew she could clean their clocks at bridge.

About three o'clock Kermit Kaiser emerged from his office stretching and yawning. He had a fist full of papers that he dropped into Teresa's "in" basket. "God I'm punchy from plowing all this garbage," he said in a mumbling voice. "Teresa, you can type out short memos to report most of what I have written, like you usually do. Please call John Beckins in Personnel and tell him that the report on the Johnson accident is coming right away. It's two days overdue and I don't want Wallace to have a conniption fit about it."

Teresa nodded a 'yes' and said, "Kermit, Mary McCulloch told me the old Maytag is broken down until Orrin can fix it. I really need to do some laundry today. Could I use your machine for a couple of loads this evening ?"

"Sure," said Kermit, almost too quickly. "Bring your quarters, though! The tariff is two bits a load!" They shared a smile and he continued, "I'm going down to the cookshack to see Marlin and have a cup of coffee. Be back in a few minutes."

Kermit Kaiser went down the narrow stairs to the office's basement and out the lower back door. As he crossed the compound to the cookshack, he was thinking furiously about Teresa. Holy Shit, he thought, I wonder if this is a signal she wants it? Well, it was up to her. She had to make the move. He was available, but she had to make the move. He entered the rear of the cookshack to find Marlin and Elron busily preparing the evening meal for the crews. Tonight it would be roast beef, mashed potatoes, corn on the cob, salad, and apple pie with ice cream. The work the young crewmen did really burned up the calories and they had to have substantial food. Marlin looked up from his work and said, "Howdy, Kermit! Coffee's where it always is. Want a piece of hot pie?"

Kermit smiled back and, while he poured himself a cup of coffee, said, "Thanks, Marlin. Coffee will do. We bachelors must keep out girlish figures if we are to cut a swath with the ladies. Have you seen Orrin? I was wondering if he was back from Lundy Lake yet."

"Not yet, and I don't expect he will show today, Kermit," said Marlin. "That's because that parasite on the public purse took his fishin' pole and a sleepin' bag with him! I expect we will see him about noon tomorrow, mebbe' later if the fishin' is good."

Kermit laughed, "That just proves once again that he is smarter that any of the rest of us."

Marlin replied, "Yep! So's young Joe McCulloch. He went fishin' today. Wouldn't say where. Musta' discovered a new, secret place full a' lunkers."

That evening Kermit had just shaved off his five o'clock shadow and was putting on his best cologne when there was a soft knock at his back door. He hurriedly threw a sweater on over his undershirt, strode over, and opened the door. Teresa Jacks was standing there with a large bundle of clothes in her arms.

"Come on in, Teresa", Kermit said. "The washing machine is right in here." He led her into a longish narrow room containing a laundry sink, an old 1950-ish Westinghouse front-loading automatic washing machine, and a narrow table for folding clothes. "The soap's in that little cupboard up there if you need some. Have you used a machine like this before?" he asked.

She put the clothes on the table and said, "Yes, my mother has one like it. I hope this is not too much of a bother, Kermit. After you work so hard all day you deserve your privacy."

"Teresa," he said, "it's no bother at all. This old house gets pretty empty sometimes. I'm glad to have your company. Start the machine and come on out to the kitchen. I'm making some snacks made for us."

The old Westinghouse front-loader had a 45-degree sloping front with a door that hinged down to reveal an opening to put the clothes into. There was a smooth glass window in the door to allow viewing of the washing action. Teresa loaded it with the first load of her laundry, added soap, closed the door, and dialed the machine into action. Then she walked into the kitchen where Kermit was busily preparing a tray of cheese, summer sausage, crackers, olives, and celery, gherkins, and carrot sticks. "Just a minute and I will have this finished," he announced. "What would you like to drink? I have juice, soda pop, liquor, and some good California wine."

"You pick out what you want and that will be fine for me too," she said, standing by the kitchen table. "Do you mind if I look around the house a little?" she ventured.

"Help yourself, but don't be put off by the single man's messes that you see!" he said, not looking up from the food preparation.

Teresa slowly wandered from the kitchen though the dining room and into the living room. The furniture was Spartan, sturdy, and utilitarian. Numerous scratches and dents gave testimony of its being bounced over many rough roads in the back of Forest Service trucks. There was a big cherry wood upright piano in one corner. The house itself was spic and span. There were a few pictures of forest scenery on the walls. On top of the piano stood a silver-framed picture of a handsome couple standing in front of an old automobile. She was studying it when she realized Kermit was standing next to her.

He handed her a goblet of chilled white wine and said, "My mother and Father. It was taken just after they were married, on their honeymoon to Lake Tahoe in 1930. He was a Professor at Stanford. They are both dead now. Plane crash ten years ago."

"I'm so sorry," she said. "You must miss them terribly."

"Yes, still do. Probably always will," he said. "Come, let's sit down at the dining room table and avail ourselves of the food I have so lovingly prepared!" They smiled at each other, walked over, and sat at the table. They filled delicate small white plates with food from the tray in the center. On the way to the table he had started a hi-fi and it produced a wonderful rendition of "Embraceable You" played on a twelve string guitar. She noticed there were white candles burning on the table. The table was covered with a lace tablecloth. She fingered the lace.

Noticing the gesture, he said, "My mother's. It was one of her hobbies. I have three of these tablecloths. I bring then out for special occasions."

She turned her gaze from the cloth to his eyes and said, deliberately and innocently, "Oh, is this a special occasion?"

He looked down at his hands for a moment and then back into her eyes, "My dear Teresa, this is the pinnacle of my social year!" At that she dropped her eyes to her plate and blushed like a maiden.

Collecting himself, he said, "Is the food alright? Can I get you anything else?"

Recovering, she said, "It's wonderful and you shouldn't have gone to the trouble". They ate in silence for a few minutes while listening to the music. Then she said, "Do you play the piano? I noticed the upright in the living room."

"A little," he responded. "I have taken many, many lessons. My mother had great musical aspirations for me, but my talents contained no genius, just mediocrity. Would you like for me to play something for you?"

"Yes, that would be wonderful", she said.

Rising, he said, "Bring your wine and sit in the lounge chair in the living room. Let's see. I must have something appropriate here." He went to the piano bench, lifted the lid, and rifled through a pile of sheet music stored there. "Ah!" he exclaimed, holding up a sheet. "Here's one that Beethoven wrote for his wife. It's a delicate and a fitting tribute to a sophisticated and beautiful woman. Its called "Fur Elise". Would you like to hear it?"

"Oh, please, yes, Kermit", she said, like a younger girl.

He played the piece and he played it well. As the music filled the room they were transported from a rude backwoods dwelling in Idaho to the baroque majesty and refinement of southern Bavaria at the pinnacle of that State's power and prestige. The music completely conveyed a great man's love and tenderness for his beloved and faithful wife. When Kermit finished playing Teresa said nothing for awhile and then said softly, "That was lovely, Kermit. Thank-you very much. Do you play often?"

"Everyday if I can", he replied. "Moose Creek is a great place to practice. No telephones or traffic noise. More wine?"

"Yes, Please", she responded. She heard the final spin cycle of the Westinghouse end and she went to reload the washer. That finished, she rejoined him in the living room and they shared another glass of the excellent Chardonnay he had opened for the occasion.

He explained, "It's a 'Fetzer' from California. I have always found they produce an excellent product and it's not exorbitantly expensive."

"It's very good," she said. "A little fruity and not too dry".

"Oh, do you know wines?" he said leaning forward with interest.

"Only a bit," she said, smiling at his interest. "I once spent a few weeks in the Sonoma wine country visiting a girlfriend who had moved from Idaho to California. We toured the Sonoma and Napa vineyards some. I'm afraid it's hard to become sophisticated in any way in north central Idaho."

While they talked, he set "Embraceable You" to playing again. Turning from the hi-fi, he walked to her chair, held out his hands, and said, "May I have this dance?"

A wave of excitement washed over her. She put her hand in his and stepped into his waiting arms. Immediately they were cheek to cheek and swaying to the intimate music. He was taller than she thought he was. How wonderful his cologne smelled! She could feel his shoulder muscles under his lambswool sweater. She hugged him tighter almost involuntarily and caressed the back of his neck. He pulled his face from hers and looked her in the eyes and she looked back into his. Then she kissed him softly on the lips.

Kermit could not believe what was happening, but he was ecstatic. He gently returned her kiss. Then they stood for a long time, swaying to the music and holding each other tight, experiencing the closeness. Then, he slowly kissed her again, more passionately. Her mouth opened a bit, their tongues met. They both instantly flooded with passion. The room seemed to be reeling and only partly because of the wine. As they drew apart a bit to catch their breath, the Westinghouse washer emitted a loud, rhythmic thudding noise that signaled an unbalanced load of wet laundry.

Teresa quickly turned and went to the laundry room. She had opened the door of the washer and was bending over, redistributing the clothes, when she felt Kermit's hands on her waist. She slammed the washer door shut, restarted the machine, stood up, and leaned back against his body. He circled her waist with his arms and began caressing her breasts.

"Kermit, Kermit", she whispered, as she turned to face him. They embraced and she felt the pressure of his erection against her. They began to intimately caress each other. At the same time, they awkwardly began shedding their clothes, helter-skelter.

"I want you, Teresa," he whispered in her ear. They were both naked now, except for Kermit's white work socks.

Oblivious to where they were, he pushed her back on the inclined door of the Westinghouse, pulled her legs up and entered her as she gasped, "Do it! Take me!"

The Westinghouse was trying to accelerate through a spin cycle with an unbalanced load. The laboring machine incidentally became a vibrating mechanical enhancement to the lovers' passionate intercourse. Teresa shrieked, "Kermit, Kermit, give it to me, all of it!" just as the still unbalanced load caused make the washer to jump, in wild gyrations, across the floor. There was no imbalance shut off switch on the elderly machine!

Kermit gripped the back control panel of the washer, spasmodically clawing the big red control knobs from it. He emitted a loud, animal "Aarrguhh!"

At the same time, Teresa was shrieking "Yes! Yes! Yes!"

The Westinghouse hopped across the small laundry room and gave a last shuddering bound and, just as it riders sexual frenzy climaxed on top of it, the machine tore its hoses from their connections and pulled the power plug. Teresa, Kermit, and the Westinghouse all collapsed in an exhausted heap while scalding and ice cold water sprayed from the ruptured hoses.

After a short while, Kermit, wheezing and naked, got up and turned the water off. On unsteady legs, he looked at the washer and at Teresa Jacks, on the floor, nude, in front of it. Then he said, "Godalmighty, Teresa! I'm never going to get sell this Goddamned 'ol washing machine. That's the best sex I have ever had in my life!" They laughed and laughed.

The windows of Kermit's house were open. In the summertime the Station was hot during the day, but cooled quickly. In the evening, the residents of the compound opened the windows to cool the houses and trailers off. Tom and Donna Rankin, the nearest neighbors of the Ranger, always did this. They usually sat out on the front porch a while until the house cooled off, then went to bed. When Kermit Kaiser played his piano in the evening Tom and Donna enjoyed it. It was like having a private concert right outside their bedroom window.

Tonight, however, Kermit had only played one song. They heard the hi-fi playing faintly. Then, just as they were both beginning to drift off to sleep, they heard a strange yelling and banging that developed into what sounded like a fight. There was definitely something wrong. Donna rose on an elbow to look out the open window in the direction of the Ranger's house. "Should we go and see what's the matter, Tom?" she said.

Tom Rankin replied, "Listen." They both lay still for a few minutes, listening. Tom smiled. He turned his head toward his wife. She was smiling too. She put her arm across his chest and kissed his face. "Want to make some noise of our own, Big Boy?" she said with a conspiratorial chuckle.

# Chapter 10 - Loose Lips

The old Chevrolet sedan Joe McCulloch was driving was heavily loaded. Its rated weight capacity was about 800 pounds and he had loaded over a thousand pounds of gold dust into it. There had been much more gold in the cache than he had first thought—over two layers of the little bags!

The old car lurched like a punch-drunk fighter as he drove it slowly over the washboards of the Moose Creek road. He was exhausted. Moving the gold from the old cache to the car had taken numerous trips up and down the hill in Independence Creek. Also, the fear of being discovered had made him drive himself hard.

As he maneuvered the old car, he wondered what he should do with the gold now. He wanted it close to the Station and home and he wanted it well hidden. Somewhere close to the road, but not too close. Then he could get it into town somehow and then, somehow, convert it into currency. He estimated he had about $600,000 in gold in the car. Jesus, he thought, that's enough to take care of me the rest of my life, if I properly invest it!

About a mile above the Station, an abortive miner's road ran up the hill south from the main road. Joe turned onto it, went about 100 feet, and stopped. The car was now just out of sight from the main road. He got out and pulled a shovel from the trunk. He knew no one ever came here except a few wintering deer. The area was a sparse stand of stunted lodgepole pines. The soil was poor and the trees just did not grow well here.

After finding a suitable place about 50 feet up the hill, he dug a pit the size of the original cache. He lined the hole with an old piece of canvas, then hauled the bags of gold from the car to it. It took a number of trips. He packed the gold into the hole, wrapped the loose ends of the canvas over the top of the bags, and shoveled the dirt back on top of the cache. He carefully covered the top of the cache with needles and debris until it matched the surrounding area. Retreating to the car, he brushed out his tracks with a pine branch. He backed the Chevy to the edge of the main road, then got out, and raked out the car tracks up to where he had been parked. Then he pulled the Chevy a few hundred yards down the road and stopped in a pullout.

As he rested, he opened a bottle of beer and slowly drank it. He just could not believe he was going to be a wealthy man. He grinned to himself. As he finished his beer a dirty, green Forest Service pickup came down the road and stopped next to the Chevy. Billie Rae reached over and wound down the right window of the pickup as the cloud of dust he brought with him settled around both vehicles. "Just fuckin' off as usual, huh?" he said in a yell.

"Yeah, but you got paid for it today, Dickhead, and I didn't!" Joe retorted. They both laughed. "Want a beer, Bill?" Joe said.

"Sure!" Said Billie. He pulled the pickup off to the side of the road and shut the engine off. Getting out of the pickup, he said, "Let's go down by the creek and drink it. John Q. Public would not like to see one of their beloved Civil Servants swilling demon rum while leaning against their fine vehicle."

Joe laughed and grabbed his small steel icebox. They walked over the side of the road and into a willow patch. Fifteen feet further they emerged on a sand and stone bank of the fast-running creek. They both sat down with grunts, and grabbed and opened a bottle of beer. After a short quiet, while they drank the first swallow of the brew, Billie said, "Catch any fish, Isaac?"

"Nope. Isaac Walton I'm not. Had a good day, though. It's good to break the routine sometimes. How was your day?"

"Same old shit," Billie said. "Kermit the Kaiser's got a flea up his ass to get the China Creek Sale up by mid-September. I'm pushing the timber crew hard to finish the cruise. Oh, I saw a lynx in the road in China Creek this morning. Beautiful cat!"

"No kidding?" Joe reacted. "I have never seen one. Big?"

"Not especially, but big ears and feet," said Billie. They both sat and silently drank their beers for a few minutes.

"Billie, you ever wonder what it would be like to have money?" Joe said, musing.

Billie looked up and said, "Not really. Never figured I would have to worry about that. Why?"

"Well, I was just wondering what I would do if I had it", Joe said. "I sure wouldn't stay with the Forest Service. Would you?"

"Shit no!" Billie snorted as he took another swig of beer. "I would live in town and come to the woods just for recreation. I probably wouldn't have time, though, because I would have to be playing golf and planning my winter in Florida. Then, of course, there would be my active intellectual life, my cars, and all my girls. I guess I'd have to come to the woods once in awhile to rest up!" They both laughed and opened another bottle of beer.

The next day Joe McCulloch stayed in the office to catch-up on the paperwork for the sale he was preparing. He also had to complete some special use permit applications for submission to the S.O. At coffee break he went to the cookhouse with Tom Rankin. Entering at the rear, Tom said imperiously to Marlin Stelges, "We are ready for our coffee and pie, Marlin!"

Marlin slowly wiped his hands on his apron and turned to face Rankin. The retort was predictable: "You Forest Service office weenies think all you got to do is waltz in here any time a' the day and place an order like this was a Goddamn short order café, huh! Well, I'm here to tell you, Mr. Big Deal Forest Officer, that it's not that way it is here; not for you and not for that pimply-faced teenage flunky you brought along with you!"

By this time, Marlin was getting a pie out of the refrigerator and slamming plates down to hold the pieces of pie he was going to cut. "No sir," he continued, "just give some woolly-headed cluck a college degree and a title and they think that they control the earth. Elron! Elron, you lazy little fart, get some ice cream out of the freezer for this pie!"

As Tom and Joe ate their pie and sipped their black coffee, Tom said, "I'm going up to Fly Hill tomorrow to check the Hoodoo range allotment's condition. Want to go with me?"

"You bet!" Joe quickly answered, for this meant a fun day in the high country with a man he respected and liked. It also meant a day with a colleague and not one of lonely individual work in the deep timber.

"I figure we will also take the binoculars and the photos of the Comet Creek area," continued Tom. "While we are up there we can visually reconnoiter Comet Creek for a possible sale next year."

They finished their pie and coffee and carried the plates and utensils to the dirty dish tray. "That was mighty fine pie, Marlin. Thank you very much", Tom said, patting the Cook's thick shoulder as he went by him on the way out of the cookhouse.

"You are very welcome, Mr. Rankin!" said Marlin. "It tastes that way 'cause I use good 'ol fatty lard in the crust!" he

111

bellowed after them. "Good 'ol lard that coats the insides of your arteries with about a half inch of waxy cholesterol each time you eat a piece!"

Both Tom and Joe were chuckling as they walked to the office. They, and everyone else in the camp, could hear Marlin shouting at Elron to put the 'Goddamned' ice cream away before it melted and ran all over the 'Goddamned' floor.

The next day Tom and Joe had lunch at the old fire lookout site on top of Fly Hill. They had a spectacular view of the whole central part of the District. Rank upon rank of wooded ridges of the Bitterroots rolled away to the south toward the Lolo Pass and the Selway country. The sun was bright and the sky was the deep, deep azure blue it only is at high elevations. Up here it was just late spring by mid August. The ground was covered with a riot of wildflowers. Myriad insects frantically buzzed from flower to flower gathering nectar. They knew, from the shortening daylight, that the first frosts of the new winter could come any day.

Joe and Tom sat on an old log. They were leg-weary. They had examined most of an extensive high country sheep allotment that morning on foot. After while Tom rose and walked slowly to the truck. He returned with a set of high powered ex-Navy binoculars and a fist full of aerial photographs. Sauntering over to the edge of the drop off into the steep canyon of the North Fork, he stopped. From there he could see into the wooded north slopes on the south side of the River, below. Joe joined him. Tom handed Joe the photos. Then he began to scan the south side of the drainage of the canyon through the binoculars. After a short time he handed them to Joe, took back the photos, and sat down, cross-legged, on the ground. He began making marks on the photos with a soft, colored pencil. Joe was looking through the binoculars at the same places Tom had scanned.

112

As Tom marked the photos he said to Joe, "See that stand of white pine, cedar, and grand fir in the middle of Comet Creek? It wraps around on into Lightning Creek. I'll bet there's 20 million feet of timber here. If we extend Road 789 in there for a main haul road, the appraisal should work out good."

"Yeah," said Joe, as he looked at the area Tom was talking about. "We can harvest that 100 acres or so of mature stuff in Cougar Creek on the way in. Funny how the 1919 fires jumped some of those patches and didn't burn them up". As he scanned the area he also looked into Independence Creek and spotted about where he had found the gold.

Soon they both went over to the shade of a bushy mountain hemlock tree. The mid-summer sun of the high country was brutally intense. Tom continued, "Joe, plan to go into that area and recon it on the ground next week. I'll go with you if time permits, but someone needs to be sure to look it over before snow falls. Measure how steep the slopes are and see if any rock formations will foul up the road location. Also, bore some of those trees and estimate how rotten that old timber is. Then we can get a better handle on what the logging might really produce in the way of wood. Sometimes those old 'punkins' are not even worth cutting down."

"I will, Tom", Joe said, "but you had better make sure you or someone else goes with me".

"Why?" said Tom, looking up curiously.

"Because," Joe said, "I might not be here next year when the cruising and layout really starts. You will want one of the original recon men to be around to help plan it and guide the timber crew."

"You planning on getting a promotion and going to another District, Joe?" said Tom in a slightly needling manner.

"No, I would never count on that sort of thing", smiled Joe. "Actually, I don't think I will be with the Forest Service much longer, Tom. Just between you and me, I have come into some money. I have plans to do some other things. I'd appreciate you keeping it quiet for now. I haven't even told Mary yet, but I figured that you should know."

Tom Rankin didn't rest well that night. Something about what Joe McCulloch had told him that day just didn't add up. He did figure out that he would have to tell the Ranger. Kermit and he were responsible for staffing the District and getting the work done. Losing one of their two foresters was a big impact and they had to plan for a replacement.

Tom met with Kermit the next evening. He started by saying, "I promised McCulloch to keep this quiet, but I thought you should know, Kermit." It was late evening. The two men were standing in Kermit's front lawn, leaning on the front fence and looking over it into the running water of Moose Creek. "Joe's planning on leaving before too long," continued Tom. "He hasn't told his wife yet, but I expect he will soon. Damn, I hate to lose a good man like him."

"You know why he is leaving?" said Kermit. "Is it something we have done wrong?"

"No. Evidently he has come into some money lately," Tom said. "I don't think it's anything we have done and it looks like there is nothing we can do to get him to stay. Might not hurt to talk to him a bit, though, Kermit. Just be sure and keep it between you and Joe and me for now."

"Sure. I'll talk to him soon," said Kermit Kaiser.

Saturday morning after breakfast Joe McCulloch said to Mary, "You know, Tom and I were up on Fly Hill day before yesterday and it was just beautiful—flowers and all. How about us jumping in the old 'Chev' and driving up to Gorman Hill for a picnic today? If we don't do it soon the snow will keep us from it until next year."

Mary was delighted. They didn't get out together much, and she loved to go to the woods. She said, "I'll fix the lunch if you will get Little Joe ready! We will need his toys, blankets, and diaper bag. The only lunchmeat we have is Spam. Will let the all right?"

He said, "Well, I eat it nearly every day for lunch, so another day won't make much difference!"

They both busied themselves with getting ready and soon bundled Little Joe, his toys, blanket, and a hamper full of food into the old sedan. Joe started the car and headed up the steep grade up to Gorman Hill. The "Hill" was about five miles from the Station and directly above it. On top of the Hill was a dilapidated old fire lookout tower. The District staffed the old tower only when the woods were really dry or if a lightning storm happened to hit the area. It was one of the few lookouts on the District that could be driven to. Most were accessible only by foot or horseback.

They drove slowly to enjoy the day and preserve the internal workings of the arthritic car. As he drove, Joe couldn't help but think that he would not have to drive an old wreck like this Chevrolet much longer. He was busting to tell Mary of his good fortune. He intended to share his secret with her today. The picnic should create the right privacy and atmosphere for it!

The Chevy's radiator was just starting to boil as they coasted to a stop at the base of the tower. Joe let the car's engine run for several minutes to allow it to cool down before he shut it off. Meanwhile they unloaded the picnic supplies and put Little Joe on the blanket in the shade below the cab of the lookout. Then they took time to look around. They had the whole mountaintop to themselves and they could see for miles and miles in every direction. It was a brilliant sunny day. Before long Little Joe had fallen asleep and Joe and Mary were lounging beside him on the blanket in the cool shade of the lookout.

115

Joe, wishing he had wine, opened two bottles of beer and handed one to Mary. He said, "I know you do not normally drink beer, dear, but today is a very special day for us, so you must. Right now we are going to toast ourselves."

Surprised, she clicked her bottle against his as he indicated she should, and said," What's so special?"

He looked into her wide eyes with an intensity unnerving to her and said, "Mary, I told Rankin yesterday that he shouldn't expect me to be on the District next season. I told him to keep it a secret for now. What has happened to us is beyond all belief. I don't believe it myself! You must keep this part of what I am going to tell you secret. Our very lives may depend on you doing that. Can you do that?"

She looked at him, completely puzzled, and said slowly and softly, "Yes".

"Mary, you and I are rich!" he exploded.

"Whaaat?" slowly dribbled from her open mouth.

"Yes, Mary, rich, rich, rich!" he laughed.

"Hooow?" she mumbled, blank-faced and incredulous.

"Mary, I found a ton of gold," he said, unconsciously looking around. "Old gold dust that was cached by miners a hundred years ago! I found it! Literally fell into it. Into a hole in the ground—full of gold!" He went on to tell her the whole story.

Gradually she realized he was not kidding. She became excited and hugged and kissed him. "Oh Joe, it's wonderful! We can have all the things we have wanted and we won't have to scrimp anymore!" she whooped.

Then he told her that he still had to sell the gold. That was why keeping the secret about the gold was so important. She nodded soberly at this, fully understanding his concern. "As far as anyone else knows we just came into "some money" and that's all they need to know, Dear," he emphasized.

"Where will we go, Joe, and what will we do?" she asked.

Kissing her on the lips, he said softly, "We have the rest of our lives to decide that. I'm so glad it happened. What makes it perfect is that you love me, too."

At the same time Joe and Mary McCulloch were having their picnic, Teresa Jacks was laying on her back, spread-eagled and naked, on Kermit Kaiser's double bed. She was sweaty and still trying to catch her breath. She and Kermit had just finished a lusty bout of sexual intercourse. Kermit came out of the bathroom, also nude, toweling himself off and smiling at her. "God, Teresa, you are a beautiful woman!" he exclaimed.

"I'll bet you say that to all the girls," she said, smiling.

He laughed and lay down beside her. "Can you keep a secret?" he said, as he stared at the ceiling.

She quickly turned and propped herself up on one elbow and looked at him, curiosity written all over her face. "Of course," she said. "Don't I keep all the nasty District personnel stuff to myself?"

"Well," he said, "Rankin told me yesterday that Joe McCulloch would be leaving before too long. Evidently he has come into a big sum of money and will be quitting the Forest Service."

"Where did the money come from? Do you know, Kermit?" she asked eagerly. "When will they be leaving? Has he told Mary yet?"

"As far as I know, Teresa, its 'no' to all those questions," said Kermit. "Remember you swore to keep it a secret."

Rolling on to her back, Teresa looked at the ceiling and said, "Oh, I will, Kermit. Don't worry." Her mind was churning with questions and she was visualizing Joe McCulloch in a business suit.

117

Tom and Donna Rankin were sitting in aluminum lawn chairs on the shady front porch of the old bungalow they lived-in. She was knitting and he was reading a book about how to train hunting dogs. The kids were playing in the front yard. In the background a record was playing and Nat King Cole's dulcet voice provided a soothing atmosphere. It was a lazy summer afternoon. They were enjoying it. Looking up from her knitting, Donna said, "Was it pretty up in the high country last week?"

Tom responded, "It was. You should have seen the flowers—penstemon, scarlet foxfire, buttercups, Indian paintbrush, all of them."

"Well, Joe McCulloch must have liked it", she said. "He took Mary and Little Joe went up to Gorman Hill this morning for a picnic. Mary was so excited. I'm glad to see him taking more time for her and the little boy. He works too hard."

"Well, Donna, you know everyone does that in the Service when they start out. I wouldn't worry too much about that, though," Tom said. "Just between you and me, it looks like Joe is quitting the Service."

Mary straightened up and looked intently at her husband. "No!" she said. "Why in the world is he doing that?"

"Well, again, just between you and me, he said he has come into some money, He figures he can afford to go now."

"Was it an inheritance? Where are they going? When are they leaving? Does Mary know?" said Donna, in a rush.

"I don't know. Donna, and don't you be prying," Tom said, looking at her for the first time. "Keep it under your hat. We will know what we need to know when it all comes out"

Donna did not say anything else. She began knitting furiously, knitting as fast as her brain was processing the new information. I will find out what's going on tonight, she thought. I'll invite the McCulloch's for dinner. How many pork chops were there in the freezer, she wondered?

# Chapter 11 – Friends

That night at the Rankin's dinner table Donna Rankin asked Joe and Mary when they were leaving. Joe McCulloch nearly choked on a mouthful of pork chop. Recovering, he looked at Tom. Tom shrugged and said to Donna, "Donna, you know that that is supposed to be confidential! Although I shared it with you this afternoon, you had no right to ask Joe the question. I makes me look like an untrustworthy motor mouth."

Unabashed, Donna said to her husband, "Tom, we are all friends here. When someone leaves, it affects all of us. Joe and Mary are special friends of mine. I have no secrets from them."

Yeah, big mouth, no secrets except that your idiot Aunt Josephine's the leader of the rocking chair brigade down at the State Mental Hospital in Orofino, Tom thought. He turned to Joe and said, "I'm sorry this leaked, Joe. As far as I know, only the people at this table and Kermit Kaiser know about it. I felt that I owed it to Kermit for personnel planning purposes."

Joe nodded and said, "That's O.K., Tom."

By the end of weekend, the fact that Joe McCulloch was leaving the Forest Service was common knowledge around the District. Joe was very well liked and most of the friends he had at Moose Creek were sad and a little upset that he was leaving. When his friend Orrin West heard it he stopped rolling the cigarette he was making and simply said, "Ah, shit! You get one good one and then he quits!"

All the inevitable questions about where they were going, and when, were building up. Out of respect and courtesy, though,

119

most did not say anything immediately, but they were very curious. Joe McCulloch could feel it when he walked into the office Monday morning. As he entered, Teresa Jacks gave him a super big smile and inspected him like he was a weird laboratory specimen. Al Fife stood up from his desk and watched him walk down the hall. As he entered his office and sat down, Billie Rae, already there and waiting for him, quickly closed the door behind Joe.

"Jesus Christ, Fella! What's this shit about you leaving?" he said sotto voce.

Joe simply said he had come into some money, had some other opportunities, and wanted to make a change.

At this Billie snorted, "So you are leaving me here with these Goddamn brush apes and going to seek your fuckin' fortune, huh? Well, 'ol buddy boy, when I retire in 35 years on a big fat 'ol Gov'mint pension and you are scrapin' a grill in some hamburger joint, don't blame me!"

They both laughed. There was a knock on their office door.

Teresa Jacks opened the door and said to Joe, "Kermit would like to see you when you have a moment, Joe." He thanked her and told her he would be there in a minute.

When she had closed the door behind her, Billie said to Joe, "Ah, the Big Boy wants to see you, Joseph, you naughty, naughty boy! I'll bet he wants to know if you are leaving because you are pissed that we have a totally inept, pompous shithead of a Ranger! He especially wants to see if you know he is banging the pee-waddin' outta' the District Clerk every night. He desperately wants to know if you'll be tattling all this to Big Daddy Supervisor Seward down in Orofino town!"

They both broke up laughing.

Finally, Joe said, "I better get in there."

Kermit Kaiser asked Joe to sit down and to close the door behind him. "Joe," he said, "I hated to hear you might be leaving. Is it for sure?"

Joe said, "That's right, Kermit. Things are right for me to make a change. I want you and Tom to know that I really appreciate the support you have given me while I learned the trade here at Moose Creek. I don't necessarily want to leave the Forest Service, but it's just the right thing for me to do now."

Kermit said, "Joe, each of us has to make choices like this. If you are that set on it I will go ahead and plan to fill behind you. Any idea of when you might actually be going?"

"In about two months, I think. I can finish the field season for you," said Joe.

"I'm thankful for that, Joe", Kermit Kaiser replied. "I'll need to begin to line up a replacement before too long, but I don't need to let the S.O. know for a few weeks. Now remember, if you need a recommendation for employment later on, just ask and it's yours. Let me be the first to wish you all the luck in the world!" Kermit Kaiser extended his hand and they shook cordially.

About 10 o'clock, Joe and Tom Rankin walked to the cookhouse for coffee. Marlin Stelges was not his usual ebullient, insulting self. He looked at them seriously and self-consciously wiped his hands several times on his long, white apron. Then he walked up to Joe, took his hand, and escorted him to the coffeepot. "Mr. McCulloch," he said slowly and somberly, "Elron and me are sure sorry to hear you are leaving us. We figured you would be here for a good while. We're going to miss you, my friend!" The diminutive Elron emerged from some hidden crevice and shyly shook Joe's hand too.

Joe, not sure what to say, mumbled, "I'll miss you guys too, but I will be around for a couple of months. You can't get rid of me that fast!" He awkwardly turned and went to the front of the cookhouse where Rankin was sitting with Orrin West.

The leathery old cowboy looked sadly up at Joe through a blue haze of tobacco smoke and said, "Buggin' out, huh?"

"Yep!" said Joe as he sat down with them. "I'm goin' where the cooks are friendly and the packers practice manners around their betters!"

"Well, Tom, some's got it and some don't," said Orrin, looking into Rankin's eyes, seeming to ignore Joe. "Me, I like the mountains. They build character in a man. Others just love the flatlands. They root around down there day after day and kinda rot away in that soft livin'. Sometimes they come up here and play at bein' woodsmen. Soon as they get a little bit dirty and sweaty, they run back down to their city friends and tell them that they had a big shittin' adventure."

"You called it, Orrin!" Joe said. "That soft living is what I want. You know what I mean: no packrats to keep me awake at night, no mice crawling into bed with my baby, drinkable water and electricity that works, roads that don't tear you to pieces, and decent pay for your work!"

"You really expect a lot, don't you?" Orrin said as he put his huge arm around Joe's shoulder. As he gave Joe a gentle squeeze, he said, with tears welling up in his eyes, "Me and the mules is gonna miss you, Son. It's just a Goddamn pity the Service loses folks like you at a time when we're turnin' into a mob of paper pushin' pen wipers."

That afternoon Joe noticed that Vic Castellano was working by the fire cache across the compound. He hurried over to see him. He liked Vic and learned a great deal from him. Vic was unloading rolls of dirty fire hose from the back of his pickup. Looking up from his work, he said to Joe, "Hear you are going on to better things! More power to you. They don't let you guys use your education anyway. It's O.K. for me, with no education and four kids to feed, but not for you, Joe."

Without a word, Joe began helping him unload the pickup. The heavy rolls of hose were still wet and filthy with mud and ashes. "Vic, you know its a funny feeling," Joe began, " I know its the right thing to do, but I sure will miss the woods and the people out here. Its a way of life, I think, not just a job."

"Yeah, I know what you mean", Vic responded. "I can't imagine doing anything else, but, hey, you can come see us anytime!"

"Well, spare time stuff is what I wanted to talk to you about, Vic", Joe said. "I know you pan gold for a hobby and pocket change. I've tried it myself a few times lately. I've got a little dust. What if I wanted to actually sell the gold dust I panned?"

Vic smiled and said, "Getting hooked, huh? It's a good hobby. I pan enough on weekends to take the family out to dinner several times during the winter. If I go into Orofino, I take the gold dust I pan down to an assayer and buyer there. His name is Dobbins and the business is 'Dobbin's Precious Metals'. He's a small time guy, but he will buy up to a thousand dollars worth at a time. If I go to Superior, I take my pannings to Joe Elias at 'Montana Metals' on Main Street. He's a bigger dealer than Dobbins because he takes in gold from all the small miners in western Montana."

When you sell gold to these guys, where does it go after they buy it?" Joe said.

"I'm not sure," said Vic. "I think it goes to Portland or Denver. Why?"

"Well, I'm just curious," said Joe. "Hell, I might hit the mother lode!"

Vic smiled hugely and said, "You might! You might! Just take old Vic with you when you do! Being an optimist when you pan gold is essential!"

Joe was thinking hard about Dobbins and Elias as he walked away from the talk with Vic Castellano. It sounded like Dobbins was not the man that would or could buy over a half ton of gold dust. Elias in Superior was probably his man. With only the forest radio in the office for communication to the outside world, there was no way he could talk to Elias from Moose Creek. He decided that he, Mary, and Little Joe would drive to Superior the next day. Still thinking about all this, Joe climbed into his Jeep, started it up, and headed for Spotted Bear Landing Strip. He had promised to help Orrin West repair fence there that afternoon.

Vic Castellano was Al Fife's boss. They had come to an understanding about work a long time ago. Al manned the dispatcher's desk during the summer, received and carried messages, and did other odd jobs around the District headquarters. In the fall and the spring, Al helped on the timber crew. In the winter he drew maps for timber and fire purposes and, frankly, dozed a lot. Vic, being the hard driver that he was, used to get upset that Fife didn't do more, but he gradually came to understand that Al wasn't paid much and he did pretty much what he was capable of. Over time, their relationship became one of habit and comfort. Vic had learned that Al performed best if he was encouraged and not pressured. He tended to fall apart under pressure. Vic tried to make sure that he visited Al at least once a day to see how he was doing and to reassure him. So, when he finished unloading the fire hoses he walked to the Office to see Al. Al knew that Vic was in the compound so he was sitting upright at the dispatcher's desk busily filling out forms when Vic arrived. "Hey Al!" Vic said as he entered. "What's cookin'?"

Al smiled as he looked up. He really liked Vic Castellano. Vic was kind and thoughtful. Not many people were

124

kind to Al. "Just gettin' my paperwork caught up, Vic," Al said, "and I'm doing Marlin's grocery order now. Then I have to do the fire cache status for Orofino."

Vic sat down in a wooden chair by a small table in the corner of the room. This was his "office". He didn't keep a regular one. He really had little use for a desk except in mid-winter. "Good! Good!" he said to Al. "Any fires on the forest?"

"Two over on the Canyon District and one on the Lochsa. All spots," said Al. "What about Joe McCulloch leaving? Isn't that something?"

"Yeah," Vic said. "You know any gold dealers around besides old Dobbins in Orofino and Elias in Superior?"

Al thought a few seconds then said, "No. Why?"

"I guess Joe has done some hobby gold panning like you and me. He wanted to know where he could sell any metal he finds," Vic said. "Old Dobbins is the only buyer I have ever used."

In the front office Teresa Jacks was listening to the conversation through the open door. She was filing her carefully kept fingernails in preparation for a careful buffing and painting. Her father used to pan for gold, she remembered. He used to show the little vials of nuggets to her when she was small. She did know it was worth 35 dollars and ounce, so a pound was worth $550.00 and, as heavy as gold was, a pound was a small volume. She remembered that from high school. She looked at the clock. In forty-five minutes the coffee that Donna was having for the District's women was being held. Normally Teresa Jacks did not attend these functions on Monday afternoons, but today she was. There was a lot going on and she wanted the latest news. The women were the ones that knew about real current events here. In addition, she wanted to see how they reacted, now that they knew she and Kermit were 'serious'. I'll bet I get more respect from the stuck up bitches now, she thought!

Donna Rankin checked to see if the coffeecake she had baked was cooling as it should. It was and it would be just right when the "girls" arrived at 2:00 o'clock.

"Do you want to use paper plates or china?" asked Rita Lou Rae from the dining room. Rita Lou was Billie Rae's wife. She was a slender, tall woman with honey blonde hair. An ex-Homecoming Queen at the University of Mississippi, she still had a very heavy southern accent. "Piper," replied Donna, mimicking her friend's accent, "and put on the niiiipkins, too, Riiiita Looo."

"Well, all right, you 'blackie-lovin' Yankee scum!" Rita Lou laughed back. This was her usual retort, among friends, when she was teased about her accent.

Donna said to Rita Lou, "You suppose Teresa Jacks will show up now that she and Kermit Kaiser are sleeping together?"

"Betcha' she does!" said Rita Lou. "Jus' to rub it in to us that she is doin' it! I spec' she wants to be sure and let us know she may be becomin' a Ranger's spouse and all. Is Mary coming?"

"Definitely," said Donna, "and I hope she will tell us all about their plans and their money!"

The raisin-cinnamon coffeecake was delicious. Donna was complimented about it far beyond what was appropriate. The four women, Mary McCulloch, Donna Rankin, Rita Lou Rae, and Teresa Jacks knew each other well. They normally would not have been particularly close, but the isolation and the close working relationships of their men made them close. They had to depend on each other in ways neighbors in towns did not.

"Tell us about your moving plans, Mary", Donna said, starting the serious talking.

"Well," Mary said, composing herself, "there's not much to tell. We leave in about two months, after the field season is over. We plan, right now, to go to Moscow, Idaho. Joe will re-enter the University. He plans to study Business Management for an MBA. We will buy a house there. We are going to leave what furniture we have in the cabin and buy all new in Moscow. Joe's Master's degree should take about two years to finish, then who knows where we will go!"

They seriously sipped their coffees almost simultaneously as they digested this new information. Then Rita Lou said, "My word, Mary McCulloch, it sounds like you'all struck it rich, what with the new house and furniture and all that you are going to buy! You must just be excited to death! We are all so happy for you, Darlin'!" They all concurred and smiled at each other.

Mary then said, "Thank you. We are very happy. We will have enough money for Little Joe's education, too, and we plan to get a new car as soon as we get to town. A Buick, I think, is what Joe wants."

"If you don't mind me asking, Mary, what happened to make such a big change all of a sudden?" asked Teresa Jacks. "It sounds like a dream came true!" They all hesitated and the three women all looked at Mary, waiting for a response.

"Joe had a rich Uncle that died and left us a bequest," She said, looking at her cup.

"Marvelous! Honey, we are so happy for you!" gushed Rita Lou.

At the same time Teresa Jacks was thinking: rich Uncle my ass! I smell a rat here.

Donna Rankin sipped her coffee. She wondered if this young couple was getting into trouble.

The next day Joe McCulloch was sitting in his Forest Service Jeep shivering convulsively, smoking a Viceroy, and drinking a steaming cup of coffee. The engine was running and the anemic heater was on full blast. Joe was soaked and cold.

127

He had just come back from a tough three-hour reconnaissance of the nearly vertical Comet Creek area. He had wound up doing the 'recon' alone. Billie was sick. The icy rain, steep terrain, and thickets of down timber had made it a miserable job. He was reflecting that he would not have to do any more of this miserable shit after a few weeks time.

A sudden wind gust shook the tall trees hanging over the Jeep causing a cascade of water to fall and pound on the sheet-metal top of the cab. He barely noticed. He was planning a trip to Superior, Montana, Saturday to check out Montana Metals. He would take a modest amount of gold in and sell it. They needed the cash! The main thing, though, was to see if the buyer could, or would, take a large amount of gold.

To Hell with this, he concluded, I going home for a hot shower. Gulping the rest of the coffee, he screwed the cup back on the Stanley, jammed the Jeep into reverse, turned, and backed up the narrow road's cut bank. He wrenched the wheel in the opposite direction, slammed the transmission onto first gear, and guided the Jeep, slithering and careening, back out the narrow logging road.

"When do you think you might be promoted again, Kermit?" Teresa Jacks asked the Ranger, as they sat cuddling on his sofa that evening.

"I don't know," he said. "The Outfit is growing pretty fast. I told Ralph (Ralph Seward, the Forest supervisor. Kermit's boss) that I wanted a Regional Office Staff job next, if possible."

Teresa Jacks was already imagining herself as a Regional Staff Officer's wife in Missoula Montana, or one of the other Regions. She snuggled closer to him and, remembering the McCullochs, said "What about Joe McCulloch leaving? At the old hen's party Monday Mary McCulloch told us they are going to move to Moscow so he can go to graduate school. They are buying a new house, car, and furniture. She also told us that the money he is getting is coming from a rich Uncle who died."

"Well, I just wish I had an Uncle like that!" Kermit said.

"Kermit, that money did not come from an 'Uncle'! I know for a fact that they did not get any news by mail or by radio this last week. I did hear Vic and Al talking about telling Joe where to sell gold. Do you think he possibly could have found gold?"

"Teresa, I guess anything can happen, but I doubt it," Kermit said, but he was thinking about where Joe had been working. Independence was in the old gold strike area on the District.

# Chapter 12 - Sorry, Joe

Early the next morning, Joe McCulloch was in the District's barn with Orrin West. Orrin was the only man that Joe McCulloch had ever fully trusted. He felt he could discuss anything with him. They talked while he helped Orrin feed the stock and tidy the barn up. "Orrin, I've got a problem and I need someone to talk to about it. What I say has to be just between you and me," said Joe.

Orrin did not stop working or look up, but said, "Never knew a man with money that didn't have a problem. As far as keeping anything quiet goes, you insulted me by even saying I have to keep it secret if you tell me something in confidence. After that, I'm not sure I want to know."

"Orrin, I need your advice bad and I need someone to watch my back", said Joe, earnestly.

Orrin sensed that his young friend was really concerned, and the implied threat he was worried about sounded serious. He stopped what he was doing, slouched down onto a haybale, tilted his old Stetson back, and said, "Shoot".

"Orrin", Joe blurted, "I'm rich because I found a cache of 100 year old gold up in Independence. I reckon there's about $600,000 dollars worth. I'm trying to figure out a way to get it from here to a buyer and keep it quiet. Everyone around here seems to know everything that I do as soon as I do it.

"Orrin whistled softly, rubbed his forehead with a horny hand, and said, "I'll be damned. You do have a problem."

Joe went on to tell Orrin about his plan to go to Superior on Saturday and then move the whole load of gold in for sale if it all looked O.K. Orrin had no better idea about what to do. He concurred with Joe that people go crazy when gold is around. He had seen it before. He promised Joe that he would try to cover his back as best he could. Joe told him the only other person that knew about the gold was Mary. Orrin's last bit of advice was for Joe to move fast to keep ahead of the gossip mill and be damned careful what he said to the potential buyer.

Wednesday, about an hour before lunchtime, Joe McCulloch pulled his tired old Chevy sedan up to the front of the establishment called "Montana Metals" in Superior. He had left Mary and Little Joe at the J.C. Penny's store three blocks away so Mary could shop. He entered the small, grubby shop and walked to the counter at the rear of the front room. No one seemed to be around. "Hello?" he called.

There was a rustling in the back room and a small hunched man appeared and said, "Yes?"

Joe explained who he was and asked if he could sell some gold dust. The little man said that it was his business and to let him see the gold. Joe produced one of the old leather bags of gold dust and the man emptied it onto a pan on a balance beam scale, put some lead and brass weights on the other pan and announced that the pannings of gold weighed 25 pounds. He looked at the dust though a magnifying glass and told Joe he roughly estimated that the volume was about 95% pure, but that an assay would be required to be sure. That would take an hour. Then he could give Joe the accurate amount of money for the gold. Joe said, "O.K., I'll be back in an hour".

An hour later Joe returned to the shop and the little man, who now introduced himself to Joe as Joe Elias, said, "My assay estimate was right Mr. McCulloch. There's 25.25 pounds of pure gold and, at $35.00 an ounce it comes to $883.75. Will a check be all right as payment?"

"Sure," said Joe, giddy at the prospect of having the equivalent of three months hard work handed over just like that. Mr. Elias made out the check and handed it to Joe. Joe stood awkwardly for a moment and then said, "Mr. Elias, may I have a few moments of your time? And may I ask you the favor of having our talk out of sight in the rear of your store?"

Elias looked at Joe McCulloch thoughtfully, gauging if he might be the type that would rob him, then said "Surely. Please come back and sit down."

After they had both settled into a pair of old black leather chairs in the cluttered rear of the store, Joe said, "Mr. Elias, would you be prepared to purchase a large sum of gold if someone brought it in to you?"

"Please, call me Joe, Mr. McCulloch", the little man said, looking hard at Joe. "How much gold do you think "someone" might want to sell?"

"Perhaps as much as 1,200 pounds," said Joe. "and please call me Joe, too."

Joe Elias leaned back in his chair and rubbed his stubbly black beard. Then he murmured, "That works out to something around $650,000. Yes, Joe, I can handle that, given a little notice. For that amount what I have to do is take out a short-term bridge loan that covers me and the check I would give to the "seller". Then I pay back the loan when I sell the gold to my commodity buyers. The loan has to be arranged before I do an assay and purchase the gold."

"How soon could that be, Joe?" said Joe McCulloch.

"Tomorrow morning," said Elias. "Would that be all right for the "seller"?"

"Yes, I think it will be," said Joe. "You said if the "seller" had the gold here in the morning you would be ready?"

"Yes, I would have the cash in my account by then and be able to write a check," said Elias. "If I do arrange such a loan, can I count on the gold being here then?"

"For sure," said Joe McCulloch. "I presume that this discussion will be held strictly confidential?"

"Of course," said Elias, " and may I ask if the "seller" has considered the tax consequences of this sale?"

"No, I doubt it," said Joe. "Do you report the sale to the IRS?"

"I have to," said Elias.

When Joe McCulloch exited the front door of Montana Metals Joe Elias closed the door behind him and watched through the window as McCulloch got into the old Chevrolet and drove off. Then Elias bolted out the front door of his shop and ran to the Stag's Head Saloon. When he entered the dingy bar, he looked around wildly. The barkeep saw him and asked who he was looking for. "Jesse! Who else?" Joe answered.

"The bum's asleep in the back room", answered the barkeep in a bored tone. "He passed out last night and I dragged him back there. Far as I know he hasn't stirred since."

Joe Elias hurried into the back room of the bar, where illegal card games took place weekends. There, on the floor behind an old round oak table and a set of chairs, lay his operative and partner, Jesse Jamison. Jesse's head was lying in a pool of vomit. He was snoring loudly.

"Jesse, Jesse!" Joe said, shaking the man violently. "Wake up, you worthless piece of shit! You have work to do! Dammit, wake up!"

The high country on the Montana-Idaho divide is mostly open. You can see for miles. If Joe McCulloch had looked back along the road as he drove home over the high pass between Montana and Idaho, he would have seen an old red Ford pickup a couple of miles behind him. Such a sighting would not have been unusual, though. Many loggers and tourists drove the road.

In the old Ford, Jesse Jamison was hunched over the steering wheel. Jamison was 47 years old. He lived in a dirty room upstairs over Montana Metals. He helped Elias occasionally, but never worked a steady job. He lived by his wits. He had been in the State penitentiary in Deerlodge twice for robbery and once for manslaughter. He was tall and wiry. He was dressed in old blue jeans and a dirty flannel shirt. As he rubbed the week's beard on his face, he wondered if the dumb ass in the old Chevrolet up ahead really had half a million in gold. Something had really excited old Elias, that was for damn sure! He rolled down the window of the truck and spewed a stream of tobacco juice out of it, then rolled it back up. Well, he sure as Hell would find out, and pronto.

Kermit Kaiser had had it after being in the office all day Tuesday and Wednesday. This Thursday, by God, he had to get out into the field and get some fresh air! He got up from his desk, grabbed his hard hat, and headed out of the office. As he passed the door of the Dispatcher's office, Al Fife yelled, "Herb Wallace is on the radio and wants to talk with you!"

Without changing direction, Kermit said, "Al, I'm in the field. Tell him that and that you will have me call him later". Teresa Jacks smiled at him as he went by. He winked at her and went out the door. He relaxed as he drove slowly up Moose Creek away from the Station. There was a small campground alongside Moose Creek about a half-mile above the Station. He wheeled into it to check its condition and cleanliness. Braking to a stop, he got out and walked around it. As usual, Vic Castellano was doing a great job. The place was clean as a whistle and the tables had just been treated with shiny brown Madison Laboratory Stain to preserve them.

As he turned to get back into the pickup, he heard someone shout "The Hell I will!" up on the hill above the

134

campground. He wondered who would be up on that barren hillside in the lodgepole, so he walked up onto the road above the campground, looking upward. From there he could see up an old mining road. He could see an old red pickup parked there, and beyond, barely visible, Joe McCulloch's old blue Chevrolet sedan.

Joe McCulloch had had most of the gold out of the cache and was carrying it to the Chevy load by load when he heard a voice saying to him, "What you got there, Boy?" Joe nearly jumped out of his skin. He looked up to see a tall man in blue jeans standing by the Chevy. The man was holding an old lever action Winchester rifle. It was aimed at Joe. The man continued, "You just take it easy now and you won't get hurt. Take that gold and put it in that pickup and keep your mouth shut."

"The Hell I will!" shouted Joe McCulloch.

The stranger jumped at the loudness of the yell and straightened up to hold the rifle to his shoulder and aim down its barrel at Joe's belly. "You shut up, asshole", he said. "One more sound like that and I will blow you to Kingdom Come! Now load that fuckin' gold and do it NOW!"

Joe could see the man was serious so he began to carry to gold toward the old pickup. He put the four bags he was carrying into the truck's box and retraced his steps to the cache up the hill. The stranger stayed about ten feet away from him and kept the gun carefully aimed at him all of the time. Joe made three trips with armfuls of gold. As he reached the back of the red pickup the third time, he heard a loud crunching sound and a moan. He turned to look at the stranger just in time to see him collapse onto the ground, rifle falling to the side. Standing where the man had stood was Kermit Kaiser. Kermit dropped the bloody rock he was holding. He looked up at Joe McCulloch and said, "You okay?"

Joe said, "Yes! Thank God you showed up! I'm sure he would have killed me after the gold was loaded." Joe hurriedly told Kermit the whole story about the gold. While he did they checked the pulse of the stranger and found that he was dead. Kermit had caved the whole back of his head in with the stone. They loaded all of the gold into the Chevy. Kermit told Joe that he had to go back to the Station and inform the S.O. of what had happened and get the County Sheriff started out to the District. "Do you think the gold will still be mine?" Joe said.

"I don't see why not, Joe," said Kermit. "I'll be back in just a few minutes. Wait for me right here." Kermit walked back down the road to his pickup and began driving back to the Station. For some time his brain had been working furiously. If he had $600,000, he would be fixed for life! He and Teresa could go anywhere and do anything they wanted! This was a chance of a lifetime! The question was, did he have the guts to take the necessary steps, and would she join him if he did? He had 25 years to go to retirement. Shit, he would be an old man by then!

When he entered the office he asked Teresa Jacks to come to his office and to bring a pen and paper with her for dictation. She gave him a quizzical look, but quickly did what he asked her to do. When she closed the door behind her he said, "Sit down and listen to what I have to tell you. This may be the most important discussion of our lives, so pay strict attention." She nodded and he began talking in a low voice. It did not take much convincing for her to agree to help him.

In a few minutes they came out of Kermit's office. Kermit said to Al Fife, "I'm going up to Fly Hill to look over the Comet Creek Sale proposal. Teresa doesn't get out of here much and she's all caught up on work, so I am taking her along. See you about 5:00 o'clock, Al."

Al said, "O.K. and have fun!"

Teresa said, "We will! Bye!"

And have a nice roll in the meadow too, thought Al.

Joe was surprised to see Teresa with Kermit when they drove up. She came up and gave him a hug and said, "Kermit thought you two should have another person here as a witness." Then she walked over and looked at the body of Jesse Jamison. She also looked at the gold in the Chevy.

Kermit said to Joe, "I think that we need to get the gold to town as soon as we can. I makes me nervous to have it here. The Sheriff is on the way, but it will take him at least three hours to get here from Pierce. I suggest we drive to Superior and put the gold in a bank safe right now. Rankin knows about this and he will be here soon. We can leave that scoundrel's body and the truck he drove right here."

Joe hesitated. He wanted to get rid of the gold too, but it didn't see quite right to leave the scene of the conflict. Rather than argue, though, he just said, "Well, O.K., Kermit, if that's what you think is best".

Soon Joe was driving up Moose Creek with Teresa Jacks sitting in the Chevy beside him. Kermit was following in the Forest Service pickup. Teresa Jacks was chattering away about the money and what Joe McCulloch could do with it. He heard little of what she said. He was thinking about Joe Elias and the connection he must have had to the dead man. They came to the top of Independence Saddle and started down the other side.

About a half-mile down the other side of the steep grade Teresa said, "I think Kermit is trying to signal you to stop!" Joe McCulloch looked in the rear view mirror and saw Kermit waving his arm. Joe pulled off into a turnout being careful to not get too close to the edge. The shoulder was soft and it was a 500-foot drop to the bottom of the canyon. He set the brake and got out to walk back to the pickup.

Kermit got out too and said, "This damned engine is missing, Joe. What a time to have car trouble!"

Joe said, "Did the temperature gauge look O.K.? Let's look under the hood." He unlatched and raised the hood of the pickup and began to look for anything obviously wrong. He felt the radiator and it didn't seem overly hot. He raised up, turned toward Kermit, and said, "Ker—" He never finished the sentence. Kermit Kaiser struck him as hard as he could on the side of the head with an axe-like Pulaski fire-fighting tool. Joe McCulloch went down and out.

Teresa Jacks ran up beside Kermit and said, "Is he dead?"

Kermit Kaiser said, "No, but he will be soon. We have a lot of work to do. Let's get it the gold into the pickup and get out of here before someone comes along."

They dragged Joe's body up alongside the old Chevy and began carrying bags of gold from the car to the truck. They transferred it all to the pickup's box and in covered it with a canvas. Then they put Joe behind the wheel of his old car, took off the parking brake, put the transmission into neutral, and pushed Joe and the car toward the edge of the canyon. The old Chevrolet hung up on the edge of the road for a moment, slid a little bit, and then plunged over the edge. It rolled over several times before it landed, with a rending crash of metal and the jingle of broken glass, in the streambottom. There was no fire. The car and Joe were resting about where Sam Burbidge had run his rocker box 100 years before.

Two hours after Teresa and Kermit left the District Office, Orrin West slowly walked into it and sat down at Vic Castellano's 'desk'. "Just got back from takin' the trail crew its grub," he drawled. He pushed his hat to the back of his head, put his boots up on Vic's little table, and pulled a bag of Bull Durham from his shirt pocket. "Those boys was sure glad to see me! Been outta' toilet paper for three days." He and Al both chuckled.

"I'll be sure to tell Vic when he comes in!" said Al. "You know a funny thing happened here a little while ago, Orrin.

138

Kermit left in a rush and then came back in about a half-hour. Then he gets Miss Teresa and takes her in his office. Then about ten minutes later they came outta there and got into his pickup and left. He said they were going to Fly Hill to look at the Comet Creek Sale area. They acted real funny, you know?"

"Is Joe McCulloch here?" said Orrin, looking very intently at Al.

"Nope, he headed for Superior on "business" earlier today," Al said. "He's been gone since about 7 a.m."

Orrin suppressed the chill that ran down his spine and made himself slowly finish rolling his cigarette. He lit it, and then he got up and sauntered away, saying to Al Fife as he left, "I been doin' Uncle's business since three this mornin'. See ya, Al."

Once out the door he quickly got into his old Ford pickup and drove off up Moose Creek. While he drove he was thinking that he should never have left Joe McCulloch alone with all that gold. He was angry with himself.

Meanwhile Teresa and Kermit had returned to where Jesse Jamison's body and pickup was. Nobody had been there, apparently. They unceremoniously buried Jesse's body in the old cache that Joe McCulloch had dug and tried to wipe away all traces of their tracks and any disturbance. Then, again, they drove up the Moose Creek road toward Independence Saddle. Kermit Kaiser drove Jesse Jamison's old red Ford and Teresa followed in the Forest Service truck.

Not far from the Saddle, Kermit drove the old red truck off onto an abandoned logging road. After about a mile it petered-out. He left the red pickup there. Then he got behind the wheel of the Forest Service rig, reached over, and gave Teresa Jacks a big kiss. They both heaved a sigh of relief and began driving back to the Station. The further they drove the more elated they became. Soon they would be rich and they would be far from Moose Creek! They began to laugh hysterical, nervous laughs of relief and happiness.

# Chapter 13 – Swift and Sure

Orrin West met Teresa Jacks and Kermit Kaiser, coming from the opposite direction, about half way up Moose Creek. He waved his arm to stop them. When the two pickup trucks were stopped side by side, he said, "Kermit, I'm driving over to Superior for the night. Al said you two went up to Fly Hill. Was it nice up there?"

"Oh yeah," said Kermit. "Great view, you know. That Comet Creek Sale will be O.K., but it's mighty steep in there."

"Sure is," said Orrin. "Anything you want from town that I can bring?"

"No, thanks, Orrin," Kermit said. "Grocery truck was in yesterday. I'm all fixed, I think. You, Teresa?" She nodded her head to indicate that she had what she needed.

"O.K., see you tomorrow", Orrin said and drove off.

Teresa Jacks and Kermit Kaiser looked at each other. "Nothing suspicious was there?" Kermit asked.

"Not that I could see," Teresa Jacks said, "and I am sure that they won't find Joe for sometime. By then we will be long gone, Kermit!" They drove on, making plans to clear up affairs and leave in two days. They were confident of themselves.

Orrin West drove slowly up Moose Creek, partly to take it easy on his faithful old pickup and partly because he was looking hard for anything unusual along the way. For some reason, things just didn't feel right. Al Fife could not put two and two together, but he was very sensitive to any changes in routine around the District, for routine was his security blanket. Changes or the unexpected made Al nervous and, often, when Al was nervous, so was Orrin.

A pile of gold can make people do weird things, he thought, for the one-hundredth time.

Topping Independence Saddle, Orrin shifted into second gear and started slowly down the other side. After going a few hundred yards, he slowly braked to a stop. At the lower edge of that turnout across from him, some dirt was freshly turned up. He backed up and pulled over into the turnout, stopped the truck, and got out. He was already hoping he was wrong, dead wrong!

He walked slowly to the edge of the road where the dirt was newly scraped away and the brush below the edge was scarred-up. He looked over the edge. Far below, half hidden in the alder and willow brush along the creek, were the torn remains of Joe McCulloch's old blue Chevrolet sedan. Orrin squeezed his eyes shut. No! He didn't want to see this! He looked again. The twisted body of the old car was still there. He would have to go down. Before he did, though, he turned and walked around the turnout.

Orrin West had been a woodsman for 40 years. He was a sharp observer. He could see two vehicles had been parked here today. There had been lots of foot traffic back and forth between them. The tracks of the Chevy did not wander off the road gradually, as if the driver had fallen asleep. The car had been stopped, then went over the side with a sharp left-hand turn. He noticed a small area where the dirt had been smoothed out with something.

He squatted down by it and ran his finger through the dirt. He then looked at his fingertip. It was dark, gooey, and wet. He tasted it—salty. It was blood. Someone had killed poor Joe and then tried to make it look like an accident! Tears came to his eyes. Goddamn it, he thought, I have just lived too damned long.

It took him nearly an hour, and several falls, to get down to the Chevy. Joe McCulloch was in it all right. A bunch of bones ticking though flesh and limbs pointed in unnatural angles, but he was not quite dead. There was no way to separate him from the metal of the car, so Orrin wet his handkerchief in the creek and gently wiped the dirt and crusts of blood from Joe's battered face. Joe gurgled a bit at the touch of the cold cloth and the one eye that was still in place opened. "Orrrr," he wheezed.

"Easy. Easy, Son," whispered Orrin.

With a monumental effort, Joe McCulloch's eye rotated to glare at Orrin West. With a great groan, he wheezed one barely recognizable word: "Kaiiiiiiserrr!" The eye clouded. Joe McCulloch wheezed a death rattle, twitched spasmodically, and was dead. Orrin West sat by the battered car, holding and patting what was left of Joe's hand. He sobbed and cried for a long time. Then he began the arduous ,steep climb back to the road, far above.

Late that night, after the Station was asleep, Orrin unsheathed the fire tools that were kept in the box in the back of the Ranger's pickup. The beam of his flashlight revealed a smear of dried blood and some hair on the head of the Pulaski. He also noticed that the canvas he had seen in the back of the pickup earlier that day was gone. He put the tools back and sadly walked to his trailer house. Inside he pulled off his old cowboy boots and threw his Stetson in the corner. Then he opened a bottle of Jim Beam whiskey and proceeded to drink himself unconscious. For Orrin West the day had been too much to deal with. He needed to obliterate it from his memory. He wanted to be unconscious for the night.

About ten o'clock Friday morning, Orrin walked into the District Office. Teresa Jacks was busy at her desk and did not even look up as he entered. Al Fife looked at him as he came into the Dispatcher's office and said, "Jesus, Orrin, you look like livin' death today. You and 'ol Jim Beam have a tussle last night?"

"Yeah", Orrin replied, "and I lost". He sat down in Vic's chair and took the cup of coffee Al handed him. Neither man spoke for some time. Finally, Orrin said, "Ranger in?"

Al said, "Yeah".

Orrin sipped the coffee, then got up slowly. He wobbled a bit, straightened, and walked to the Ranger's office door.

Kermit Kaiser was planning his and Teresa Jack's getaway. Orrin knocked, then entered, and closed the door behind him. For Orrin West to come into his office was unusual. Kermit said, "What can I do for you, Orrin?"

The leathery old cowboy didn't sit down. Instead, he looked at Kermit Kaiser coldly for several seconds. Then he reached slowly under his wool Filson cruiser coat and pulled out an ancient Colt .45 caliber long barreled Buntline Special. He cocked it and placed the end of the long barrel right on the end of Kermit Kaiser's nose. Then he said forcefully and quietly, "You let out a peep, you murderin' sonofabitch, and your fuckin' brains will cover half this District!"

Kermit Kaiser's eyes bugged out and he began to quiver like a reed in a wind.

"Now, Kermit, what we are going to do is walk out of here and get into the stake body truck out front. All you are going to say to the folks outside is that we are going for a ride up to Scurvy Mountain Lookout. Don't even think about getting smart. If you do, I'll kill you and then I'll cap that vicious twat of a fuckin' clerk, so help me God!"

Kermit was thinking fast. He said, "If you do that, you will be signing your own death warrant".

Orrin smiled grimly at Kermit and said, "I often think that I've lived long enough already. With slime like you around,

144

I'm sure of it, so try it if you want-to! Its all the same to me, you miserable asshole."

Teresa Jacks looked up as Kermit Kaiser and Orrin West came out of the Ranger's office. She was going to speak, but Kermit, who seemed flushed, spoke first, saying, "I'm going with Orrin up to Scurvy Lookout. Be back later tonight."

He and Orrin went out to the two-ton truck parked in front of the office, climbed in and left. She noticed that Kermit was serious and that Orrin was even more dour than normal.

Al Fife came to the door of the dispatcher's office. She looked at him and said, "Did you know they were going horseback riding today?"

Al lit a Lucky Strike, took it out of his mouth, picked some loose bits of tobacco from his lips and tongue, and said, "Nope. I saw Orrin had loaded the stock in the truck, though. Figured he was taking someone for a ride 'cause there was two horses."

Teresa Jacks sat down at her desk. She was worried. She knew Kermit didn't like to ride horses. He normally avoided them. Just then Mary McCulloch came in the office door and said to Teresa, "Hi! Have you heard from Joe? He should have been back by now, don't you think?"

Teresa smiled. "Oh, I'm sure he is O.K., Mary."

Orrin West stopped the truck as soon as they were out of sight of the Station. He had the pistol in his left hand pointing across his lap at Kermit. His right hand was on the wheel. Trouble was, he couldn't shift the transmission and keep the gun hand free, too. He said to Kermit, "lock that right hand door will you?" When Kermit turned to do it, Orrin grabbed the back of Kermit's neck and smashed his head, hard, against the metal dashboard of the truck. Kermit was out like a light. Orrin put the pistol into his belt. From behind his ear he retrieved a cigarette he had rolled earlier, lit it, and drove off up the mountain.

Five hours later the sound of the radio jerked Al Fife awake. He jumped and sat bolt upright at the desk for a second, not knowing where he was. Then he heard Orrin West on the radio calling the Station. Al seized the nearby pedestal microphone and squeezed the 'push to talk' button. "Orrin West this is Moose Creek", he responded.

"Al, I'm in the truck up in South Saddle at the Scurvy trailhead. There's been a bad accident. Ol' Red ran off with the Ranger. They both went over that cliff above the little lake 'bout halfway up. Both are dead at the bottom of the cliff. Send some help up as soon as you can. I will go back up there and keep the critters away from 'em 'til you get here. Be sure and bring a tarp or something to bring the Ranger back in."

"10-4 Orrin, Moose Creek out!" Al said shakily. Shit, Oh-Dear, he thought, what the holy Hell was he going to do now? Before he could do anything, Tom Rankin came on the radio.

"Al this is Tom. I copied that from Orrin. I'm on the way in, about 10 minutes away from you. While I am getting there, call Orofino and have them get the Sheriff and the Coroner headed out here. You might suggest they use a chopper. Copy?"

Al responded, "I copy. 10-4, Tom. Will do!" He called the Supervisor's Office just as Rankin had told him too. When he finished, he was still upset at what had happened so he sought some company. He said in a raised voice, "Teresa, GodAlmighty, what do you think of that?" There was no reply from the front room. Al got up and went into the front office. No one was there. Teresa Jacks was nowhere to be seen.

Orrin West sat on the edge of the cliff looking down at the small lake below. Three-fourths of the way down, among the boulders at the toe of the cliff, were the intertwined remains of Kermit Kaiser and a big red horse. Orrin was smoking a roll-your-own when Tom Rankin came puffing up the trail from South Saddle. He was alone. The recovery crew was being

146

formed up at the Station and would be another half-hour getting to the South Saddle trailhead. Tom flopped down beside Orrin, breathing heavily.

Orrin pointed at the bodies far below and said, "There they are." He waited while Tom caught his breath, then said, "Tom, I'm going to tell you something you will not want to hear, but you have to. I don't need to tell you to keep it under your hat." Orrin went on to tell Tom the whole story. By the time he finished, Rankin's head was down and tears were dripping from his eyes.

"Poor Mary," Tom said softly.

"Yeah," said Orrin. "It's just a crying shame." After a pause he continued, "I figure the gold is around the Station somewhere and that little shit, Teresa, knows where. We will need to handle that when we get back. I reckon you should be the one that discovers poor Joe, maybe tomorrow. Not me".

They sat quietly for awhile. Tom Rankin lit a Lucky Strike and slowly got to his feet. Then he said to Orrin, "Show me where the horse shied and ran over the edge, Orrin. I want to have it straight. I'm sorry about Ol' Red, but not about Kaiser. The murdering fucker deserved a helluva lot worse than this."

# Chapter 14 - Credit Suisse

Teresa Jacks was sitting at a little mahogany desk in a small room in the Brown Palace Hotel in Denver, Colorado. She was registered under the name of Sandy Johnson. She had been gone from the Moose Creek Ranger Station for two weeks.

During that time she had bought a 1960 Oldsmobile sedan from in Missoula and abandoned Kermit Kaiser's Mercury in a parking garage there. She swapped cars again in Billings before heading south to Denver. She was terrified that the police would be conducting a vast hunt for Kermit's accomplice in the murder of Joe McCulloch. All this car swapping was hard work. At each swap, the gold dust had to be transferred. She had cleaned out her bank account while she was in Missoula. She thought she had her trail covered well, but she still jumped every time she heard a police siren on the street below.

What she could not have known was that she was not being looked-for at all. Joe McCulloch's body had been 'found' by Tom Rankin two days after she left. No one suggested he had been murdered. The authorities had called it an accident. Teresa's abrupt disappearance had been chalked up to a fit of sudden depression and hysteria at hearing of her lover, Kermit Kaiser's, death. Although everyone thought it was strange that she had disappeared so suddenly, no one connected it to Joe's accident. She was listed as a 'missing person'. Several District people scoured the area around the District compound looking for a body. They thought she might have committed suicide. Her family in Weippe was distraught. They worried and asked around, as best they could, to see if anyone had seen or heard of her, but that was all. No one even thought of hiring a private detective to find her. They didn't have the money for a search anyway. The whereabouts of Teresa Jacks became a mystery.

Orrin West and Tom Rankin knew that she was a murderess, of course. They also knew she probably had the gold. They couldn't do anything about it, though, because they were co-conspirators in the 'accident' that had killed Kermit Kaiser. Overall, both Orrin and Tom were satisfied that the greater justice had been done, because they figured Kaiser was the primary perpetrator of the crime. Meanwhile, they both were concentrating on helping Mary McCulloch and Little Joe.

They saw to Joe's burial and helped move his wife and son back to her folk's place. Regarding the gold, they simply told Mary that Joe had never told them where it was. Sometimes they got drunk together in private, made solemn toasts to Joe McCulloch, and hoped Kermit Kaiser was turning on a spit over Hell's hottest fires.

In her small hotel room in Denver, Teresa opened a bottle of white wine she had purchased that afternoon. In the course of drinking it, she seriously considered her plight and what she had to do. She was a very bright woman; far brighter than her background or education signified.

She knew instinctively that she needed one thing right now and needed it badly: a new identity. She knew you had to be a crook, or know a crook, to get a new Social Security card, driver's license, and all the rest. She would have to find someone to help her. Second, she needed to convert the gold she had to cash and put it away somewhere secure so the authorities could not find it or her or trace the gold sale. Both of these needs were 'tall' orders for a young woman from Weippe!

Having eaten no dinner and drunk a full bottle of wine, she began to get drowsy. She walked over to the bed and laid down on it. Soon she was fast asleep.

Evelyn Murdock had enjoyed her lunch. Once a week the "girls" from her office met at Murphy's Shamrock Bar in downtown Denver to visit and eat lunch. Murphy knew this pattern and expected them. They didn't tip much, but they were young and pretty and he liked them and their cheery banter and laughter. He usually sprung for two bottles of cheap champagne for their table and got a couple of kisses on the cheek for that.

Today the young women had consumed the wine and had just finished their entrees'. They were giggling and debating about what desserts to have. There were several "Oh, I shouldn'ts" and a corresponding number of "Oh, If you are, I will's" around the jolly table.

Evelyn had had three glasses of the Champagne and had no room for dessert. Anyway, she was getting a bit tipsy and the Irish corned beef sandwich she had eaten was not mixing well with the alcohol. "Girls, I have to go," she said.

There was a chorus of "Oh, no's" and "Stay awhile longer, please's", but she was adamant. She said her good-byes and retrieved her coat. She thanked Mr. Murphy for the Champagne on the way out and kissed his cheek as she usually did. He beamed and opened the door to the street for her.

On the street the fresh air revived her. She noticed a 'Giant Sale" sign across the street in the window of the Denver Department Store. She needed a new sweater, so she stepped off the curb between two parked cars and into the street. She might have been just careless or a bit wine-befuddled, but she never saw the speeding red sports car that hit her. The impact flipped her into the air, back over the sports car. She landed, in a distorted pile of flesh and clothing, in the next lane. She was dead before she hit the pavement. People came running from all directions. Amidst the confusion, no one saw Teresa Jacks quickly pick up Evelyn's purse and put it under her coat.

Teresa Jacks now became Evelyn Murdock by virtue of the social security card, driver's license, credit cards, and other documents in Evelyn's purse. The real Evelyn Murdock was buried two days after the accident that killed her. By that time Teresa Jacks had found out that Evelyn had been single and living alone. Her parents lived in California. She had her new identity, it appeared. Luck seemed to be with her. She changed her hairstyle and color to match Evelyn's. Disposing of the gold, now in cheap suitcases in her car, was still a problem.

The next day Evelyn Murdock, for that was her assumed name now, went to the local Interstate Bank branch office in downtown Denver. There she talked to a very nice young Vice-President named Jeffrey Morgan.

Jeffrey was very helpful, even as he stole glances at Evelyn's beautiful, and elegantly crossed, legs. He explained that Interstate could indeed transfer funds anywhere in the world, but that they did not buy or trade gold. They could also help Evelyn set up an account in a Bank anywhere, but any sum transferred out of the United States would have to be duly reported to the Internal Revenue Service.

Evelyn asked about Swiss Banks and how one could contact them. When Jeffrey produced an International Bank Directory, she leaned over to look at it with him, knowingly exposing most of one breast for his clandestine examination. At her request he wrote down the name, address and phone number of one of the major banks in the Swiss list: Credit Suisse in Geneva. Jeffrey started to rise as she stood, thanked him, and left. However he quickly sat down again, in confusion, after half-rising, for his sexual arousal was only too apparent. Several females clerks, who had been watching the whole encounter, looked at each other, knowingly smirked, and rolled their eyes.

Back in her hotel room, Evelyn looked at the clock and calculated that the Banks in Switzerland would still be open.

Then, following the instructions she received from the local telephone operator, she dialed the number Jeffrey had given her. The receptionist at Credit Suisse greeted her with a friendly "Bon Jour!" and transferred her to an Account Executive.

She let him know, in no uncertain terms, that she wanted to do business with the Bank and that it involved a large sum of money. She also told the Executive that the business she wanted to conduct would have to be absolutely confidential and private. If Credit Suisse could not do what she wanted, she announced, she would look elsewhere. The young Account Executive told her that the Bank could comply with her wishes, but that he would have to transfer her to the Senior Account Executive for Confidential Accounts.

Soon she was talking to a Herr Helmut Schmidt, whose heavily accented English exuded confidence and experience. She explained to him that she wanted to rent a large safety deposit box. One large enough to hold a volume equal to approximately one cubic meter. He hesitated for a moment, as this request was a bit unusual, and then said, "No problem, Madame".

She then said, "I plan to send you a number of small packages that you are to store for me, unopened, in my safe deposit box. I want only the bank and me to know about the box and about the shipments. You are to call me when each package arrives and has been stored. I will number each one, sequentially. I will send them, intermittently, over a period of time, by first class mail. Can you do that?"

"Yes, Madame," replied Helmut. "I will establish a confidential number that you can put on each parcel. That way, when it arrives, we will know that it is yours and what to do with it. It will be the same number you use in any other contacts with us. I will also need to know your mother's maiden name. We will need, also, to decide on a personal account identification name or number that will be known only to you and us. What would you prefer to use for that personal identification?"

Evelyn Murdock hesitated for a moment. Then she said, "My mother's maiden name was Iverson. The secret identification we can use is to be "Kaiser".

"Very good, Madame", Herr Schmidt said. " The safe deposit box and our services will cost you approximately 1,000 Swiss Francs each six months. Is that satisfactory?"

She answered yes and waited while Herr Schmidt registered the information about the account, the account number, and the secret identifications for it. They agreed she would wire the money to pay for the six months storage and services when the U.S. banks opened the next day. "It has been a pleasure doing business with you, Ms. Murdock," Herr Schmidt said in closing. " Please call me if you have any questions or if I may be of any other service to you."

She thanked him and told him to expect the first package in about a week.

"Very good!" he responded, "Bon Jour".

The next several weeks Evelyn Murdock would periodically fill a small cardboard box with one bag of gold, label it with the address of the Zurich bank and the transaction number that Herr Schmidt had given her. Then she taped the box securely shut, and mailed it via first class 'Par Avion' to the Credit Suisse Bank in Zurich. When it arrived and was safely stored in her safe deposit box in the Credit Suisse vault, Herr Schmidt would telephone her to let her know it had arrived. As soon as she knew that the parcel had arrived safely, she prepared another one and sent it off.

By the start of the new year, 1965, the gold was all stored safely in Switzerland, unknown to the United States Government or anyone else but Evelyn Murdock. This done, Evelyn sold her car to a young man on the street for cash, signing the back of the car title on the line 'Owner Transferring' as Sandy Johnson. She then packed, checked out of the hotel, and took a cab to the Denver's Stapleton Airport. Using a passport that she had acquired earlier under the name of Evelyn Murdock, she boarded a jet plane on the first leg of a journey to Zurich. As she sat in a first class seat on the airliner and sipped Champagne, she bid a private and solemn good-bye to her former identity. Signing the car title release had been Teresa Jack's last act in this world, she hoped, and the true beginning of Evelyn Murdock's new life. She truly relaxed for the first time in months. She fell into a deep sleep to the dull thrumming of the plane's turbojet engines before cruising altitude was reached.

Later, on board Swissair flight 1708 from Boston to Zurich, smoothly cruising through the black Arctic night over Greenland, Evelyn Murdock had considerable time to think about her next steps. Once in Zurich she would, with Herr Schmidt's able assistance, sell the gold and convert it into a cash account in the bank. Again, with Herr Schmidt's help, she would put the money into several safe investments. That would make the wealth begin to appreciate. Later she might secretly bring some of the money back into the United States and make non-taxable or cash investments of various sorts that would capitalize on the rapid growth of the American economy.

Personally, she had decided to go to a continental polishing school. That would help remove the 'Idaho" from her and allow her to move comfortably in moneyed and high-class circles. Some liberal arts education and foreign language training would help too. Eventually she hoped that she would find a rich and sophisticated man to marry, have a family with, and live a beautiful life.

At about the same time Tom Rankin was sitting uncomfortably in the Forest Supervisor's office in Orofino, Idaho. The room was in the top floor of an old gray stone Post Office Building. The floor was gray marble and the walls were painted a pale, sickly green. The old oak furniture and everything else in the office smelled like "O Cedar" furniture and floor polish. The odor of the polish mixed sickeningly with omnipresent stale tobacco smoke.

Ralph Seward, the Forest Supervisor, was in a meeting. He was late for the appointment with Rankin. Seward had asked for this meeting and Tom had driven in over the 100 miles of rough road from Moose Creek Ranger Station last evening. There had been no reason given for the summons, but Tom knew that this was not unusual in the 'Service'. He had concluded he was in big trouble about something, but he could not, for the life of him, guess what it was.

Ten minutes later, Seward came in carrying a handful of papers. He shook Tom's hand and sat down, saying, "Jesus Christ, Tom, all I do is go to meetings anymore! Sorry I kept you waiting. I only have a few minutes before I have to go back in there, so here's the deal. You know John Bucks, our Timber Staff Officer, had a severe heart attack two weeks ago. I want you to be the new Timber Staff Officer. I personally want you in here to help me on other things, too. You can't sit out at Moose Creek forever. You need to get ready for your own Forest soon." Seward looked at Tom and waited for a reaction.

"O.K., Ralph," Tom said, "but what about all the others you are jumping me over? Won't they be pissed?"

"To Hell with them", snorted Seward. "Until those other assholes grow a brain and get off their duffs, they don't have any bitch coming." Seward stood up, shook Rankin's hand, and said, "I'll expect you here in a week. Glad you're coming, Tom. I know you will do a great job!"

Tom Rankin went down the hall with his head spinning. Jesus, he thought, I'd better talk to a real estate agent right now! Then I will head home and tell Donna that we're moving again.

# Section 3 - 1988

> **"And earthly power doth then show likest God's, when mercy seasons justice".** — William Shakespeare (Merchant of Venice, Act I, Sc. 1, line 163.)

# Chapter 15 - The Life

John Rothchilde looked across the bedroom at his wife. She was sitting at her dressing table preparing for the dinner party. He smiled to himself. She was still stunningly beautiful even after 20 years! He felt that he was indeed a fortunate man. The fact that Evelyn was his wife, that he was one of the richest men in England and America, and that that he had a fine home and friends, all made him feel very happy and self-satisfied.

He couldn't help humming happily to himself as he carefully finished tying his black bow tie and adjusting the satin cummerbund around his middle. As he did, he criticized himself for eating too much. He was very definitely getting a middle-aged 'spread' in spite of his exercise routine. He turned and walked over to where his wife was sitting, bent over and carefully and tenderly kissed her on her bare shoulder. She stopped applying her make-up and turned her head to smile at him.

Evelyn Murdock-Rothchilde was indeed a very beautiful woman. She was tall and slim and had beautiful facial features and striking large brown eyes. Her glossy dark brunette hair contrasted perfectly with her light cream complexion. On top of all that, she had a regal air acquired from some of the best finishing schools in Europe. Her skin was wrinkle free, thanks to the ministrations of the finest plastic surgeons in Hollywood and Switzerland.

She said to her husband, "John, are you dressed already? How handsome you are! Be sure to use some of that cologne that I brought to you from Paris last month. I love it! Now, let me finish so we do not keep our guests waiting."

He stood up straight, saluted in the best British Army manner, a gave a mock leap toward his dresser, saying, "Love doth propel me like Cupid's arrow, Ma Cheri!"

"Oh, John", she giggled, "let me finish up here and stop your British music hall routine. Why don't you go down to see who is here and be sure that Barclay is serving them drinks? Then come get me."

"I will do that, my dear," he said. Then he put on his tuxedo jacket, expertly shot his shirt's cuffs in its sleeves, and went out the door.

Evelyn Rothchilde continued to carefully apply her makeup. While she did so, she reflected on how lucky she was to be John Rothchilde's wife. She had met him at a resort on the Costa Del Sol in Spain in 1968. Three months later they had been married in the small village church near his ancestral home in Kent. His family had been in money and banking in England for ages. He was a Baron of the Realm. His father had wisely invested heavily in American industry and had doubled the family fortune in the 15 years after World War II. Her thoughts were interrupted by a soft knock at the bedroom door.

A beautiful woman walked in and said, "John asked me to come help you. He said a whalebone corset and bustier are hard lace up all alone. I volunteered to help!" They laughed.

157

The woman, Lily Vanderlinden, was Evelyn's best friend in the entire world. Contrasting with Evelyn's dark eyes and hair, Lily was blonde and fair, with startling dark blue eyes. She was the wife of Roger Vanderlinden, who was the scion of one of the oldest families in New York and John's partner in many business ventures. The Vanderlindens owned more shipping, in the form of oil tankers, steamers, and cruise ships, than they could keep count of. Roger's great-great-great grandfather had been one of the original 'Patroons' of New Amsterdam in the 1600's.

"Help me get into my dress, Lily," Evelyn said. "Then I need help with final touches! Are George and Gloria here yet?"

"George is into his fourth glass of John's Bell's 25 year old Scotch," Lily responded. "I only hope he does not get sick at the table again. The last time I swore off Welsh Rabbit forever!"

Evelyn's dress was an elegant, but simple, white silk affair with silver threaded accents. It set off the diamonds around her neck and on her wrists and fingers and was a perfect complement to her complexion, eyes, and hair. When she had it on and fully adjusted, she sat back down at the dressing table while Lily made the final adjustments to her coif. That finished, they both checked the other over and left the bedroom.

The entrance of the two beauties, as they slowly descended the ornate spiral marble staircase of the Rothchilde mansion, was everything that they could have wished. Lily, the fair Nordic type, and Evelyn, a brunette in the best Continental sense, were even more stunning together. All twenty gowned and tuxedoed guests interrupted their conversations and turned to look up at them. The women on the floor below were all jealous and the men were all entranced. Only the baroque chamber music, being played by a string quartet in the next room, disturbed the silence.

As they approached the bottom of the stairs, John Rothchilde stepped up onto the bottom step, raised his glass, and announced, "How privileged we are to have the two most beautiful women in the world here to grace our humble table tonight! Then, in a manner of mock seriousness, he went on, "I give you, ladies and gentlemen, Madame Rothchilde and Madame Vanderlinden, the two people in charge of the arduous task of disposing of the revenues of the houses of Rothchilde and Vanderlinden!"

The guests all laughed and clapped with abandon. Evelyn took John's arm and they led the guests to the brightly lit, crystal chandeliered, dining room. Roger and Lily Vanderlinden were right behind them.

Nearly all their guests were old friends who traveled and lived in the same elite circle that the Rothchilde's did. Most had mansions nearby in the Hudson River Valley, at least one home in Europe, and a winter resort home in the south of France, Spain, or the Caribbean. Most were from 'old money' families, but a few were 'noveau riche'.

Once they all were seated at the huge, silver-laden table, there was considerable toasting of one another and gay talk. Dinner courses came and went. The finest wines and liquors flowed in rivers. Expert servants bustled about the table making everything go smoothly.

In the middle of the main course, one man began to lower his head to his plate. His neighbor caught him just before his face encountered his duck a' la orange and two of the men sprang up and half carried him to a sofa in a nearby sitting room. He reposed there in a peaceful alcoholic coma the rest of the evening. His embarrassed wife said to the group, " George has such a passion for good Scotch whiskey, it is a pity that he has so little capacity for it!"

The table chuckled and Roger Vanderlinden stood, hoisted a glass of champagne to head level and said, looking at the embarrassed lady, "A toast to George! His Scotch capacity may be lacking, but his taste in ladies exceeds that of all the men here!"

"Hear! Hear" the men at the table chorused and beat on the table with their palms. George's faux pas was forgotten. Everyone renewed their previous conversations.

The dessert course brought an immense multi-tiered cake to the table. When all was prepared, John Rothchilde again stood with a glass in his hand. Much experienced at this sort of thing, he waited patiently until he had everyone's attention and all talk had ceased. He began, "Ladies and Gentlemen and my most beloved friends, I have been exceedingly fortunate in my life. I inherited wealth and have had the best education money can buy. I also happened to have a very handsome physiognomy and superior intellectual and sexual powers."

At this point he was interrupted by several boo's, hisses, and "Says Who's?" from the men at the table.

Holding his hands up theatrically, John waited again for the clamor to stop and then continued, " I acknowledge the jealousy and envy exhibited by my less fortunate colleagues, but please let me continue. As I was saying, I have much to be proud of and thankful for. However, there is one element in my life that I never fail to marvel about; one element of good fortune that transcends all others and one that I am totally at a loss to explain. This element is what has made me complete and is the precious jewel at the center of my being. This all-valuable and treasured element is Mrs. John Rothchilde, my beloved wife and my best friend." He was interrupted at this point by applause and much nodding in agreement.

Resuming, he went on, "Now, I had the great good fortune to meet Miss Evelyn Murdock over 20 years ago as she was sunning herself in a beach chair on the Costa del Sol. I was immediately attracted to her. Most notably by her lack of any apparel except a string bikini bathing suit bottom! But, once our relationship progressed beyond my animal lusting for her body, I found her to be irresistible in many ways!"

160

He paused, again, to let the laughter subside, then continued, " I found her to be intelligent, cultured, and in possession of a formidable Swiss bank account! However, the most amazing thing about her was that she actually seemed to like me; even my flabby adipose love handles and my prematurely thinning hair! My analysis was that, before she came to her senses, I would try to get her to the altar as rapidly as possible. I succeeded, believe it or not"

One guest injected loudly at this point, "It is incredible, John!"

Undeterred, John plunged on, " Now, we have been married for 20 years. Years I would never in the world have foregone. I can truthfully say that I have been a happy man ever since that glorious day when we wed in that little chapel in Kent. Friends, I have already exceeded my year's quota for droll wit tonight. Now let me be serious and propose a sincere toast. Here's to Evelyn, the light of my life, the blood in my veins, the breath in my lungs. God Bless you, Dearest. Happy Anniversary!"

A shout went up from the group, "Here's to Evelyn! Happy anniversary and long life!" Evelyn rose, thanked them, and made the first cut in the immense cake. The servants then smoothly took over the serving. As they still stood at the head of the table, George hugged her and produced a black velvet covered box. Everyone stopped talking to watch her open it. She drew out a diamond necklace with magnificent emerald at the center. The group applauded again as John fastened the necklace around her neck.

She kissed him tenderly and said, "I love you, George! Thank so much for everything, Dear."

He could only whisper in her ear in return, "I can never do enough for you, Evelyn."

161

Later that night, after all their guests had departed, they were back in the bedroom relaxing in their dressing gowns.

John said, "Evelyn, I am going to Washington tomorrow afternoon. There is a reception and dinner being held by the Forest Industry Association. I need to see several of the people there regarding our interests in Oregon. Also, there is rumor that Senator Blanchard might be there. I want an introduction to him. If he decides to run for President in 1990, he will become a very influential man." He checked himself and said, "Sorry. I didn't mean to get into all that detail, Dear. What I was beating around to was to ask if you might like to fly down with me?"

She thought for a moment and then said, "Yes I would. It fits nicely into the time I have before the Crippled Children's Charity Ball preparations begin. It will be good to see Jason and Gloria again too. What time do we leave?"

"I told Dave to have the plane ready about three o'clock. Is that alright for you?" he said.

"It's a date!" she said. Then she slipped out of her light nylon robe and, nude, sat on his lap, held his head in her hands, and kissed him on the lips. "John," she said, seriously, "you simply must come to bed with me now. I have to start paying you back for that emerald and it may take all night!"

"All night?" he said quizzically. "You will be paying for it longer than that, given the price of it!"

She laughed and said, "Let's see if you feel the same way in a few hours, Tarzan!"

162

from Oregon, Chairman of the Forestry and Federal Lands Committee, and an, as yet, unannounced Presidential aspirant. The forest industry representatives immediately engulfed the legislators. The Congressional staffers and aides, who had been gorging themselves at the buffet tables, were now at the elbows of their Legislators, notebooks, calendars, and pens at the ready.

It was the time for Jason Creadmore to earn his pay. He left the Rothchilde's as they talked to a grossly fat Interior Department Assistant Secretary. He maneuvered to the side of Senator Blanchard's Chief of Staff and whispered in his ear.

A short time later John and Evelyn were interrupted by a booming voice saying, "Mr. and Mrs. Rothchilde, I'm Bill Blanchard. Its great to finally be able to meet you in person!"

They turned to face the Senator and shook hands with him. Blanchard was a large, ruddy-complexioned man with a forceful, direct way about him. He continued, "Your and my friend here, Jason Creadmore, has kept me fully informed of your views on the Yachats land exchange out in Oregon. I want you to know, right off the bat, that I will do all I can to help to make it happen."

"I am very glad to hear that, Senator," said John Rothchilde, "and I am sure that with your help, and that of Congressman Tallford, it can be passed through both houses. There are some details I want to discuss with you, tomorrow, if possible. I would also like to find out what I might be able to do to help the Republican cause in 1990."

Blanchard looked at his aide, who was standing a foot or two away and said, "Dennis, what time would be best to meet with Mr. Rothchilde, given the voting times coming up on the floor tomorrow?"

Dennis replied, through a mustard and barbecue sauce-laden beard, "I suggest two o'clock, Sir. Thirty minutes?"

Blanchard looked back at John Rothchilde and said,

"Does that work for you, John?" John Rothchilde replied in the affirmative. After some "Thank-you's", and "See you tomorrows's", the Senator moved on, working the powerful and influential people in the group like a skilled matador works bulls.

"Nice work," John Rothchilde said to Jason Creadmore. "Let's meet in the morning to decide what to say to him and how much is appropriate to donate to the 'cause'."

As the reception went on Jason escorted John and Evelyn through several other introductions and brief discussions. Evelyn was relaxed and enjoying herself as Jason led them up to another small group of people. Distracted by a burst of laughter across the room, she faintly heard Jason say, "John and Evelyn, I would like you to meet the Chief of the U.S. Forest Service, Mr. Ralph Seward." Her head jerked to look at the man. What she saw was an older, grayer version of a face that she had seen over 20 years ago in Orofino, Idaho.

The man smiled, apparently not recognizing her as the former Teresa Jacks. He said, "I'm delighted to meet you, Mr. and Mrs. Rothchilde. I understand you have forestry interests related to several National Forests out in Oregon. I hope that you will feel free to discuss those interests or other, related issues, with me or my staff at any time."

Evelyn relaxed. There was no glimmer of recognition in the man's eyes at all. John thanked the Chief and he mentioned his concerns about the Yachats land exchange. The chief replied that he was aware of it and said he was not up on the details. Then he turned and motioned to someone in the crowd to join them. Turning back to them he said, "I do happen to have the man here who knows all about it. I would like you to meet him. He is my assistant in charge of National Forest System Resources, Mr. Tom Rankin."

Evelyn was frozen at the sound of the name. An older, grayer, stockier Tom Rankin walked up to the Chief and the Chief said, "Tom, meet John and Evelyn Rothchilde. Mr.

Rothchilde is interested in the Yachats exchange and has a few questions about its status."

"I would be pleased to try to answer any questions that you have, Mr. Rothchilde," said Tom Rankin. John Rothchilde and Tom Rankin visited for a few moments about the Yachats exchange. The Forest Service Chief excused himself to continue to circulate through the crowd. Evelyn watched Tom Rankin closely as he talked to her husband. Beyond the normal courtesies, she could not detect any sign that he recognized her as anything but the wife if John Rothchilde. In a few moments, John and Tom Rankin concluded their short business discussion. Evelyn and John moved on.

"Is anything the matter? You don't look well," she heard her husband saying.

"Just a bad headache, Dear," she replied.

John Rothchilde turned to Jason and said, "Mrs. Rothchilde is not feeling well, Jason. We have accomplished everything we came here to do tonight as far as I can see. I think its time we left."

As they moved toward the door Evelyn thought she saw Tom Rankin looking at her.

# Chapter 17 - Quandary

When Evelyn and John returned to their hotel suite, she told him that a hot bath might help her headache. Excusing herself, she went into the bathroom, started the water running, undressed, and immersed herself in the hot water of the suite's large Jacuzzi tub. Amid towers of bubbles and the circulating, soothing hot water, she tried to collect her thoughts.

Running into those two men from her past life in the Forest Service after over 20 years had completely nonplussed her. Was she afraid of them? Not directly, she decided. Even if they recognized her, they could not really know if she had been an accomplice in Joe McCulloch's murder. No, what was frightening about them was that they might ruin the wonderful life she had so carefully constructed for herself. More than anything else she loved how she lived, her husband, and her friends. She knew she would do anything to preserve that.

Moreover, if that was her fear, was there any reason to think that the two men could or would do anything to hurt her or disrupt her life? Probably not, she thought, but there was always some remote chance something could happen. They were really "little fish" in a big, big pond, even if they had become prominent bureaucrats. John could squash them in a minute with his influence and money. But, John must not become involved at all!

There was always the chance that Tom Rankin harbored ill will toward her or felt that she was an accomplice in Joe McCulloch's murder twenty years ago! She decided that even a remote chance of something happening was not tolerable. The bathroom door opened slightly and John's voice intruded into her thoughts.

"Are you alright, Dear?" he asked in a concerned tone.

"Much better, Dear", she said back. "I plan to take a couple of aspirin and go to bed as soon as I get out of this tub."

"Good," he said. "Do you mind if I drop down to the bar for a nightcap with Jason so we can plan tomorrow's work?"

"Of course not," she replied. "I will probably be asleep when you come in, though, Dear, so 'good night' and remember I love you very much!"

He said, "I love you too, Evelyn. Good night". The door to the bathroom closed.

Late that night Evelyn Rothchilde lay in her bed, wide-awake. She had pretended to be asleep when John came to bed at midnight. She had decided that she needed more information than she had about Tom Rankin. She needed clues about what he might do, if anything, about meeting Teresa Jacks after so many years. She also now needed to know what had happened at the Moose Creek Ranger Station after her abrupt departure. In other words, she thought, she needed to fill in some blanks. Then she might be able to decide what to do. Hopefully she would not have to take any action and it would all blow over.

She slowly relived the events of that time back in 1964, going from event to event. She knew nothing of what had happened after her departure. She had necessarily cut off all communication with everyone she had known in Idaho, even with her parents and relatives. She had assumed that all they knew was that she was a missing person, and probably dead. Since there was no way she could contact them directly, she would have to find someone else to get the information she needed. A professional investigator would be best. She needed someone extremely discreet. Who would know such a person? She vaguely recalled that Lily Vanderlinden had used a private investigator a couple of years before.

Lily had been receiving unwanted and insulting calls from a disturbed man she had known when she was in college. Eventually the fellow began to follow her and yell insults at her. She kept it all from Roger. She did not want him to worry about her. She did retain a private detective to deal with the situation. Evelyn could not remember any specifics, but she did recall that the problem was settled quickly and discreetly. When she got home she would talk with Lily Vanderlinden and see if the detective was still in business. Yes, she would call Lily tomorrow when she was back in New York. This brought some comfort to her worried mind. Most of all she would have to move quickly. For all she knew, Tom Rankin was on the telephone to the FBI right now!

They flew home the next day. That afternoon Evelyn was on her own. John Rothchilde was playing golf with his cronies. She had called Lily Vanderlinden that morning and arranged a late lunch with her at "The Point". It was a restaurant overlooking the Hudson, upstream from the West Point Military Academy. The place was a popular getaway restaurant for the gentry of the Hudson Valley. Its excellent views of the River were bolstered by a fine French cruisine. The place's architecture featured dark stonework and walnut paneling. Each booth was very private, just as if they had been constructed for the sort of thing she was up to.

When Lily arrived, she was conducted to a secluded booth overlooking the majestic gorge below. She took one look at Evelyn and knew she was very worried. This place and the timing of the meeting were unusual, too, so Lily, being no one's fool, knew something was going on. Evelyn had Lily's drink waiting for her on the table. Seated opposite Evelyn, she sipped her vodka gimlet and said, "Now, Evelyn, what's is this all about?"

Unable to resist being coy, Evelyn looked at her drink and said, "What makes you think something is going on?"

Lily wanted to get to the point, so she said, "All right, forget it. Did you shop in Washington at all? I hear all they have is the stuff that doesn't sell in New York."

That tactic smoked Evelyn out and she said in a hurried and low confidential tone, "I need your help, Lily. What we discuss must be kept absolutely confidential. Do you promise that?"

Lily downed the last of her gimlet. Now they were getting down to business! Leaning forward and speaking in the same tone of voice Evelyn had used, she said, "Of course, you dolt! Am I your best friend or what?"

They both jumped involuntarily when a man's voice interrupted, saying, "Would you care for another drink, ladies?"

They both ordered refills and the waiter left to fetch the drinks. When he was out of earshot, Evelyn said, "Lily, I have a situation with a former beau similar to the one you had two years ago. I ran into him in Washington and he made a nuisance of himself. I don't want John to know about this fellow or to worry about it at all. What did you do about your situation? Perhaps I can do the same."

They were both silenced for a few moments, again, while their drinks were delivered. As the waiter disappeared, Lily looked into her drink, raised it, sipped it slowly, and said, "I did just what you are doing, Evelyn. I went to a good friend who had had a similar experience and asked her what she had done. It turned out she had used a professional investigator and she referred me to him. He turned out to be very efficient, effective, and discreet. He was also expensive, but I credited part of the cost to buying his silence."

Evelyn Rothchilde digested this information briefly and said, "Is he still around? I mean, can you refer me to him?"

"I think he is still in business in New York City," Lily said. "His name is Joseph Smeltzer. You would find his name in the phone book. Evelyn, honey, I hope this all works out for you. Please feel perfectly free to lean on me if there is anyway I can help beyond this!"

Evelyn replied, "I really appreciate that, Lily, Dear. I know I can always count on you when the chips are down. I would tell you more, but the less said now the better, in case it ever leads to litigation."

"Smart girl!" responded Lily.

Joe Smeltzer's greatest secret was that he looked like everyone else. No one would have picked him out of a crowd. He was medium height, medium build, medium everything. His clothes were medium priced and fit moderately well. People like him, and even strangers would voluntarily tell him things they would not admit to their best friends. However, behind this diffident 'everyman' manner and open-faced friendliness, Joe had a mind as sharp as a razor. Time and hard work had also given him the trained observational skills and intuition of a hungry panther. These attributes were the keys to his successful business.

He had survived by his wits for years and years and made darned good money doing it. New York City and Hudson's Valley gentry had come to know his name and now used him a great deal for investigative work that they needed. He was especially appreciated because be was extremely discreet and preserved client-investigator privilege scrupulously.

When Joe Smeltzer was led to Evelyn Rothchilde's lunch table at the small Chez Moulin restaurant in Catskill, New York, he looked like a moderately successful salesman. He shook her hand as he stood by the table and sat down when she invited him to. He already knew as much about her as could be found in recent public records and the society pages of the New York papers. While they sized each other up, there was polite conversation about the weather, his drive up from New York City, and her appreciation for his prompt response to her call. He then suggested that they drive separately to a nearby resort where they could sit on a veranda overlooking the River and do business with assured privacy. A long talk was called-for and such a location could be made to look casual and informal while being far out of hearing range of others. She agreed.

The Buck Springs Resort had been built in 1914. It had been designated a "grand" hotel similar to the Grand Hotel on Mackinac Island, Michigan, and several others of that type and vintage. It had the mandatory wide veranda with small tables. From the veranda, guests could see far over the River and down the Hudson Valley. It was seldom busy and it was perfect for their meeting.

They chose a table near one end of the veranda. She allowed him to order the drinks for them and was surprised when he ordered Kir, white wine with a touch of Creme de Cassis liqueur. Few Americans knew about Kir. She had learned about it in France. It was named after, and in honor of, a brave Second World War French resistance leader that was caught, tortured and killed by the Nazi Gestapo. In America, knowledge of it usually meant that the person who ordered it was traveled and somewhat cultured. Joe Smeltzer didn't seem to be that type of person. She concluded that there was more to him than met the eye.

"What can I do for you, Mrs. Rothchilde?" he asked, after they had received their drinks.

"It is a very personal matter," she said, "that must be handled with the utmost discretion, Mr. Smeltzer."

He nodded solemnly.

She continued, "My husband cannot know. I want to protect him from any concern or worry. Do you understand?"

Joe Smeltzer said, "Of course, Mrs. Rothchilde".

173

"Also", she went on, "my husband knows nothing of my early life. None of my friends here do. Please keep what I tell you strictly to yourself. Only we will know what you find out. Is that clear?"

"Perfectly", he responded, "and let me assure you, Mrs. Rothchilde, this sort of arrangement is not unusual when I deal with people of your stature. Believe me I am highly motivated to be exceedingly discrete in such matters. My whole reputation and business is built on the fact that I honor confidence. You need have no concerns about this in the least."

She looked into his eyes for several seconds and then replied, "Thank-you. I believe you." She then went on to explain how she had run into Tom Rankin in Washington and how he was linked her to her past in Idaho. She gave him her background up until she left Moose Creek Ranger Station, with no mention of her complicity in the murder of young Joe McCulloch, of course. She went on to explain how she had fled at the shock of Kaiser's death and for fear of having her reputation ruined because of her affair with him. Rather than go home and face questions and embarrassment, she had disappeared and created a new life for herself.

She explained that she had assumed another name, worked, attended finishing school, and been lucky enough to meet and marry John Rothchilde in Europe. No one in Idaho knew her whereabouts and she wished to have it remain that way. Now she had encountered a man from her former life and she was afraid he had recognized her. This contact might open her whole past up or, at least, generate embarrassing questions. Most of all, she did not want the issue to reach her husband and friends here in New York.

Joe Smeltzer was silent for a few minutes when she finished her monologue. Then he said, "I understand what you have said. I infer that, as a first step, you wish me to see if this

174

Tom Rankin is pursuing the matter in any way, or, even better, to see if he did, indeed, recognize you in Washington?"

"Exactly," she said, "and I would also like to know if he has contacted anyone in Idaho to tell that he has seen me alive and living another life!"

"Yes," said Joe, "that is the real way to find out if he recognized you. Now I need to ask you a series of questions to facilitate my work. Do you mind?"

"Of course not," she said, "but may we have another drink first?"

As soon as the waiter departed with the order to bring fresh drinks, Joe Smeltzer produced a small, leather bound notebook and began asking Evelyn Rothchilde questions about her former life. He wrote her answers in the book. The fresh drinks came. He continued to ask questions. These were mostly mundane, such as, 'What is your father's full name and where do your parents live?' et cetera. When he could not think of any more questions he said, "Mrs. Rothchilde, how should I contact you if I have further questions, we need to meet, or I have a report for you?"

She thought for a few seconds, then said, " I have voice messaging on a private 800 number that is secured to my own password. You could use that and only I would ever hear your messages. The number is 800-777-2321."

"Perfect," he said. "I will be in touch soon. I expect the first part of this work to go quickly, but being sure Mr. Rankin did not make the connection to you and your past may take a little longer. You can expect my first report in a week with, I would guess, a full report in three weeks. Will that be satisfactory?"

"Wonderful," she said. "Knowing that you are working on it has already put my mind a little more at ease, Mr. Smeltzer. What about your compensation?"

"My normal charge is $500.00 per hour plus incidental expenses, like travel. I would estimate that this work would take less than a full week of my time. If I run into unexpected difficulty and find that more time may be needed, I will let you know. If that rate is acceptable, I will plan to start today. We can settle up when I finish, if you like."

"If you erase my concerns, like you have those of my friends in similar situations here on the Hudson, Mr. Smeltzer, it will be a bargain. Please proceed and call me at my 800 number as needed."

They both stood up. Evelyn Rothchilde shook his hand and turned to leave, but he held her hand and she looked back at him questioningly. He let go of her hand and said, "One more thing, Mrs. Rothchilde, before we part. Please call me 'Joe', just like I am a good friend of yours. I certainly intend to be just that. Don't worry about a thing. Good day".

She smiled at him and said as she turned to leave, "Thank you so much, 'Joe'. Good day to you, too."

Joe Smeltzer watched the tall, elegant woman walk away down the veranda and over to her car. When she had driven away, he sat back down at the table they had shared. What a fine lady, he thought, and what a talented liar! There was much more to this than she said, for sure. She and Rankin had been tied together in something dirtier than a mere illicit 'Affaire de Coeur' back in the Idaho woods. He smiled to himself. It would not be too hard to find out what it was in this age of technology.

He bent down and opened the old-fashioned British-style brief case that was next to his chair. He extracted a laptop computer and plugged it into the 110-volt outlet on the wall behind the table. Then he motioned for the waiter and asked to have a telephone brought to the table. The waiter returned with a telephone that he plugged into a wall jack nearby. Joe ordered coffee and a cheeseburger. Then he booted up the computer and got onto the "Web". By the time he finished the burger and was downing his second cup of coffee, he knew more about Evelyn and John Rothchilde, their friends, John Rothchilde's business, the Forest Service, Teresa Jacks and her family, Tom Rankin and his family, than Evelyn Rothchilde knew. He also had the newspaper accounts of the deaths of Joe McCulloch and Kermit Kaiser, too. Very interesting, he thought, that those two deaths coincided with the disappearance of Teresa Jacks! This was shaping up to be an interesting, and possibly very lucrative, assignment!

# Chapter 18 - Old Friends

A couple of days before Joe Smeltzer met with Evelyn Rothchilde, Orrin West was sitting enjoying the evening on his back porch. He was living in the tiny town of Greer, Idaho, in the Clearwater River canyon a few miles above Orofino. The old apartment building he lived in faced right onto the one road through the tiny town. Its secret bonus was that it backed out over the lime-green westward running Clearwater River, 100 feet below. There was a wide deck at the back.

He often spent the evenings sitting there, like he was this evening, rocking in an old rocking chair and looking westward down the steep canyon. He would watch the canyon walls shade to deep purple and the river turn to molten gold in the sunset. It was at these times he was most content. Life had been long and good. The beauty and peace of these evenings assured him that God was in his heaven and all was well.

Orrin had aged, but not well. He considered this a consequence of doing wild things and avidly pursuing the various sins. Even with the pounding he had given his body over the years, he was a tenacious fellow. He had survived two heart attacks that would have killed most men. Now he spent most of his time on this deck or at the saloon four doors down the street.

A few years back he had married the only widow in Greer. Her name was Marge and she was his age. The marriage had been mostly for convenience and companionship. They were surprised when they came to love each other very much. She owned the apartment building they lived-in. She maintained it and Orrin West very well.

When the telephone rang a day earlier, he had been astounded to hear Tom Rankin's voice. Tom said that they needed to meet right away. "That would be wonderful," he had responded, "but what's so urgent?"

"Teresa Jacks," was the terse reply. "I ran into her at a reception in Washington yesterday. I couldn't believe it. She's married to a financial mogul named John Rothchilde. If it's all right with you, I'll fly out tomorrow and be in Greer early the next morning. I need to talk to you about what we should do, if anything, Orrin."

"Well come ahead," said Orrin. "I'll be thinking about the whole deal while you travel."

"Oh," said Tom, "there's one other thing, Orrin."

"Yeah?"

"I'm planning to have Joe McCulloch's grown son join us. He's become a big shot lawyer in San Francisco. I figure he has a right to be in on our discussions and might also help us out. Any objections?"

Orrin paused and then said, "Does he know how his Dad died?"

"No," said Tom, "but I think he should know. Now is as good a time as any."

"You're right, Tom. Remember where I am? It's Marge's Apartment House, Apartment Number One. The latch string will be out."

Since Rankin's call, Orrin had been reliving the events of the summer of 1964. Now he tried to put them into perspective, given the time that had passed and things that had happened since. Both Tom and he had kept an eye on McCulloch's widow and young son. They had helped Mary move back to her parent's home in San Jose. They had been glad when she eventually

179

married a man named Lebowitz. He turned out to be a good person and he was kind to the growing boy. The boy won a scholarship to the Stanford Law School. He had lost track of the boy, Little Joe, who's real name was Daniel, about that time. Now he would meet him again. He and Tom would be telling the young man the truth about his Dad's death. He worried some about how the young man might react, but remembering he was Joe McCulloch's son, he figured the boy would be all right.

Teresa Jacks' resurfacing was the dilemma. Should they seek revenge or justice or simply do nothing? What would be best for all concerned? Who should call the shots? Orrin West rocked and rocked and thought and thought until long after the sun had set and the gold on the river had faded to black.

About 10 o'clock in the morning a day later, a black Mercury Marquis with a Hertz sticker on the bumper, stopped in front of Marge's Apartments. Daniel Lebowitz and Tom Rankin got out. They knocked on the door of Apartment Number One.

A smiling, vigorous, plump, gray-haired woman opened the door. She shook hands with them and said, "Orrin told me about you boys coming! Go on in the living room. He's waiting for you there. Breakfast will be ready in about a few shakes. You haven't eaten have you?"

They both swore that they had not eaten, for they immediately knew she would be upset if they had. They went inside to see Orrin.

The living room was filled with old, comfortable furniture and several reproductions of Charlie Russell's western bronze sculptures. Orrin rose when they came in, hugged Tom and solemnly shook hands with Daniel. The craggy old man towered over both of them. Daniel noticed his gnarled hand was twice the size of his own when they shook. He could not remember ever meeting him before.

Orrin got each of them a mug of coffee and, at his suggestion, they went out and sat down on chairs on the rear

180

deck. Awkwardly at first, Tom Rankin and Orrin renewed their old, close relationship, Then they brought Daniel Lebowitz into the conversation. They asked him lots of questions about the welfare of his mother and what he had been doing with his life recently. They reminisced a bit about his father and told him some tales of things that they had done together before he died.

While they were laughing together about one of these stories, Marge announced breakfast was ready and ushered them to a table groaning under a huge load of homemade biscuits, sausage gravy, grilled pork chops, scrambled eggs, ham, bacon, and waffles. "We eat this way every day!" said Orrin.

"If we did, he would have been dead a long time ago!" said Marge, from the kitchen. "That man would eat a truckload of biscuits and gravy every morning if I let him."

"Please, Mrs. West, come and join us," said Daniel. He had noticed that there was no place set at the table for her.

"Thank you for the invitation, son, but I come from a generation where, if there's company, the women eat after the men", Marge said. "I just feel more comfortable cleaning up out here in the kitchen while you eat. Go ahead. Go ahead and eat!"

What they consumed scarcely made a dent on the food on the table. As they ate, Orrin said, "When I was working in the woods in the '30's, we ate this way every meal and we never got fat. Just burnt it all up swingin' axes and pullin' misery whips! We used to horse log then, too. Daniel, I remember tellin' your old man, when he was still wet behind the ears, that I used to work a four-dog team pulling logs outta' the woods. I remember his eyes got real big and he said "Jesus! They musta been big sonsabitches!" Orrin laughed to himself at this.

Tom, seeing Daniel's blank look, said, "You see, "dogs" are metal devices that hook the logs to the tow chains behind a team of horses. Your Dad assumed Orrin meant that canines were pulling the logs instead of horses."

"I get it now," said Daniel, chuckling. "Mr. West, they don't teach much about logging in law school, I'm afraid."

After they had eaten all they could hold, Orrin stood up and said toward the kitchen, "Marge, that was mighty fine. Thanks, Dear. If you will wait 'til later, I'll help you clean up." Then he turned to the two men and said, "Fill your cups and let's go back in the out on the back porch and get down to business."

As they did what Orrin suggested, Daniel detoured to the nearby kitchen door and said to Marge, "Mrs. West, that was a fine breakfast. Thank-you very much." With her hands deep in the dishwater in the sink, she smiled and nodded. Then Daniel followed Orrin and Tom to the rear porch.

Orrin settled into his rocker and the other two each sat down in comfortable wicker chairs nearby. Orrin looked at Tom and said, "How much does Daniel know?"

"Not much, Orrin", Tom responded. "We need to go back to '64 and tell him what happened from the start." That they proceeded to do, especially the part about Orrin finding Joe McCulloch dying and his last words incriminating Kermit Kaiser. They could both see tears well up in Daniel's eyes as he sat with his head in his hands and looked at the floor.

Orrin went on to tell how he had put Kaiser and the red horse over the cliff on the Scurvy Mountain Trail and how Teresa Jacks had disappeared that very day. Until Tom had seen her at the reception in Washington, DC, they had both figured she was dead. "We never found the gold. We thought she might have gotten away with it, but never knew for sure," he summed up the old story.

Tom Rankin took up the narrative at this point. He described the meeting at the reception and what he had learned about the Rothchildes. "They are really big deals in the financial circles of the Country. I would guess that bitch, Teresa, changed her name, used some of the gold to educate herself, and married this guy Rothchilde. She always was a darned good-looking woman. She has changed a bit over the years, but it was Teresa Jacks for sure. No doubt about it! The real question before us now is: do we do anything about it?"

There was a silence for a few minutes as the three solemn men looked at each other and sipped their coffee. Finally Orrin spoke, "There's no use going to the authorities. That would just mess up things and probably would result in Tom and me going to jail for doing in Kaiser. If we do anything, it will have to be below the surface. We don't have to do anything, I guess, but it galls the shit out of me to have her get away Scot-free. I am sure she helped Kaiser murder your Dad, Daniel."

Tom Rankin looked at the young man. He said, "I feel the same way as Orrin, Daniel. We don't have to do a thing, but I thought you should know the whole story, at least. If you decide to do something, we will stand with you on it. My main fear is that Orrin and I could go to jail if we do it wrong."

Both Orrin and Tom watched as Daniel slowly raised his head from his hands. The handsome young man looked at both of them. Then he looked over the railing at the green river below. Staring at the river, he said slowly and softly, "I want to take some action. I'm not sure what it is right now. Whatever it is I will make sure you are not involved in anyway that will endanger you. Since this is all such a bunch of new facts for me to absorb, I don't want to make any hasty, emotional decisions. I'll need some time to research the Rothchilde's and figure out what to do. I do want to do something, but, like you say, it will have to be done 'sub rosa'."

"If you will permit me to give a bit of advice, Daniel, I might be able to help", said Orrin slowly, as if he was venturing onto dangerous ground.

Daniel sat up and looked at the old man. He said, "There's no one I would rather have the counsel of, Mr. West. You and Tom were my Dad's best friends. Thank you for including me and allowing me to take action as I see fit."

Orrin West looked down at his gnarled hands and rubbed them slowly together. He then said slowly, "I've been thinking about this since Tom called. Here's what I came down to. She's not worth killing. Killing her might result in more trouble than its worth and it won't bring your Dad back or make up for what you and your mom have suffered. I figure a good way to get even is to take a lot of money from her and her husband.

I doubt that he even knows who she really is. That is her weak point. She is probably scared to death of his finding her out. Another way to get even is to have her worry the rest of her life about being exposed for the murderer that she really is.

Finally, I suggest, if you do anything, you do it for justice and not for revenge. Revenge tends to damage those who do it more than those who receive it. You and your mom have had enough bad stuff happen to you. I would try to be sure whatever I did would not be a negative for you in the end."

Tom Rankin looked at Orrin and appreciated his down-home wisdom more than ever. Then he said to Daniel, "That is good advice, Daniel. Orrin has evidently thought this through carefully. I would only add a couple of things to what he has said. First, take some time to think this all over, then let us know what you decide. If we can help you in any way, we will.

Second, be very careful. They are very powerful people with widespread influence and connections. I would be surprised if Evelyn Rothchilde has not already retained an investigator to watch me. That's why we needed to do this quickly and why I built in considerable 'cover' for this trip."

Daniel had never known strangers could be such friends so suddenly. He wanted to hug them. Full of emotion, he simply said, "Thank you for everything. I mean taking care of Kaiser and all. I value your advice. It's worth a lot to simply now you are here for me. I will need your advice. I suspect you are certainly right, Tom, that these powerful people really know how to take care of themselves. We need to be very careful."

"Well, son, you know where to find this old horse," Orrin said. "As for my high ranking bureaucrat friend here, I know he is never at home. He just jumps on and off jet planes. Do they really pay you for what you do, Tom?"

How adroit the old man is at changing the subject and inserting humor, thought Daniel. With a good education, the man would have been the president of a corporation. Through his thoughts he heard Tom saying, "Orrin, I make one big decision a month. Then I have to rest for a month to get ready for the next one, you know!"

A little later Daniel and Tom were driving down the twisting river canyon of the Clearwater River to Lewiston to catch their planes home. As they passed the town of Orofino Tom said, "This is the County seat of Clearwater County. It's where the Supervisor's Office of the Clearwater National Forest is. Your Dad and I used to work here in the winter when the snow chased us out of the Station at Moose Creek. You lived here a couple of winters as a baby. The town began as a jumping off place for gold miners to go to the backcountry. This was the end of civilization in those days."

Daniel looked at the small town across the River as they whizzed past. He thought to himself that it must have been the end of civilization in 1964 too. He said to Tom, "Was Orrin West here too?"

"Off and on," replied Tom. "He was in the mountains with us all summer. In the winter he usually stayed in the really small towns like Pierce or Weippe. He always said he didn't like the 'big city'."

"So he stayed outside of "civilization"?" said Daniel.

"In a manner of speaking," said Tom. "He tends to have a fair disregard for his fellow humans. I guess he has seen them do so many bad things. He figures the fewer of them he has to deal with the better. You know, Daniel, Orrin West is one of the only genuinely honest human beings I think I have ever met. I have never known him to compromise his principles or go back on his word. The mistakes he makes are innocent and he doesn't make many. I wish to hell there were more people like him. The world would be a better place if there was."

# Chapter 19 – Daniel

Two weeks after their initial meeting, Evelyn Rothchilde received her first report from Joe Smeltzer. Joe reported that, as far as he could tell, Tom Rankin had not made any connection between seeing Evelyn Rothchilde at the recent Washington reception and the Teresa Jacks he had once known in Idaho.

He did not tell Evelyn Rothchilde how he had reached this conclusion. She did not need to know. In fact he had bugged the Rankin's house and tapped their telephone. Then he had reviewed their recent telephone bills for possible calls to Idaho or other old friends connected to Rankin's assignments in Idaho in, or about, 1964. The rest he had gleaned from public records, old newspapers, and the like. The less Evelyn Rothchilde knew about all these things, the better, he felt.

He did tell her about the public details of the accidental death of Kermit Kaiser and her family's consternation at her disappearance. He informed her that her father was now deceased and that her mother lived with her sister in Pierce, Idaho. Most of the older Forest Service people she had worked with in Idaho were now retired or dead. He mentioned, incidentally, that the Joe McCulloch's widow, Mary, had remarried and currently lived in San Jose, California.

Joe Smeltzer recommended continued surveillance of the Rankins for another week or so, just to be sure. She concurred. He promised to report in again in about two week's time. Evelyn thanked him profusely.

What Joe Smeltzer did not bother to tell Evelyn was that he continued to "smell a rat". Intuition and experience told him that this issue closed off too smoothly and neatly. The coincidence of this Mr. McCulloch's death and Teresa's flight was disturbing. It sounded to him like money or something else was involved. He could not put his finger on it. However, he planned to continue the investigation, on his own, even if it was just keeping the bugs in Rankin's house for a couple of months more.

Greatly relieved by Smeltzer's call, Evelyn Rothchilde immediately arranged a lunch with Lily Vanderlinden. She owed it to Lily for the wonderful referral to the investigator. At noon that very day they were sharing an expensive bottle of champagne at "The Point" and two squabs were being poached for them by the chef. Evelyn raised her glass to Lily and said, "Here's to good friends like you, Lily! Thanks so much for the advice and help!"

Lily smiled and replied, with her glass lifted toward Evelyn, "It's a privilege to be able to help you, Evelyn. I'm so pleased Mr. Smeltzer was able to help."

"Well, it's all over and done now, thanks to you and your knowledgeable friend."

Lily Vanderlinden waved her hands in the air over the table and said, "Enough of this. I want to talk about pleasant things, especially your husband's new associate!"

"What new 'associate'?"

"Roger mentioned it last night to me. His name is Daniel Lebowitz. Roger said that they were planning a reception for him before too long. I guess he is from a law firm on the west coast and is Stanford-trained in business law", Lily replied.

188

"Oh", Evelyn said. "I didn't have a chance to talk to John this morning. I'll ask him about the reception tonight. Will you help me with it, if need be, Lily?"

"Of course, Dear," Lily responded. " Roger said the young man is only about 28 years old and very handsome. I understand he will be doing legal work for both Roger and John. Evidently the amount of work they now have is enough to keep a private lawyer busy full time, so they decided to hire one and bring him in-house."

As she drove the winding river road on the way home, Evelyn thought about the new lawyer. A new person, especially a young man, would be nice to have in their social circle, she decided. Nearly all the men and women that she and John associated with were either their age or older. Having a bright, young person around with fresh outlooks and opinions would be good for them all. She hoped that he would not be a dullard or so intimidated that he would be mute. In addition, Lily and she could have fun trying to find him a nice girl his age from among the Hudson's gentry!

That evening when Roger had half finished his usual Glenmorangie on the rocks, Evelyn brought the subject of Daniel Lebowitz up. "Oh, yes, Dear", He said, "I meant to say something to you about that this morning. I hope you were not too surprised to hear about it from Lily."

"No, no, John. Not at all", She answered, "but do fill me in now, Dear. Lily said something about a reception and Lily and I would be glad to take care of that if you and Roger would like us to do it."

"That would be ideal!" He responded. "It would help Roger and me get him introduced around. All of the ladies could size young Daniel up. We need to know what all of you think, too. The sooner the better! Perhaps this very weekend?"

Evelyn paused and then said, "I think we can do that. Yes, four days to set it up should work. Saturday night here at our place—all right?"

"Wonderful!" He smiled and gave her a big hug. Then he said, "You know, Evelyn, I just don't know what I would do without you sometimes. You are such a help and comfort to me everyday!"

She pulled away, walked to a nearby chair, and sat down. With mock seriousness she said to him, "Well, now you have to pay for my help by telling me all you know about our young man."

"First", he began, "he is a west coast lawyer from San Francisco. Comes highly recommended and with exemplary credentials: Summa cum laude in business law from Stanford. Finished high school and law school early and has been working for a prestigious old banking and financial management house, 'Pong and Lee', in San Francisco the last two years. He has done a lot of fine work for them, particularly regarding foreign trade arrangements between U.S. companies and Asian ones."

At this point John sat down beside her, took a sip of his Scotch, and continued, "That is what really attracted us to him. In addition to the fact that the President of the banking house, Dr. Huang Lee IV, called me personally to recommend him. He thought Daniel was ready for a new, more challenging assignment. Both Roger and I have done business with Lee and Pong before and trust their judgement implicitly. Dr. Lee knew from an earlier discussion that we were considering hiring a lawyer to work for us full time.

Following up, we briefly interviewed the young fellow early last week. We liked him immediately, and offered him a job with us on the spot. You can't imagine happened then! It flabbergasted Roger and me, considering how young the fellow is! Well, we made the offer of employment, with no mention of remuneration. This fellow looked at us for a few seconds, got to his feet, and said, "I'm your man if, for no other reason, because of the fine and immaculate reputation of you two gentlemen. It will be, in my estimation, the highest privilege to work with you both. There is no need to discuss my pay. I know you will be fair and honest."

Evelyn, we both got up and walked to where he was standing and shook his hand. Then he looked straight into our eyes and added, "I hope you both will consider me, from this point forward, not only your employee and lawyer, but also your friend." You know, Dear, I have not encountered such sincerity and honest good will from another person since we married. Both Roger and I think we have found a fine lawyer and a fine person. I'm sure you will agree when you meet him Saturday."

Daniel Lebowitz arrived a little late at the reception in his honor. Not seriously or insultingly late, but just late enough for a fine entrance. Roger and John introduced him to their wives and allowed them to introduce him to the other couples. All the guests were into their second drink. This slight alcoholic lubrication allowed them to emit a joviality that fully accepted this minor faux pas, especially since he made a good impression immediately.

He was tall, athletic, and shockingly handsome. All the women in the room had one thought occur as they met him: he looked exactly like a very young Alec Baldwin, the movie star! A dark mane of hair parted on one side and combed back on the other, the same cleft in a masculine chin, and a smile that could melt an ice goddess. As the introductions went on, they noticed that he spoke quietly and respectfully to everyone and was liberal with compliments. Within a few minutes, all the men in the room liked him like a son. All the women adored him. Those with daughters of marriageable age were furiously calculating how they could set up a meeting between Daniel and their offspring.

The Rothchilde's butler, Barclay, announced dinner. They assembled at the large table in the dining room. When they were all seated and had full glasses of wine before them, John

191

Rothchilde rose. He began, "Before I propose a toast of welcome to our new friend and colleague, Daniel Lebowitz, I am taking the privilege, as host of this event, to make a few comments".

This elicited a few moans and a muffled, "Not Again", followed by snickers.

Undaunted, John Rothchilde continued, "Daniel, both Roger and I want to say how pleased we are that you have joined us in business. Moreover, we look forward to having you join our circle of friends and acquaintances, many of which are at this table. I also want to let you know that you should, in no way, feel obligated to associate with any of these people if you don't want to. In fact I wouldn't myself except that it has become a habit and it would be too much work to form another circle of acquaintances."

He was interrupted at this point by several of the group who interjected, "Don't trust this villain, Lebowitz", "He only likes us for our whiskey and our wives", and "We associate with him because his wife is nice and we feel sorry for her, Daniel!"

Daniel smiled broadly, looked around the table, then back at John. He said to Mr. Rothchilde, "I see you have them in your pocket, Sir!" Everyone laughed.

John Rothchilde plunged on, " So, if you all will raise your glasses, save Daniel, I propose we toast our new friend and bid him welcome! We will not invoke a request for his success, for we know his talent and character makes it axiomatic! Welcome! Welcome!"

They all drank the toast and called, "Speech!"

Daniel Lebowitz stood before them, immaculate in a finely tailored tuxedo. Fingering the label with one hand he said shyly, "You do me great honor. I do not quite know what to say. Thank-you, in any event, for the fine welcome and encouragement". Then he went on with more assurance, "I was a bit late tonight in my arrival because I was researching the background of each of you. I am aware of just what a distinguished group this is. You are all people that I am proud to be associated-with. I cannot express my satisfaction at being allowed to work with John Rothchilde and Roger Vanderlinden. I hope my work will justify your good will. I intend to be a good friend and colleague to each of you.. What I did not expect tonight was the degree and universality of beauty exhibited by the ladies! Gentlemen I congratulate each and everyone of you on your fine taste and your ability to induce such beauties to marry you!"

At this point all the women at the table were beaming. Several husbands made comments like: "And they will make sure you are caught before long, Laddie!" and "Daniel, they are setting tender traps for you right now!"

Daniel smiled and continued, "Please accept my thanks for this fine welcome. I want to especially thank our host and hostess. Thank you very much." With that he sat down and everyone at the table clapped politely.

During the evening, Evelyn Rothchilde had plentiful opportunities to talk to and observe Daniel Lebowitz. He certainly was a handsome young fellow, she thought, and very smart, too. She felt that there was something vaguely familiar about him. It was something about the way he moved, walked, spoke, but she could not put her finger on just what it was or why it he familiar to her.

Soon the evening was ending and she and John were saying good night to the guests at the door. When it was Daniel Lebowitz 's turn to leave, she shook his hand and said, "I'm so glad you could come tonight. You made a great hit with the group. Come and see us again soon, Daniel."

He squeezed her hand gently and said, "Thank you for having me and giving me such a grand welcome. I hope to see you again soon, Mrs. Rothchilde. Good night".

She watched him walk down the steps to where his car, an ancient Porsche, was parked. What was it about him that seemed familiar? She could not determine what it was. She closed the door, wondering.

# Chapter 20 - The Report

Ten days after the reception for Daniel Lebowitz, Evelyn received a message on her voicemail that she should contact Joe Smeltzer. She immediately called him. He said, "Are you in a place where you can talk openly, Mrs. Rothchilde?"

"Yes, go ahead", She said.

"I'm afraid that I have some disturbing news to report, Mrs. Rothchilde. Tom Rankin has made and received several telephone calls to Idaho and to California over the last two months. I did not know this when I last talked to you because he had used a separate personal calling card. I won't go into the details of how I know this now, but take it for granted that I know and have evidence to this effect.

Logic then dictated that I try to see if any of these calls might be connected to people you know or knew in 1964. Indeed, they were, but I wanted to check with you to validate these were people you knew then. Several calls were to a Mr. Orrin West, a retired Forest Service employee, who now lives in Greer, Idaho. There was also a call to a Mrs. Mary Lebowitz of San Jose, California. She was the wife of a Mr. Joe McCulloch in 1964. He worked at the Ranger District you did then. Mrs. Rothchilde, do you know this Mr. West and Mrs. Lebowitz?"

Evelyn Rothchilde began to feel faint as Joe Smeltzer talked. It was obvious that Tom Rankin had recognized her and called McCulloch's widow and his old friend Orrin West to discuss it. When Joe Smeltzer said Mary McCulloch's name was now Lebowitz, she had almost shrieked. She realized Joe Smeltzer was still on the line and was talking.

He was saying, "Mrs. Rothchilde, are you still there?"

"Yes. Yes, Mr. Smeltzer. I was just shocked at the news. I'm sorry. Yes, I knew both of those people back in 1964. West was a packer and Mary McCulloch was the wife of a young forester. It seems apparent to me that Tom Rankin did recognize me. I'm at a loss as to what to do now. I hope that my relatives in Weippe have not been told!"

"I understand your concern, Mrs. Rothchilde," Joe Smeltzer said. "It's hard to tell how far the information has been disseminated. That is why I called you right away when I acquired this evidence. I have a suggestion as possible course of action for you now, if you are interested."

"Please feel free to advise me," Evelyn said.

"Have a neutral party, perhaps a lawyer, approach Tom Rankin, explain your predicament, and offer to pay for his silence and his recanting of the story to the people he has contacted. That may work, since, from what you have told me, he has no particular axe to grind as far as you are concerned."

Evelyn Rothchilde knew better than that. Kermit's untimely and freak accidental death had linked her, West, Rankin, and Mary McCulloch together. She was not sure Rankin or West had figured out her role in the murder of Joe McCulloch, but she could not take a chance that they had. She needed time to think, badly. She said to Smeltzer, "I need some time to think, Mr. Smeltzer. This has all come on me so suddenly I am overwhelmed."

"Its natural that you should feel that way", he responded sympathetically. "Why don't we discuss this again tomorrow morning at the same time? I would advise, however, that we not take too long to decide on a course of action, Mrs. Rothchilde. We may be able to nip this in the bud now and not later."

"I understand," she said. "I will call you at 10:30 tomorrow morning. Thank you for the advice, Mr. Smeltzer, Good-bye".

Joe Smeltzer hung up the telephone and leaned back in his office chair. He raised his feet and rested his heels on the corner of his desk. Suspicions confirmed, he thought. She does not want to enter negotiations with Rankin because there is more at stake here than just her privacy. I'll bet, he thought, she and that Ranger were involved in the death of the McCulloch kid! But why? A love triangle? Probably not. The boy had a wife and child right there. It must have been money. What money? From where?

Evelyn hung up the telephone and sat on the edge of her bed, staring into space. As the shock of the news wore off, her brain began to function again. Lebowitz, Lebowitz, she thought. Could it be possible Mary McCulloch/Lebowitz and Daniel Lebowitz were connected and knew about her? If he was connected to Mary why was he here, working for John now? It was too much of a coincidence! She had to find out if there was a connection.

She could not ask Joe Smeltzer to do it for her. In fact, she had to dismiss Smeltzer immediately; pay him off and dismiss him! She certainly did not want him to start to put two and two together and link her to a criminal act. Until she knew for sure that Rankin or West had figured the murder out, there was nothing to act on. Daniel Lebowitz might be the key to finding that out. Rankin's phone calls might have been coincidental—just calls to old friends, but the timing, coming right after he saw her in Washington, made her think it was no coincidence. She decided not to have anyone talk to Tom Rankin for now. That would be an admission of her identity. She would look into Daniel Lebowitz's background and get to know him better. Then she would decide what to do next.

The next day, just before lunchtime, Daniel Lebowitz's office intercom came to life. His secretary announced that Mrs.

Evelyn Rothchilde was in his front office and would like to see him. Daniel quickly ushered Mrs. Rothchilde into his small, but elegantly walnut paneled office. She walked to the east window that overlooked the Hudson River and said, "What a nice view you have, Daniel!"

"Yes", he answered, "the view and the woodwork is supposed to impress any businessmen I have in here. I chose to locate in Albany because I can drive to your and the Vanderlinden's homes easily and, at the same time, get scheduled air service, too. That way, I can be anywhere in the country, including New York City, quite rapidly. What with your husband and Roger Vanderlinden working a lot at home and their travelling a lot, it seems ideal."

"I agree," she responded, "and it sounds like you thought it out like a smart man would. I am here in Albany for some personal business today. I thought you and I could take time out for lunch. It would give us a chance to get to know each other better. I always make it a habit to get to know my husband's close associates well. It facilitates me helping him and anticipating his needs. Are you free to go with me to lunch?"

"Am I! I skipped breakfast today and I am ravenous!" he said. "Shall we leave now?"

"I'm ready if you are," she said, smiling at his boyish enthusiasm. "There used to be a little English-style pub around the corner from here. Shall we try it?"

He was already putting on his overcoat and holding the inner office door open for her. "I know it," he said, "and it is still open for business". As they left he announced to his secretary, "Mrs. Rothchilde and I will be at lunch until, I think, about 1:30, Cindy."

Within minutes, they were occupying a booth at the "Fox and Hounds" restaurant and pub around the corner. They each had ordered a crab sandwich special and had pints of Newcastle Brown English ale before them on the table. "Now," Evelyn said, "tell me about yourself, Daniel. Not all the credentials, but about your family and where you were raised, et cetera."

Daniel looked at her for a moment. Then he took a sip of the ale, and began, "I was born in a small Idaho logging town called St. Marie's. My father worked for the U. S. Forest Service. When I was two years old, the family moved to a remote Ranger Station in the Bitterroot Mountains in north central Idaho. Two years later, in 1964, my father was killed in an accident. I don't remember any of that. We moved to live with my mother's parents in San Jose. That's where I was raised, so I consider California home. You know most of the rest as far as school goes. After graduating from Stanford, I went to work for a financial house in San Francisco. That way I could stay close to mom and make sure she was all right. She seems to be doing very well now, so when this opportunity came up, she all but ordered me to take it for career development reasons."

Evelyn successfully contained her first alarm. Daniel was, indeed, the son of Joe McCulloch! Without visible hesitation, she calmly went on to ask, "What about your personal life? Do you have friends and what do you do for recreation?"

"I'm afraid I haven't had much time for anything but education and work. You saw my hobby at the reception: the old Porsche. I am gradually reconditioning it as time and money permit. I play a little tennis and handball to keep in shape. Most of the women I have dated are as busy making a career as I am. There's no one special. I figure I will get to that when I have cleared away some of the other things I need to do."

"It sounds like you know what you want. Just what is that?" she asked.

"For now it's just progress and learning as I go, I guess. Eventually I would like to become a professor, I think, in a prestigious law school like Harvard. The academic atmosphere and life has a lot of appeal to me. Honestly, Mrs. Rothchilde, that is about as far as my thinking has progressed."

"Please call me Evelyn, Daniel. Do you plan to bring your mother east?"

"Not for now. She has established a good life for herself. She remarried a number of years ago to a fine man named Saul Lebowitz. I took his name after they married. Saul helped put me through school. He ran a medium sized moving and storage business in San Jose. He died a few years ago of cancer. Mother sold the business. It brought enough for her to buy a nice annuity. She gets by very well. Now that I am out of school, I think I help her out best by being a good son and achieving things she can be proud of. She keeps busy doing volunteer work and with her hobbies and friends. I will probably have her come for a visit sometime later, though. That is if she is willing to leave California for a little while."

Their lunches arrived and he ordered another ale for each of them. While they ate, the discussion languished. Evelyn was thinking that she had confirmed who he was and where he came from. He was, indeed, Joe McCulloch's son. That answered the strange familiarity she felt when she saw him. It was the McCulloch walk and broad shoulders; she could tie it together now.

He seemed to be completely innocent of her true identity. She felt he could not have the innocence and equanimity he exhibited if he suspected that she was an accomplice in his father's murder. Indeed, if he did know, he was a better actor than anyone she had ever met! On her best intuition, she decided to take him at face value. Perhaps, in some small way she could repay him some for his father's death and absence during his formative years. She would call Joe Smeltzer off the case tomorrow morning and pay him.

As they finished their lunches, she said, "Daniel, Lily Vanderlinden and I are planning a social at her house for some of our friends about a week from now. We would be very pleased if you could attend. Would you like to?"

"Of course, 'err, Evelyn," he said.

This was the first time he had said her first name and, for some reason, it made her excited and a bit giddy. Hiding unsettled feelings, she said, "Wonderful! Please bring a date if you wish. It will be Saturday afternoon, weekend after next. We plan to brunch about eleven and then break up after tea about four o'clock. You can expect to meet the sons and daughters of several of our friends. Many of them are about your age."

She looked up at him as she spoke the last of the invitation and found him looking directly into her eyes. Then he said, "With you and Lily Vanderlinden there, Mrs. Rothchilde, a date would be an unwanted distraction, so don't count on me bringing anyone with me. Besides, I know very few people here, so it would be a problem even if I was inclined to do so. I assume the dress will be casual?"

She could feel herself blushing at his compliment. She said, in a slightly elevated voice, "Oh heaven's yes. Just a sport jacket and slacks will be fine, Daniel. We might even play some badminton or croquet after brunch, so be prepared for that!"

"It sounds like fun, Evelyn," he said. "If my classic car will run right, I will be there at eleven sharp! Thank you so much for the invitation. I suspect my bachelor apartment will be getting pretty lonely and boring by that Saturday."

Driving home down the River, Evelyn thought long and hard about Daniel Lebowitz. He seemed to be no danger to her at all. While it was disconcerting to have someone so closely connected to the late Joe McCulloch in her current family life, Daniel had certainly given no indication of knowing she was Teresa Jacks or that she had any connection to their former lives in Idaho. Evidently his mother had told him nothing or had nothing to tell him about her, Teresa, or his father's death.

There was some risk to keeping him around, so close to her, because someone could always inform him of the historical connection. On the other hand, she reasoned that that chance was remote and, after his sterling impression on everyone, it would be very difficult to logically get him out of her and Roger's life right now.

She thought about the other things that Smeltzer had told her earlier. She decided that, rather than taking any overt action for now, she would let the Rankin threat ride. The odds were that noting would happen. In her estimation, opening up the whole thing was filled with risks too; risks she didn't want to take now.

Apparently the thing to do was to bide her time and keep an eye on Daniel and the overall situation. If the thing in Idaho blew up, she would deal with it then. If Daniel became a problem, she would try distance herself and Roger from him if the situation got too risky or uncomfortable. Remembering her invitation to Daniel regarding the social, she made a mental note to call Lily Vanderlinden as soon as she got home and have her add him to the guest list.

Following the lunch with Evelyn Rothchilde, Daniel Lebowitz walked back to his office deep in thought. As he passed through the front office on the way his private room, he said to Cindy, "No calls, please, for an hour, unless it is Mr. Rothchilde or Mr. Vanderlinden."

Once in the office he took off his overcoat and went to stand at the window. As he gazed across the Hudson, his mind was going a mile a minute. He could not stay still. After a few minutes he put his coat on, left the room, and told Cindy he was leaving for the day. She knew his beeper would be on if anything urgent came up.

Soon he was zooming down the Interstate toward New York. The familiar purr of the old Porsche's engine calmed him a bit. By the time he turned into the private drive of his apartment community, he knew what he had to do.

In the apartment he tore off his tie, poured himself half a highball glass of Glenlivet, picked up his telephone and dialed a 202 area code telephone number. A secretary answered and

Daniel said, "Please let me talk to Tom Rankin. Tell him its extremely urgent."

Tom Rankin was sitting in the third excruciatingly boring Forest Service meeting of the day when the secretary tapped him on the shoulder and whispered in his ear, "There is an urgent call for you, Mr. Rankin. It's a Mr. Lebowitz." No one in the meeting seemed to notice as he rose and quietly left the room. The secretary directed the call to his office telephone and he recognized Daniel's voice at once.

Daniel said, "Tom, I have been invited to a social this Saturday after next at the Vanderlinden's. The invitation was from Evelyn Rothchilde. Based on discussions I had with her today, I am sure she knows I am Joe's son, but she doesn't appear to think I know about her or that I know anything about her past. I plan to play my card with her that Saturday at the social. Then I will involve her husband on Monday of the following week. Let Orrin know what's up, please. I will need you with me for the meeting with her husband. Can you make it?"

"Just let me know the exact time and place, Daniel," said Tom.

"Tom. I think you should plan to come to Albany that Sunday morning. Plan to stay three or four days. The tickets for the flight will be waiting for you at U.S. Air at National Airport. I'll let you know exactly which flight is booked I'll pick you up at the Albany airport. Figure on staying at my place. That way I can discuss my plans with you and have your advice before we meet Rothchilde on Monday. Sound alright?"

Tom said, "O.K., Daniel. Be careful, son. For your information, I have had the "insurance policy" papers you prepared stored in a safe deposit box here. If the worst happens my banker, or I, will see they go to my lawyer immediately. I know its a small chance, but you never know for sure how people will react under stress."

203

"I appreciate that, Tom," said Daniel. " Pray for me. I think that, if we handle this right, it can turn out well for all concerned. Good-bye". Daniel hung up the telephone and stared at it for awhile. He was committed. It was a relief. He sipped his Scotch slowly and thoughtfully.

# Chapter 21 - Social

Daniel Lebowitz arrived at the social at the Vanderlinden's at 11:15 Saturday morning. The butler conducted him to a huge Florida room at the rear of the house. About thirty people occupied it. Some of them spilled out of the room, through a set of ornate French doors, and into a magnificent back yard boasting an artificial lake.

Over half of the crowd were young, eligible men and women; the privileged offspring of the Hudson Valley gentry. The rest were the mothers or aunts of the youngsters. These women carefully stayed on the peripheries of the mass and observed the social intercourse. No fathers were in evidence. Daniel was slightly older than the average young attendee, but not by much.

Evelyn Rothchilde and Lily Vanderlinden both came over when the butler brought him into the room. They assured him that they were 'absolutely delighted' that he could make it. They both commented on the style and appropriateness of his dress. Indeed, he did look like he was ready for a British garden party. This was thanks to the knowledgeable haberdasher at the Brooks Brother's store in Albany.

Evelyn and Lily immediately began taking him around and introducing him to the mothers present. When this was completed, they took him to meet the others his age. This must be how a young prize bull feels at a stockyard auction, he thought to himself. As soon as he had been circulated, they left him on his own with his peers. His observation, as he exchanged small talk with a pair of vacuous, but pretty, girls, was that this was the Hudson version of a mating ritual. It made him feel even more like a round of beef in a butcher's display case.

After a suitable length of time, the lunch buffet was announced and they all went out onto the lawn and filled plates from overflowing and exquisitely decorated tables. The fare was light, but very good. There was a tray of the very best champagne. The latter was undoubtedly calculated to loosen the tongues and inhibitions of the youngsters a bit, but not too much, for the amount offered was limited.

A number of tables for four were placed under a large green and white striped awning nearby. Soon these groups of four were engaged in animated discussions. Most of the matrons sat to the side and commented on the young people and their appearance and behavior. It was all very pleasant, gentile, upper class, and Victorian.

Daniel Lebowitz was bored to the core with the social. Most of his peer group seemed to be spoiled and none too intelligent. Most had, or were, attending the finest universities on the strength of their parent's donations to the school. While standing aside and looking at the Vanderlinden's house, he noticed Evelyn Rothchilde coming toward him. As she walked up she said, "You look bored, Daniel. The company not to your liking?"

"As a matter of fact, I am having a bit of trouble relating to these people", He answered. "I have little to talk to them about. I live in another world that is different from theirs. They obviously exist in a world of wealth and privilege with few real responsibilities. They are nice enough, but I have nothing to say that they are interested-in." He hesitated, worried that he had been too frank, and then continued, " I don't want to sound pompous or condescending, but that's it, Mrs. Rothchilde".

"You are certainly honest," she responded, " but consider the fact that soon they will soon have to enter their father's and mother's world of high finance, business, and business-related social activities. They will have to learn fast then and they know it will be very hard. I think, consequently, they naturally have a tendency to want to hang onto childhood and lack of responsibility as long as possible. Enough of that, though, come let's walk down to the lake while we talk."

They strolled toward the 20-acre man-made lake at the foot of the slope behind the great house. There was a bench under a shade tree and he suggested they sit down.

When they were seated he announced, "Mrs. Rothchilde, there is something that we need to talk about."

She looked at him, smiled, and said, "Evelyn. Call me Evelyn."

"As you wish, Evelyn". He began again, "Evelyn, I appreciate your invitation for me to come to this event, but I really came because I have serious business to conduct with you, personally".

"My," she said, "You sound very serious, Daniel."

"I am. I know that you were formerly Miss Teresa Jacks, of Weippe, Idaho, and that you participated, with Kermit Kaiser, in the murder of my father. I also know that you subsequently stole the gold he had found in Independence Gulch in the summer of 1964. I came to New York specifically to settle the matter with you, not to work for your husband."

His words hit Evelyn like the concussion of an exploding artillery shell. Time seemed to freeze. She felt faint. She grew visibly pale, but she managed to mumble, "Who in the world is this Teresa Jacks? Have you lost your mind, Daniel?"

"Quite the opposite," he said in a flat intonation. "I have witnesses ready to corroborate what I have just said. They can place you at the murder site with Kermit Kaiser. I suggest you do not play games. You could go to a penitentiary for murder."

Evelyn looked around like a trapped animal. She saw Lily Vanderlinden coming over to where they sat. She savagely whispered to Daniel, "Don't breath a word of what you just said to Lily. We will leave immediately and discuss this, but don't say anything to her, for God's sake!"

Lily Vanderlinden could tell her friend was very upset, just by her pale color and the wildness in her eyes. She said, "Is anything wrong, Evelyn? You don't look well, Dear."

Daniel Lebowitz said, "I was just telling her the same thing. Perhaps I had better see you home, Mrs. Rothchilde?"

Evelyn Rothchilde managed to say, "I really do feel quite ill, Lily. I hate to leave in the middle of the social, but perhaps it would be best for me to go home and lay down. Daniel can take me. I'm so sorry, Dear!"

Lily Vanderlinden said, "Don't worry about that at all! You just get home and take care of yourself. I'll call a little later and check on you. Thank-you so for looking after her, Daniel!"

As Daniel Lebowitz and Evelyn Rothchilde walked away toward the house, Lily Vanderlinden looked after them. She was wondering what could have upset her friend to severely and so quickly.

As Daniel drove his old Porsche out of the Vanderlinden's brick-paved driveway, Evelyn Rothchilde hissed, "Take me straight home and we will talk about all of this. I will not say a thing until we get there!" At least she would have a few minutes to think. Her mind worked furiously during the drive home. As they entered the house she said to Barclay, "Mr. Lebowitz and I have some business to attend to, Barclay. We will be in the study. We don't want to be disturbed."

"Very good, Madame", Barclay said, and he hastily retreated toward the kitchen.

When they entered the dark, book-lined study, she closed and locked the heavy walnut doors behind them. Without an invitation, Daniel Lebowitz walked to the bar, poured himself some of John Rothchilde's fine Bell's 25-year-old Scotch whiskey, and seated himself on the massive leather couch in the center of the room.

Evelyn took off her coat and hat, poured herself a half tumbler of Finnish vodka, added two ice cubes to the glass, and sat at the end of the couch opposite Daniel. She sipped her drink and then said, "Now, where in the Hell did you come up with the fiction you spouted to me at Lily's? Do you really plan to try to extort money from John and me? I'll tell you, if you try, we will hand you your head on a platter!"

Daniel Lebowitz, paused a moment for effect, and then replied in a low and even voice, "Please don't threaten me, Mrs. Rothchilde. I have all the information about you that I would ever need to send you away for the rest of your life. Even a half-competent, besotted lawyer could take what I have and win, in spite of your powerful husband and all his money and connections.

However, I seek justice, not revenge. If I had been interested in revenge you would be dead right now, perhaps pushed over a cliff in a car just like you and Kermit Kaiser did to my Dad! I want you and your husband to know, from the start, that I am not in this alone. The documentation and all the depositions of the witnesses are in safe keeping and the witnesses all know what is going on right now. Should anything happen to any of us, the evidence will go directly to a prosecuting attorney."

Evelyn Rothchilde glared at him and took a long drink of the vodka. Her heart was beating fast and the blood was pounding in her head. She now knew she could not intimidate him. She would try another ploy. Coolly she said, "I do not care what you have in a greasy folder somewhere or what group of rum-heads you have talked-to. None of this is true. It is not true.

209

These things happen all the time to rich people like us—accusations formulated to get blackmail money. Usually John and I find it is cheaper to pay the crooks off than to go to court. We will be willing to do that in your case, Mr. Lebowitz. We want to stay out of the tabloids. Of course you would have to sign an agreement that you would drop the accusations, once you had the money. How much will it take?"

"I'm glad you are being more reasonable, Evelyn," Daniel said, "but I am afraid it may be a bit more complicated than that. However, if you accede to my demands, I will assure you that you will not go to prison. I will not give you my demands now. I have arranged to meet with your husband on Monday and discuss the matter with him. I plan to make the agreement with both of you through him. I realize the real power in the family is Mr. Rothchilde. In addition, he has been kind to me and I do not want to hurt him any more than is necessary. I know that you do not want to hurt him either. Please do not initiate any contact with me between now and Monday. From now on I will only deal with your husband until this matter is concluded."

With that he swallowed his last bit of Bell's, sat the empty glass on the ornate coffee table in front of the couch, and got up and walked to the door to the study. There he paused, turned, and looked back at Evelyn Rothchilde and said, "Consider yourself lucky. Most people who learned what I did about you would have strangled you. You can come out of this with your life intact if you behave and cooperate." Then he walked out and slammed the heavy door behind him.

Evelyn Rothchilde sat on the couch in a state of shock. She put her head in her hands and began sobbing. After several minutes, she regained her composure. She realized that she would have to tell John tonight or early tomorrow. How? How? Was there any way that he could he love her afterward?

She thought of suicide, but put it away. She was not such a coward that she could not kill herself, but she could not stand the idea of hurting her husband. She knew her death would ruin his world. Her mind raced through improbable, desperate, possibilities. She could run again and hide in foreign countries, but she knew John, with his resources, would find her.

Lebowitz had held out a glimmer of hope, for he had mentioned justice and not revenge. She would grab for it as hard as she could. She again began to sob big racking sobs. Mascara flowed onto her handkerchief along with her tears. After awhile she got up and slowly walked upstairs. She undressed, drew a hot bath, and climbed in the hot water. John would be home in a few hours. She would tell him everything soon. She prayed to Almighty God he would understand.

That evening, about 8 o'clock, John Rothchilde came home from a trip to Chicago. He found his wife waiting, beautiful and loving. She had a special dinner prepared for just the two of them. She told him that this evening would be the best in their lives, no matter what happened in the future, and that she wanted him to remember it forever. That evening they were closer and more in love than they had ever been. He was happy beyond words. His wife was fantastic. He was happy as only a happily married man can be.

The next day, Sunday morning, Evelyn and John Rothchilde rose late. They had had a fabulous evening of good food, wine, loving, and talk. They awoke refreshed and made love again. Then they showered, had a leisurely breakfast, and read the newspapers. By the time they were dressed, it was 11 o'clock. Evelyn suggested another cup of coffee on the patio. As they sat in the sun drinking the refreshing brew, she said to him, "John, I have something very serious to discuss with you, so please give me your fullest attention, Darling."

The tone of her voice quickly pulled him from his blissful state of contentment. He looked at her. She was sitting upright in her chair and looking at him with unusual sincerity and earnestness. He sat up straight too, leaned on the table with his elbows and looker her straight in the face. He said, "Evelyn, you have all my attention."

She then continued, "John, we have had a wonderful marriage and life. I want it to go on forever, just like it is, but there is a great danger that it will not. You knew nothing of me, really, before we married. Some old things have come back to haunt me now and I need your understanding and support as never before."

John Rothchilde looked at his wife's serious face and grew even more serious. He said, "My God, Evelyn, for a moment there I thought you were going to say you had a serious disease or something like that. It's not that is it, Darling?"

"No. No. It's not that," She said. "John, it's about some trouble I was in years ago. I thought it was all behind me, but it has surfaced now and you are caught in it with me. I wish to God that you weren't, but you are. I am sick about it. We need to talk it all out today so you are ready for tomorrow."

"Well, I think we can handle anything like that if we stick together!" he said. "What's this about tomorrow?"

"You have an appointment with Daniel Lebowitz tomorrow, right?"

"Yes. Is he involved?" he said.

"Yes, Dear. Now let me tell you the whole thing from the start. Some of it is very ugly, but I am convinced you must hear the whole story. I only hope that you will not think too badly of me. Please remember that I love you more than anything in the world and I would rather do anything than hurt you." With that, Evelyn Rothchilde began to tell her husband her whole story from beginning to end. She did not shade the truth or lie a bit.

As she poured the whole tale out, John Rothchilde sat and quietly listened. A few times his brow wrinkled or his eyes watered up, but otherwise he was immobile. He looked into his wife's eyes during much of her talk. The monologue went on for over an hour. His wife came to the end by describing the meeting with Daniel Lebowitz in the study the preceding day. She finished with the words, "John, after this, if you want me to just go, I will. I love you so much I can't stand the prospect of you disliking me. If that's the way it will be it would be better for me to just go away. I'm so sorry to have to tell you this. So sorry!" She began to weep in spite of herself.

When she finished John Rothchilde sat for a few minutes without speaking, looking at the table before him. Then he looked up at her, as she dried her eyes, and said, "The first thing to do is for you and me to have a good, stiff drink! Then let me give you my thoughts. O.K?"

They got up and went into the study where she and Daniel Lebowitz had met the day before. John made a tall Scotch and soda for himself and a tall bloody Mary for her. Then they walked back out into the brilliant sunlight and sat again at the table on the patio.

"Evelyn", he began, "that is a truly shocking story. We will have to deal with the situation as forthrightly as possible. First, you are my beloved wife and you will, if I have anything to do with it, be just that for as long as I live." She looked at him with love in her eyes and then began to sob quietly.

He gave her a few minutes to collect herself, and went on, "Tomorrow I will meet with Daniel Lebowitz and work this thing out. It sounds like he may be trying to do the right thing, but feels horribly wronged. I can't say that I blame him. If the roles were reversed, I don't think I would have controlled myself as well as he did. In any event, you and I will straighten the matter out with him. We will do what we need to do and go on with our lives.

I do not recognize the person you described to me as Teresa Jacks. It is certainly not the women that I have known, and now know, as my wife. Daniel Lebowitz may ask for some things that you don't want to do, but that remains to be seen. Whatever it is, we will go through it together and come out the other side just a devoted to each other as we are now. Now, come sit on my lap, give me a hug and tell me you love me just as much as I do you, Dear!"

Evelyn rose from her chair, quickly sat on his lap, and hugged him as hard as she could. Tears flowed freely down her cheeks and onto his shoulder. At that moment Evelyn Rothchilde would have died, in a minute, for the man.

# Chapter 22 - The Price

At 10 o'clock the following morning, Daniel Lebowitz and Tom Rankin were ushered into the plush office that John Rothchilde maintained in the small town of Hudson, near his home. As they entered, they saw that John Rothchilde and Roger Vanderlinden were waiting for them. Daniel shook each man's hand and introduced Tom Rankin to them. John recalled meeting Tom in Washington.

While they were still standing John Rothchilde said, "I took the liberty of inviting Roger to attend this meeting with me. I hope that you do not mind. He is my closest personal friend and business associate. I value his opinions a great deal. What we are going to discuss today might affect our joint holdings and, also, since the subject is very personal to me, his presence will help me a great deal."

Daniel said, "It is a privilege to have him here, John, and Roger's involvement and opinions will be valuable to me, too. As you can see I have brought along a similar friend, Tom Rankin, to help me thorough this meeting. Tom was directly involved in the events we are going to discuss today and can give us a perspective few others can. I trust him to the highest degree."

After they were seated in wing-back leather chairs around a low oval coffee table, John Rothchilde began the meeting, by somberly saying, "Gentlemen, I hope what we talk about to day will stay in this room. Daniel, I appreciate your discretion in this matter up to this point."

Daniel Lebowitz looked up at him and replied, "Mr. Rothchilde, I am sorry that I had to discuss this first with Mrs. Rothchilde day before yesterday. However, I considered it essential that she fully understood the gravity of the situation. I assumed, and it appears correctly, that that understanding would allow us to come straight at the problem today without complex preliminary moves that might make a solid settling of the issue impossible. It also allowed her to tell you in her own way, I hope."

Tears welled up in John Rothchilde's eyes as Daniel talked. When Daniel finished, he said, "You are wise far beyond your years, Daniel. Evelyn gave me the whole story yesterday morning. It gave us a chance to really come to terms with the situation and ourselves. Thank-you for handling it the way you did. I have filled Roger in on the whole matter, so no repetition is needed for him." Roger Vanderlinden reached over and squeezed his friend's forearm in support and sympathy.

"If you wish, I will continue on and present our position, John," said Daniel. He knew the easy way to handle the loaded situation was to present it like a business proposition. That was what all four were used to doing and it was more comfortable that way.

"Please do, and help yourselves to the coffee", replied John Rothchilde, indicating a silver service on the table that was emitting the pungent smell of coffee.

After pouring himself a cup of the black brew, Daniel Lebowitz opened a folder he had laid on the low table earlier. He extracted four sets of print-covered paper. He gave each of the others a set and began to read aloud from the first page of the one he kept for his use. The first part of the reading dealt with his discovery of what had happened to his father when he visited Greer, Idaho, and discussed the matter with Tom Rankin and Orrin West, a few months earlier. The second part described his investigation of the matter and what he had found that supported and verified the stories of Orrin and Tom. At this point, he

216

looked up at John Rothchilde and Roger Vanderlinden saying, "The fact is, gentlemen, that there is a nearly iron-clad case against Miss Teresa Jacks, now Mrs. Evelyn Rothchilde. The evidence could put her into a penitentiary for the rest of her life for the murder of my father, Joe McCulloch, in 1964."

At this point Daniel paused and sipped his cooling coffee. John Rothchilde took the opportunity to say, "Daniel, does anyone, other than you, Tom Rankin, and Orrin West know this whole story?"

"No," Daniel replied, "but the story and all its details are stored in a place that will be accessed by a friend of mine, who is a Federal Prosecutor, if anything should happen to any one of the three of us or any of the witnesses in the case. John, I took those precautions not because I distrust you or Roger, but because I didn't know what reactions I might get from Mrs. Rothchilde Saturday. A perception of being trapped, and the associated desperation, can make anyone do strange things. However, my estimation of the relationship you two share was that she would turn to you as she did. I am happy that I was correct. So, the secreting of the case documents was done merely for insurance against a remote possibility and not as a threat to either of you."

"I appreciate your motives, Daniel," John Rothchilde said. "Please continue."

"Now we get to the hard part," Daniel said. "What to do? I have spent many sleepless nights on this question, believe me. The first thing I concluded was that I would not rush to a blind judgement of your wife, John. That is why I arranged to come here and be in your employ.

My friends, Dr. Huang Lee IV and Mr. Lee Pong, of the San Francisco Law Firm I was formerly a member of, helped in this. I hope you will understand that they did this out of sense of justice sought. They know few of the details. They have their put trust in me to handle any actions with civility and not out of any animus for you or yours. They are connected in a most curious

217

way to this whole case though; a way I could hardly believe what they told me. You need to hear this.

They think that the gold that my Father found in 1964, and that was subsequently stolen by Kermit Kaiser and Teresa Jacks, was from an old cache made by their great grandfathers in 1869. The remaining gold the two men had was carried out on their backs to civilization. That gold formed the financial foundation for the Pong and Lee fortune in California. They think this is true because the description of the cache, its construction and location, as well as the marking on the gold bags. All that matches the story of the cache that is recorded and told in their family. They even have some of the actual leather gold bags in a display in their offices!"

Tom Rankin had not heard this story before. All three of the men sitting with Daniel looked at each other with raised brows and incredulous eyes. Tom said, "That's an incredible story, Daniel!"

"Remarkable. Remarkable!" said John Rothchilde.

"But let me return to the issue at hand", continued Daniel. "The reason I came here was to get to know you and Mrs. Rothchilde. I wanted to do this before taking any action. What I found was two happy, talented and honorable people who have a great set of friends; people who have been kind and supportive of me. In a short space of time, I have come to greatly value the relationship with both of you gentlemen and with your families. Indeed, far too much to have any desire to hurt you or to devise any revenge against any of you." As he said the last few words of this, Daniel's voice cracked.

Tom Rankin put his hand on Daniel Lebowitz's shoulder and said, "Its O.K., Son. You are doing fine. Go ahead."

After a few moments Daniel continued, "But the acts of Teresa Jacks and Kermit Kaiser have caused a lot of pain and suffering and I still feel that justice should somehow be served. I know that you, as the honorable men that you are, recognize that

218

too. Therefore, I have prepared a list of suggested actions that you can take to settle accounts.

My intent is, if we are adroit about this, to have an outcome that is positive and amicable. My mother and I can never replace the years we would have had with my Father, whose young life was cut off in his prime. I can never replace the untold hours I would have spent with him learning and playing at his side." Daniel stopped, for his throat had closed again with emotion. He managed to choke out, "Please finish this page for me, Tom."

John Rothchilde rose and walked around behind Daniel Lebowitz's chair. Standing there, he put his hands on Daniel's shoulders in a silent sentiment of support and sympathy. He remained there while Tom Rankin continued the reading.

Tom found where Daniel had stopped on his copy of the paper. He read aloud, " Therefore, (a) in consideration for the of provision of the sworn lifelong silence of Daniel Lebowitz, Tom Rankin, and Orrin West regarding the preceding recorded matter, the murder of Joe McCulloch, and (b) on behalf of myself and my Mother, Mrs. Mary Lebowitz (McCulloch) for the suffering we have incurred from the actions of Miss Teresa Jacks, now Mrs. John Rothchilde, I request on behalf of myself and my Mother, the following:

(1) The creation of a trust fund for Mary Lebowitz (McCulloch) that will provide an annual after tax income to her for life of $250,000. The trust fund to revert to her son, Daniel, upon her death.

(2) The creation of similar trusts, yielding $100,000 per annum, for Mr. Tom Rankin and Mr. Orrin West for as long as they live, with right of survivorship to be determined by them. This for the grief and pain they have suffered associated with the murder of Mr. Joe McCulloch.

(3) The creation of a "Forester's" endowed Chair of $500,000 (from an independent trust fund administered by the

Harvard Foundation) per year in the Law School of Harvard University, Cambridge, Massachusetts. Concentration of the activity of the Chair to be focused on environmental law-related matters.

(4) The installation of Mr. Daniel Lebowitz as the first incumbent in the Harvard Law School's "Forester's" Chair, with tenure for life. Subsequent incumbents to be chosen by Harvard University Law School in consultation with the Rothchilde and Lebowitz families.

(5) The continued employment of Daniel Lebowitz as the Lead Lawyer for Rothchilde/ Vanderlinden Enterprises, Inc.

(6) The continued friendship for, and moral support of, Daniel Lebowitz by both Mr. John Rothchilde and Mr. Roger Vanderlinden, and, if possible, their heirs and families."

When Tom Rankin finished the list of requests from Daniel Lebowitz there was silence in the room for several minutes. John Rothchilde still stood with his hands on Daniel Lebowitz's shoulders. Tears were running down Daniel's face and he mopped them off with his handkerchief. Slowly John Rothchilde lifted his hands from Daniel's shoulders and walked around to where Roger Vanderlinden was sitting. He then said, "Roger and I need to discuss this for a moment in private. I suggest we go into the nook next door, talk and then come back. It should only take about 10 minutes."

Daniel nodded his drooped head and Tom Rankin looked up at John and said, "Agreed".

The two men returned, after only a few minutes, and sat down in the chairs they had occupied earlier opposite Daniel and Tom. John Rothchilde began, "Both Roger and I find your request to be unacceptable in some details. We wish to discuss the matter in more detail. I want to tell you that we are not far apart and the issue is not the nature of your request but some of the details of it that we want to be clear on between ourselves before a formal reply. Are you willing to meet again tomorrow at 10 a.m. to finalize this?"

Daniel Lebowitz, somewhat recovered, said, "Of course, John".

All four of the men rose to their feet and, moving away from the chairs and the coffee table, shook hands. When John and Daniel shook hands, John did not let go of Daniel's hand, but pulled the young man to him and gave him a tender hug. Then he patted him on the back with his left hand and walked Daniel to the office door with his arm around his shoulders. John Rothchilde had tears in his eyes when he said to Daniel, "See you at 10 o'clock tomorrow, Son," as Daniel went out the door.

Thirty minutes later Daniel and Tom were sitting in a small bar near the office drinking Glenfiddich Scotch whiskey, neat. It was their favorite Scotch. Its light, peaty flavor deserved savoring without water to interfere. Tom Rankin said, trying to be upbeat and supportive, "You did real good in there, Danny Boy! It was a fine thing to not want to hurt them after not having a Dad and all. I thought your requests were minimal and carried the intent well. I just can't see what they have to quibble over."

"I expect it may be a legal point or some minor control issue—a refinement, not a major change," said Daniel.

"Well, I'll tell you here and now, they should be praising their lucky stars you didn't rip their financial guts right out, after what Teresa did to you and your Mom."

"Tom, I know you were there, but I wasn't. I missed having a Dad by blood, but old man Lebowitz was O.K," replied Daniel. "I never knew Joe McCulloch. I can only guess what he was like, so its not as hot an issue with me, just a loss, I guess."

"Well, no matter what, your requests were very modest, Danny, compared to the billions these guys have. Don't let them back you off a bit tomorrow! Oh, I had better call old Orrin. I'll bet he is about to crap his pants wanting to know what happened.

By the way, why did you put that stuff in there about Orrin and me getting a trust fund?"

Daniel took a sip of Glenfiddich, rolled it on his tongue, swallowed and said, "I'm afraid you two old farts would starve before you die!"

Instead of laughing Tom looked at Daniel seriously, gulped, and quickly looked down at the wood of the bar. His chest heaved several times. Then he raised his glass and took a big swallow. As the glass came down so did a cascade of tears.

"Jesus, what did I say?" said Daniel. "I was just trying to be funny."

After a few minutes of silence, Tom Rankin mopped his eyes with his handkerchief. He looked at Daniel and slowly said, "I couldn't believe it, Danny. Right then, you looked just like Joe and you said exactly what he would've said in the same way. Goddamn it! He was such a good kid. I still miss his dumb ass every fuckin' day! So does Orrin." Tom took another long swallow of whiskey.

Daniel looked at the older, graying man. Then he rubbed Tom's broad back with his hand and said, "Don't ever ask me again why you and Orrin are getting something out of this. You guys lost a buddy for the rest of your life. You also carry the pain of that loss in a way I never will. I expect, when I get to meet my Dad at sunset, he will insist that you and Orrin will be right there with us."

Tom just looked into his empty glass, mentally miles away and years ago in another world in the Idaho woods.

Daniel Lebowitz looked down the bar and said, "Bartender! Another round here! Right away, please!"

About the same time, John Rothchilde opened the door to his house. Evelyn was standing expectantly at the foot of the staircase waiting for him. Her face was solemn because she was steeled for the worst. Her eyes bulged with the question: what did they want for their silence? John went to her, hugged and kissed her and said, "Come with me into the study".

While he mixed them drinks she said, "Are you going to keep me in suspense forever?"

He looked up, smiled, and said, "It was the damnedest thing you ever saw, Evelyn. He asked for peanuts. His main concern was to keep our friendship and respect. He made me cry with his sincerity and honesty. All this from a boy who lost his father forever. I still cannot believe what a fine, fine man he is. We owe him big time. Big time!" He handed her drink and she saw he was not kidding at all.

He went on "You know why he talked to you first yesterday instead of only to me today? To give us time to work it out, just like we did. He was so far ahead of us. By God, after being in business for so many years, I just couldn't believe it! Let me give you the full story with all the details." He went on to recount that morning's meeting in detail. At the end, they were both weeping in relief.

Then John Rothchilde said, "We owe him more than we can repay, Evelyn. I owe him. I begged off more time to think about it and what it should be. I wanted to be sure that you and me are together on whatever we decide to do. We have a bit of work to do the rest of this day. Roger and I meet with them again tomorrow at 10 A.M."

They talked all afternoon. They talked into the night. Finally, exhausted, they climbed the curving marble staircase and crawled into their huge bed. As consciousness slipped from them both, she whispered in his ear, "John Rothchilde, there is no woman in the world that loves her husband as much as I love you."

# Chapter 23 – Justice

The four men gathered, as planned, at 10 o'clock the next morning. John Rothchilde began the meeting, saying, "Thank-you for allowing Roger and me the time to think about your requests. Also, thank you for meeting us again this morning. We have studied your requests carefully. We have several suggestions for changes. I think you will find them all agreeable. Please permit me to go through them one by one:

(1) The creation of a trust fund for Mary Lebowitz (McCulloch) that will provide an annual after tax income to her for life of $250,000. The trust fund to revert to her son, Daniel, upon her death. <u>Agreed, but the amount will be $500,000 per year.</u>

(2) The creation of similar trusts, yielding $100,000 per annum, for Mr. Tom Rankin and Mr. Orrin West for as long as they live, with right of survivorship to be determined by them. This for the grief and pain they have suffered associated with the murder of Mr. Joe McCulloch. <u>Agreed, but the amount will be $250,000, for each.</u>

(3) The creation of a "Forester's" endowed Chair of $500,000 (from an independent trust fund administered by the Harvard Foundation) per year in the Law School of Harvard University. <u>Agreed, but the amount will be $1,000,000 per year for the Chair.</u>

(4) The installation of Mr. Daniel Lebowitz as the first incumbent in the Harvard Law School's "Forester's" Chair, with tenure for life. Subsequent incumbents to be chosen by Harvard

University Law School in consultation with the Rothchilde and Lebowitz families. <u>Agreed, Daniel Lebowitz will fill the Chair.</u>

(5) The continued employment of Daniel Lebowitz as the Lead Lawyer for Rothchilde/ Vanderlinden Enterprises, Inc. <u>Disagree. We require, as an alternative, that a Law firm be created called 'Daniel Lebowitz and Associates' and that it be capitalized, by us, in the amount of $5,000,000 immediately. That Law firm to be the designated Law Firm for Rothchilde/Vanderlinden Enterprises, Inc.</u>

(6) The continued friendship and moral support of Daniel Lebowitz by both Mr. John Rothchilde and Mr. Roger Vanderlinden, and, if possible, their heirs and families. <u>Agreed, with pleasure, and we look forward to the continued friendship and association.</u>

(7) In addition we have one added one more item: We require that at <u>Mr. Daniel Lebowitz accept the ownership of 50 acres of forested land immediately adjacent to the Rothchilde estate in the Hudson Valley. This ownership is conditional upon his building a home there for himself and occupying it within one year from this date.</u>"

Daniel Lebowitz and Tom Rankin sat in stunned silence when John Rothchilde finished his presentation. Neither of them had expected such generosity. They were overwhelmed. They were shaken out of their silence when John Rothchilde said, "Are those terms of agreement acceptable to you gentlemen?"

After a moment Daniel looked into John Rothchilde's eyes and said, "Mr. Rothchilde, you and Roger are more than generous. I simply don't know what to say except, of course, we accept, with pleasure."

Both John Rothchilde and Roger Vanderlinden were smiling broadly by now. John replied, "We had law clerks working last night to prepare the papers, so we can sign them right now. I want to get it over because Lily and Evelyn are

225

setting up a fine brunch for us at the house right now. I want you and Mr. Rankin to go with us and help us celebrate. Also, I know that Evelyn wants to have a few moments alone with you two."

He then went to the door of the office and called three young, and very bleary-eyed, law clerks in. They brought with them a series of documents to sign.

When all the papers were signed, John Rothchilde turned to Tom Rankin and said, "Tom, if you will be so kind, I would like to have you take these papers out to Idaho and have Orrin West sign them too. Assuming you would be willing to do that, I took the liberty of scheduling a private jet to take you and one of the law clerks out there after the brunch today. When you are done, the plane can return you home to National. Is that O.K. with you?"

"Certainly, Sir", smiled Tom. "I want to personally thank you on behalf of Mr. West and myself. Your kindness, generosity and civility are most appreciated."

Now it was John Rothchilde's turn to be a little embarrassed, but he quickly replied, "Tom, it was you and Orrin that lost a close friend and carried the pain of for so many years, not me. I cannot repay either of you for that, but I can show my appreciation for your manner of handling this problem. You made it possible for my wife and I to continue to have our life together. I can't pay you enough for that. Please extend these same sentiments to Mr. West for me." They shook hands cordially.

Tom said in reply, "You can really thank the old man out in Idaho. He had the wisdom to see that revenge is worthless, but mercy has a lasting benefit. I guess age brings that sort of wisdom to you eventually".

Roger, standing smiling near the office door, interrupted. "Fellows, we had better get going or we will be in trouble with the ladies for spoiling the food and keeping them waiting!"

The brunch turned out to be a garden party with about twenty-five guests, all friends of the Vanderlinden's and Rothchilde's. The best champagne flowed freely and everyone had a fine time. A few asked what the occasion was. John Rothchilde told them that the occasion was "being alive and well!"

After a little while Evelyn Rothchilde approached Tom Rankin and Daniel Lebowitz and asked them if they could speak privately. Leading them, she went into the same study that Daniel and Evelyn had met in two days before. Then she closed the heavy doors and asked them to please sit, which they did.

Standing, she rubbed her hands together for a moment and then said, "I want you both to know that I have relived the horrible events of 1964 over and over in my mind. I want you to know that I am so very sorry for what happened to Joe McCulloch. I also know that no amount of money can repay the pain and loss that I have caused. On top of all that, you have handled the matter in a way that allows me to continue my life and doesn't destroy John or me. How can I possibly repay you? I never can!

What I can tell you is you have made me realize that there is mercy and charity in the world. I wish I had been old enough and wise enough to know this in 1964. I might have saved your poor father, Daniel." By now tears were rolling, one after the other, down her cheeks. She went on, "I want you both to know that I will spend the rest of my life trying to live up to the standard both of you, and Orrin West, have set for me. I will be praying for your forgiveness, and for Joe's, everyday of the rest of my life." At this point, she began to sob uncontrollably.

Both men stood up. Daniel Lebowitz walked to her and put his arm around her shoulders. She put her head on his shoulder and sobbed, "Oh, Little Joe, I'm so sorry, so sorry!" and began sobbing again. They stayed by her until she regained her composure.

227

When she did, both Tom and Daniel asked if she would be all right and assured her all would be well and that time heals all wounds. Then Daniel Lebowitz said, "Mrs. Rothchilde—I mean Evelyn—your guests are expecting to see you circulate as the fine and great lady that you are. I suggest you powder your nose and see to you duties."

She looked at them both and said, "How lucky I am to know people like you. Yes, I must take care of the guests. Please excuse me for a moment. I will rejoin you outside." With that, she left the study and disappeared up the curving marble staircase to the bedrooms above.

Tom Rankin looked at Daniel Lebowitz and said, "Daniel, that is not the girl I knew at Moose Creek in 1964. She has really become a fine person. I am glad Orrin convinced us to take the moderate and Christian course to solving this situation. I think we have come out of it better. Let's go outside and put this behind us."

They walked out into the brilliant sunshine side by side. Roger Vanderlinden, noticing their approach, raised his glass to them and announced to the group around him, "Grab your wallets, folks, here comes a bright lawyer and a senior bureaucrat. That's a dangerous combination to have around capitalists like us!"

Everyone laughed and one guest shouted, "Don't you believe it, anybody! Rothchilde and Vanderlinden are the real sharks in this group!" The laughter redoubled. Daniel Lebowitz felt very fortunate to be with these people. He felt accepted and at home.

Three years later Orrin West was told by his Doctor that he had a terminal liver disease and had six months to live. This came as a surprise since Orrin felt fine and had the vitality of a man half his 80 years. Marge let Tom Rankin know. Orrin wouldn't. Consequently, one month after the bad news, they were all together - the West's, Rothchilde's, Vanderlinden's, and Daniel Lebowitz - at the dedication of the Orrin West School at Weippe, Idaho. Included in the group were two Chinese-Americans- Dr. Huang Lee IV and Mr. Lee Pong. The school was to be built and operated by the Rothchilde/Vanderlinden Foundation and would provide superior schooling for the sons and daughters of Idaho woods workers and Forest Service personnel stationed Northern Idaho.

Orrin enjoyed the festivities a great deal but was embarrassed at all the attention. After all the "Hoo-Rah", as Orrin called the proceedings of dedication, was over, he and Roger, John, Tom, Huang Lee IV, Lee Pong and Daniel boarded a Jet Ranger helicopter and flew into the Bitterroots. After an extended aerial tour the group landed and camped for the evening high on Fly Hill.

After a big steak dinner that they prepared together, Tom told them how he had first learned about the gold discovery from Joe McCulloch in this very spot in the summer of 1964.

Then Lee Pong fascinated everyone by telling them the story of his grandfather and Huang Lee's grandfather coming from China and how they were able to leave this very country with the gold that created the family fortune. He finished saying, "We are so glad we have been able to actually see the rugged country that our grandfathers overcame to become rich. Thank-you very much for inviting us to be with you!"

From where they were camped, they could look across the canyon of the North Fork of the Clearwater River right into Independence Gulch. Each of them knew that their lives had been altered by past events in this remote Idaho backcountry.

Sensing the group's feelings, Orrin poured out a glass of Jim Beam bourbon whiskey, his favorite, for each man. With the sun setting in the west, blue shadows darkening the canyons below them, and the evening chill coming down, he led them in a

229

toast to those that came before them and loved the land like they did. At the end of it Orrin said, "Lord, bless 'em all, especially Joe McCulloch, Huang Lee and Lee Pong, wherever they are. And Lord, especially bless and look out for we poor sinners gathered here, around this campfire, in our beloved Bitterroot Mountains tonight."

The other six men answered, "Amen and Amen!" Then they swallowed their whisky and threw their glasses into the darkening canyon below.

# Epilogue

Five years later Orrin West had only been dead a year. He had beaten the Doctor's best estimates of his survival potential by three and a half years. Each year most of his annuity went to the School with his name on it in Weippe. His widow continued the practice until her death several years later. The full annuity amount was then bequeathed to the School.

Tom and Donna Rankin live in a retirement home in Coeur d'Alene, Idaho, on a golf course. Their neighbors are mostly fellow Forest Service retirees.

John and Evelyn Rothchilde have continued with their lives much as they had before the events of 1988. The main change is that they spend more time together.

Daniel's mother, Mary Lebowitz-McCulloch, died in her sleep two years after the settlement agreement.

Daniel Lebowitz married the daughter of some close Rothchilde friends, Marie Hoekstra, a Vassar graduate, and heiress to a sizeable fortune. They have two children, Joseph, and Mary. They live in a fine house on land immediately adjacent to the Rothchilde mansion, where they spend much time. A year ago John Rothchilde adopted Daniel Lebowitz, who is now legally named Daniel Rothchilde and is, after Evelyn Rothchilde, the heir to the Rothchilde fortune.